Nicki Johnson 1994

D1005706

Consider
THE
CROWS

Also by Charlene Weir

The Winter Widow

Consider
THE
CROWS

Charlene Weir

St. Martin's Press
New York

Design by Basha Zapatka

ISBN 0-312-09772-7 (hardcover)

To Chris and Leslie and Bruce

With thanks to Ruth Cavin, Meg Ruley and
Patrolman David Pires of the Daly City Police
Department. Any errors are due to my poor
understanding rather than his invaluable assistance.

1

FEBRUARY WIND SNIFFLED around the police department and rattled the office window where Susan sat hunched over the desk, muttering to herself. The new budget, pages of blank spaces just waiting for numbers, rested atop the clutter of duty rosters, crime reports, and today's *Herald* with a picture of Dr. Audrey Kalazar. The vice-chancellor was scheduled to speak at a conference in Dallas.

Susan snapped on the desk lamp, adding its glow to the fluorescent ceiling fixture's, in an attempt to dispel gloom and frustration. How did she know how much should be allotted for paper towels; she could barely balance her checkbook with the use of a calculator.

"Susan—?" Hazel, the dispatcher, a stocky woman in her blue uniform, late forties with short auburn hair, stood in the doorway with a look of apology. "I know you said not to bother you, but—"

"Afternoon Miz Wren," Mayor Bakover gave Hazel a polished smile as he edged around her. "Something has come to my attention that you should know about."

He stood before Susan's desk, both hands clasped on his silver-handled cane, leaning into it with his forty pounds of excess weight. He wore his usual dark suit, white shirt and tie. Behind his back, Hazel rolled her eyes and discreetly withdrew, closing the door after her.

Susan rose. Now what? In the year she'd been chief of police, things often came to his attention that she needed to know about, and many of them made her wonder why one of San Francisco's finest didn't get herself back there.

He inched the wooden armchair a bit closer, pinched up his trousers at the knees and dropped into it, resting his cane against the side. As far as Susan knew, the cane was for effect rather than assistance. He smiled to show his goodwill, which was patently false; if there was any will at all between them, it was ill.

"Hippies are squatting at the old Creighton place," he said.

"Hippies," she repeated as she sat back down.

His fleshy face darkened. "You people in California can have all the perverts you want, but this is a nice town. We aim to keep it that way."

California probably hadn't had any hippies for twenty-five years. "What is it you want me to do?"

"Get her out of there."

"Her? One woman?"

"Girl. Young. Kids have been seen going in and out." He shook his head. "It's happened before. Bunch of freaks moved in out there. All living together. Selling drugs."

Living together and selling drugs seemed, in his opinion, equally bad. "What makes you think this girl is dealing?"

"Plants in the window."

"Plants."

He leveled a hard look at her. "They grow the stuff in pots in the house."

"I don't believe that's quite enough to arrest her."

He held the look for two beats before he smiled his practiced smile. She reminded herself not to underestimate him. She'd

2

done that once before, thought she was so smart and found he was using her for his own ends. Beneath his sandy-gray hair was a shrewd mind.

"Get out there and tell her to leave."

"I'll check her out in the morning." Tomorrow was Sunday and Susan's day off. She had plans, but not something she was eager to get at.

"I'm not asking you, Miz Wren. I'm telling you."

"Mr. Mayor, I have to meet with a group of college students in—" She glanced at her watch and saw it was three o'clock. "—one hour." She was to tell them the committee stood firm in its decision not to allow them a booth at the Crafts Fair. The kids wanted to pass out information on AIDS and if they were denied they threatened a demonstration "like you've never seen." If they even tried it, one committee member had threatened to bring his shotgun.

"You serve at the pleasure of the city council," he said.

Ah, yes. The club he held over her head. Temporary. Synonymous with "you're the wrong sex and not only that but an outsider." Martin Bakover was a tried-and-true chauvinist.

This was the beginning of Susan Wren's second year as acting chief of police. After finding her husband's killer, she'd simply stayed on, needing a place to heal. Hampstead was as good as any. In spite of the murder investigation at the start, the town was safe; Daniel's life had been here, and the job was low-key. She'd simply let the days slide one into another, dealing with a few break-ins, theft from autos, running of stop signs, loud music, barking dogs, and the occasional instance of wife-beating. To change the pattern, there were her periodic scare-sermons to various school-age groups on the dangers of drugs, exciting things like the celebration of a resident's one hundredth birthday and the odd parade to commemorate such important events as Timber Wolf Day.

She picked up her pen and shuffled under papers for her

notebook. If she moved smartly, she could just work in a visit with this *hippie* before meeting the students. "What's her name?"

"I don't know." He reached for the cane and rose, gave a little jiggle to straighten his trouser legs and rested both hands on the silver handle.

"Any difficulties with the budget?" He nodded at the forms. "Keep those figures within reason."

Ha. She wondered if there was some way to sneak in the money to hire a new female officer.

Where the hell was the old Creighton place? Another little reminder that she was an outsider. Probably property still identified by the name of some previous owner a generation or two back. She pushed a button on the phone and asked Hazel for directions.

The sky was an ominous gray when she headed the pickup across town on Rockridge and then cut north. Rain, she thought; it wasn't cold enough to snow. Must be getting used to Kansas, if she was blithely dismissing this temperature as not cold enough to snow. To her California blood, anything under forty degrees felt cold enough to snow.

Hampstead, nestled in shallow hills between two rivers, was a clean little town with wide streets and large trees that arched overhead; homes ranging from very modest to expensive; but even the cost of the most expensive was downright laughable if compared with San Francisco real estate. A pretty town in sunshine, with the overcast sky, Hampstead had a hunkered-down, closed-in look that made her feel like an alien.

Hazel's directions on the seat beside her, she drove past the fast-food places and used-car lots on the edge of town, then hit open fields with limestone fence posts and barbed-wire fencing. A red-winged blackbird took flight as she sped by. Keeping an eye on the odometer, she clocked off one mile and then swung left into a long driveway more mud than gravel and riddled with potholes.

Brush scraped at the pickup as she jounced toward what she hoped was a house. The driveway widened and on her left the brush gave way to an expanse of dead weeds; on the right beyond the house stood a thick grove of trees. A weak ray of sunshine, straggling through a dark cloud, hit on a mean little house, weathered wood frame with flaking no-color paint, that looked just this side of falling down. Incongruously, the front door glistened bright red from a recently applied coat of paint, so recent it looked still wet. She knocked.

Inside, a dog barked. A murmured voice hushed the dog and then called through the door. "Who is it?"

"Chief Wren. I'd like to ask you a few questions."

"Who sent you?"

Susan's eyebrows went up. She'd come mostly to satisfy the mayor's request but *who sent you* roused her professional curiosity. Could she have a dope-dealing, sin-living hippie here? "Would you open the door, please?"

After several seconds the door opened three inches. A large furry white dog stuck a snout through the gap. Susan was glad to see a small hand firmly attached to the dog's collar. Another second or two went by before the door opened wider.

Susan smiled in a friendly fashion. Public relations. Half the reports that landed on her desk came from citizens stopped for traffic violations and complaining the officer made them feel like criminals. "Hi. I heard someone was living here and I just stopped in to meet you."

"Oh." Still holding the dog's collar, the young woman backed away and invited her in. "You're the police chief? You're a woman."

"That's pretty much what everybody says. My name's Susan Wren." She let a slight query into her tone and the young woman obliged.

5

"Lynnelle Hames."

Late adolescence, early twenties, Susan thought. Small and so thin her collarbones were apparent beneath an over-long blue sweater that covered her jean-clad fanny. Blond curls, large green eyes and a pointed little cat's face. Also a frightened look. Not uncommon when a cop appeared on your doorstep.

"I don't think I've seen you before. You must be new. How long have you been here?" Plants in bright-glazed pottery bowls lined the windowsills of the two narrow windows.

"Not that long. Just a few weeks."

She didn't look like a dealer, or a user for that matter. Though that didn't mean anything; it was easy enough to be fooled. But this kid didn't feel right for it; no sly defiance or little click of fear in her eyes. She reminded Susan of a runaway she'd known in San Francisco; a girl who had gotten mangled by the life on the streets, abused by predators, and ended up in a drawer in a refrigerated room. "How do you like it here?"

Lynnelle nodded, then shrugged. "I like it. So far anyway. Oh, why don't you sit down." She tipped her head at the only piece of furniture in the room, an overstuffed chair in shabby gold plush with a floor lamp beside it. "It's more comfortable than it looks," she added with a quick grin.

Susan crossed the scratched hardwood floor to the windows and ran an eye over the plants; several different kinds. She had no idea what they were, but she knew what they weren't. They weren't pot. Hampstead was still safe. She settled in the gold chair and dropped her shoulder bag at her feet. Posters were thumbtacked to the damp-stained walls; a lion in a tree, snow-capped mountains, and an aerial view of a village nestled around a vivid blue lake.

With the inside of an ankle, Lynnelle nudged a guitar case out of her way and folded her legs Indian-fashion to sit on the small white shag rug in front of the Franklin stove. The dog, a

6

Samoyed, flopped down beside her with its mouth open and its tongue hanging out. Lynnelle kept her hand on the collar.

"That's a beautiful dog."

"This is Alexa." Lynnelle leaned over and hugged the animal. "Isn't she neat? First dog I've ever had. We're a team."

"She looks like she could put away a lot of food."

"Oh yeah, eating is one of her best things. Keeps me broke."

"I can believe it," Susan said. "If you're looking for a job maybe I can help. Ask a few people if they need anyone."

"Oh thanks, but I don't need a job. Well, I need one, but I've already got one. At the college? I'm a clerk-typist."

"Where did you live before you came here?"

"Boulder. You know? Colorado. I liked it there too, but here is better. This is kind of like home."

"You're renting it?"

Lynnelle nodded and looked around at the barren room with delight. "It's all mine, the whole place. Just for me and Lexi."

"It's kind of isolated out here, isn't it?"

"Yep. Abandoned. Lonely. I figured I fit right in." It was supposed to be a joke, but it didn't come off. Under the perky manner was a raw edge of pain that Susan responded to. Her own sense of isolation, abandonment and loneliness, always just under the surface, made her want to reach out to this kid. "You don't get nervous living by yourself?"

"Nope."

"What made you choose Hampstead?" Susan could almost feel Lynnelle close in as she looked away, traced a circle on the dog's head with one finger.

"Oh, you know. Reasons. And it's so pretty here. The hills and the trees and all the white houses."

Something not quite right here, Susan thought, something she wasn't picking up. Letting her emotions clog her perceptions. "What reasons?"

Lynnelle shrugged. "Just reasons."

7

"Do your parents know you're here?"

A mixture of expressions that Susan couldn't read—anticipation, apprehension, determination—flashed across Lynnelle's face. "My mother. She'll know."

The little niggle of worry gave another nudge, and got pushed aside as Susan noted the time. She was already late for the meeting. Reaching for her bag, she got to her feet. "I guess I'd best be going. I'm glad to meet you. If you need anything, give me a call."

"Hey, thanks. It's nice to meet you too." Lynnelle uncoiled herself in one smooth movement and opened the door to let Susan out, then stood watching as Susan climbed into the pickup.

There was a forlorn quality about the slender figure in the half-open doorway, a look that comes when you're lonely and you watch somebody, anybody, walk away.

Susan started to go back; ask a few more questions, stay with the kid a little longer, dig out what reasons brought her here. Glancing at her watch again, she started the pickup. The college bunch were probably painting placards and organizing their demonstration.

The sky was blacker, but the rain held off.

"Are they still here?" she asked Hazel when she got back to the department.

"In the interrogation room."

"Getting ready to riot?"

Hazel smiled, exposing one slightly crooked front tooth. "I don't know about that, but there's been a lot of giggling going on."

Susan could hear the chatter as she came down the hallway; it abruptly ceased when she reached the open door. Four bright young female faces gazed at her innocently, then darted quick glances at each other. They sat two on each side of a long wooden table.

"I apologize for being late." Susan pulled up a brown plastic chair and joined them.

"We were just getting ready to leave," Renée said with reproach. She was a sturdy young woman with a mane of red hair and cinnamon freckles.

Next to her sat Robin, thin, intense, ash-blond hair plaited into one long pigtail. Across the table was Roz, orange earrings dangling, her dark hair cropped short up the back and even all around, creating a bowl effect.

Susan thought of them as the three R's. The fourth student was Julie Kalazar, the vice-chancellor's daughter. Straight brown hair, shoulder-length and parted in the middle, framed the sharp planes of her face. All four wore jeans and the blue Emerson sweatshirt with the glittery-gold snarling wildcat.

"I spoke with the fair committee," Susan began, working out the sentence as she went along, "and their decision is—"

"No," Renée finished with a so-what-else-is-new flourish.

"They do have a point," Susan said. Although not a good one. "This is a crafts fair and the purpose is to raise money. They feel that passing out free information on AIDS isn't a big money-maker."

Robin snorted. "They just want to pretend only freaks and druggies get it."

"It is the committee's decision. And they are entitled to make it. I am sorry—" Susan was trying to think how to phrase, And don't try any kind of commotion, disturbance, demonstration, or destruction or you'll all be arrested for civil disobedience, disturbing the peace, disorderly conduct, littering and anything else I can think of.

"It's okay." Julie tucked a strand of hair behind one ear.

"We got a better idea," Roz said.

The three R's all grinned.

Julie frowned at them, then said to Susan, "If we sell something, can we give out the AIDS information to anyone who wants it?"

Feeling as though she were being set up for something, Susan said slowly, "I would think that would be acceptable. What would you sell?"

"Jewelry," Julie said.

The three R's carefully refrained from looking at each other.

"Okay," Susan said slowly. "Submit another application, and if it's turned down, let me know. You're aware the jewelry has to be something you've made?"

"Yes," Julie said. The three R's nodded.

"Well then, there shouldn't be any problem. That sounds fine."

All four of them gathered up their down jackets and their backpacks and scooted out like freedom fighters hearing the call. Why didn't it feel fine?

She trudged off to run Lynnelle's name through records and see if anything turned up. Nothing did.

The house was cold when she got home, and empty. Empty, she couldn't do anything about, but she kicked up the heat to take care of the cold and spread out the budget on the desk in the small office off the living room. The plan was to work on it a couple hours, then knock off for dinner, but the image of Lynnelle standing alone by the bright red door kept getting in the way. Susan lit a cigarette, propped her head in one hand and bent her mind around figures. A *pit pit pat* on the window made her look up. The rain had started.

2

RAIN PATTERED SOFTLY at the kitchen window and Carena Egersund, at the round oak table, looked up from the calculus exams and watched wavery streaks trickle down through her reflection. She'd planned to get the exams finished up this evening: so far she'd managed a lot of coffee drinking and no exam grading. Her mind, with equal parts irritation and uneasiness kept jumping back over the ugly scene with the vice-chancellor. Dr. Kalazar had been furious with her, furious and threatening. *Confine your interests to statistics and probability theory or you won't teach at Emerson next year.*

So much for your new life, lady. She raised her cup in a toast and took a sip. Uck. Cold. She thought of her ex-husband and wondered how his new life was going. Well, Jerry, all you dreamed it would be? She raised the cup again. May the blue bird of happiness—or as my father would say, *der blau vogel von gluck*—fly up your nose.

The doorbell rang and coffee sloshed over the exams. She glanced at the clock radio. Eight o'clock on Saturday night? Tossing down the pen, she stood, tugged the gray sweatshirt down over the sweatpants and flopped toward the door in her fuzzy slippers. On the way past, she switched on the lamps at either end of the couch, then the porch light.

It shone down on a damp waif with a floppy hat, faded jeans and blue down jacket. "Hi, Dr. Egersund," she said with a smile so careful it was almost painful. "Can I talk to you for a minute?"

She seemed familiar, but Carena couldn't place her. A student? Not one of mine, Carena thought as she unlatched the storm door and invited her in. Probably selling tickets for something or other, tickets were always being sold for something or other; or wanting to know if a math course would be available for next term. Students couldn't seem to grasp that monumental decisions could wait until office hours.

"What can I do for you?" She relieved the young lady of the jacket and draped it over a dining room chair.

The down jacket had given the girl an illusion of bulk. Without it, she looked about fourteen, small and thin. Snatching off her hat, she shook out her blond curls and her green eyes stared gravely at Carena with unnerving steadiness. She opened her mouth to speak, seemed unable to come up with anything and cleared her throat instead.

Carena was curious. Students, in general, weren't this nervous when confronting a professor, even if they were arguing about a grade they knew they deserved. If she was reduced to thinking about her ex-husband, Carena figured she ought to welcome any distraction. "Maybe we could start with something simple, like your name."

A quick spark of humor glinted in the green eyes. "It's Lynnelle. Lynnelle Hames."

The name meant nothing to Carena, but Lynnelle waited as though it should. When the silence stretched to awkwardness, Carena offered coffee. Lynnelle accepted with a grateful nod, and let her eyes drift over the furnishings; the rose and white brocade chair and matching couch, the painting of autumn trees on the wall above, cherrywood bowl on the coffee table, pale

12

rose rug, the wooden rocker. She smiled as if she'd satisfied something for herself.

In the kitchen, Carena dumped her cold coffee, refilled the cup and poured a second one. She looked through the cabinet, hoping to find a cookie or two—ever the mother, milk and cookies—but was out of luck, then ferried both cups back to the living room.

Lynnelle was planted in the chair by the fireplace, her chin firmly high; a young lady with her mind made up; whatever the cost, she was determined to get on with it.

Carena handed her a cup and sat on the couch opposite. "Are you enrolled at Emerson?"

"No." Lips pursed, she sipped tentatively. "I work in the English department. Clerk-typist."

Ah. Probably why she looked familiar. "You wanted to see me about something?"

Lynnelle set the cup down, scooted forward in the chair and fixed her gaze on Carena's face. "You don't know me, but I've thought about you a lot." The words came out as though they'd been rehearsed, then all of a sudden she seemed to forget what came next. Her glance slid away and landed on the mantle. With a soft smile, she stood to look at the small ceramic ghost crying over a broken pumpkin, a Mother's Day gift from Michael when he was little. Lynnelle held it in the palm of her hand and looked at it from all sides. "Boy, I hope this isn't an omen. Your great important moment in life and you break the pumpkin."

Carena started to feel uneasy. Her mother always said this habit of picking up strays could one day be dangerous. There was something a little looney-tunes about this young lady.

Lynnelle put the ghost back and peered at the framed picture of Michael in cap and gown for high-school graduation. "Picture of your son."

"Do you know Michael?"

13

"I know a lot of things." Picking up the snapshot tucked in the frame, she studied it closely; a snapshot of a much younger Carena and a baby Michael.

Carena was beginning to think maybe she'd better hustle this girl right on out. "Are you in some kind of trouble?"

"No." Lynnelle started to say something and once again seemed to lose her place.

"Why are you here?"

Lynnelle turned, squared her shoulders and raised her chin. "I thought you might like to meet your daughter."

Oh my oh my oh my oh my oh my. Take a breath. Well then, she knew how old this young lady was. Twenty-one. "Oh, Lynnelle. No. Child."

Lynnelle stiffened, her face went blank as though she'd been slapped. "Your very own baby. You gave away like some— puppy you didn't want. And never wanted it to turn up again. Well, guess what."

"Lynnelle, no—"

"You ever think about me? Wonder how I was? What I looked like? What the people were like you gave me to? He died, you know, my father, who I thought was my father. He fell. He was a builder. Scaffolding. Some kind of scaffolding and he fell. And she married again, my— my— I was fifteen. He'll be a father for you." Her voice took on a singsong quality. "He'll love you and you'll love him too. You'll see. We'll be a family again." Abruptly, she turned and stared down at the cold ashes in the grate, back rigid, fists clenched.

"Lynnelle—"

She spun fiercely, like a small animal at bay. "I know about the fight with Dr. Kalazar. She wants to fire you. Maybe she'd like to know. How you had a baby and you weren't married and you gave it away. I could tell her, you know. I—" Tears glistened in her eyes. Angrily, she rubbed at them with the back of a hand and darted toward the door.

14

"Wait." Before Carena could get her mind working and her muscles lined up to respond, Lynnelle had flung open the door and nipped out. Carena went after her, but by the time she got to the street the VW was already speeding away. The taillights sparkled in the light rain as they disappeared around the corner. She felt Lynnelle's pain. That lashing out with the silly threat to tell Kalazar had come from deep hurt. Lynnelle had been obviously nervous when she arrived. She'd probably thought a long time before she'd worked herself up to it; played it out in her mind, memorized the dialogue.

Oh, you poor child. I'm so sorry. I handled that very badly. I don't think fast on my feet.

Back inside, Carena noticed the down jacket still hanging over the dining room chair, the shoulders spotted with raindrops. You can't run around without your coat. She checked the pockets and found crumpled Kleenex, a stick of gum, and a paperback book, *Summer of the Dragon* by Elizabeth Peters, with an envelope as a bookmark. It was addressed to Lynnelle Hames, Seven Creighton Road, Hampstead, Kansas. Nothing inside. She reinserted it at the appropriate page and stuck everything back in the pockets, then wandered into the bedroom, where she stacked pillows at the head of the bed, kicked off her soggy slippers and stretched out to stare at the ceiling.

Here is this child, turned up after all this time. What should I do? I don't know. That's not good enough. I'm afraid of what this will mean. That won't help either. Oh God.

God? Remember me? Yes, it's me. I realize you haven't heard from me in a long time but, you see, there's this problem.

She sighed. Maybe God got bored with having it all and periodically looked around for some amusement. When she'd accepted the position at Emerson, it had seemed like some cosmic bad joke; it put her, at forty, right back in the very spot she'd spent the first eighteen of those years trying to get away from. And now here was this child.

Maybe God had an even more complicated game in mind.

Rain spattered against the window. She'd hesitated to accept this position, but she wanted to get away from Boulder, Colorado, where her ex-husband was, and jobs weren't that easy to find. There was the little matter of a roof over her head. She looked at her watch. Only eight-thirty; it felt like midnight. Swinging her legs over the side, she sat up and picked up the telephone receiver. Holding it against her chest for a moment, she took a breath and with a shaky hand punched in the number.

In Topeka, thirty-five miles away, the phone was answered by a young male voice. "Hello, Stevie, this is your Aunt Carena. Is your mama around?"

"Yep, she's here."

A clatter came through the line as the receiver was dropped and she heard Stevie yell, "Mom?"

A moment later, Caitlin said, "Carena, I'm glad you called. It's been a while."

"I guess it has."

"What's wrong?" Caitlin's ability to pick up on the emotional climate was phenomenal.

"Nothing's wrong." Carena hesitated. "It's just that—" She told her about Lynnelle appearing on the doorstep.

"Oh Carrie." Silence. "How did she find you?"

"I don't know."

"But what was she doing in Hampstead?"

"She lives here."

"In Hampstead? Where?"

"Somewhere out on Creighton Road."

More silence, then Caitlin spoke in a soft voice. "What does she want?"

"I don't know, Caitlin." Her mother; a teary reunion, stunned disbelief and joyous embraces.

"What do you think she'll do?"

"Maybe nothing. I was so surprised, I just sat there with my

16

mouth open. That might have turned her off the whole thing."
Not likely.

"Do you think so?" Caitlin's voice faded and she said something Carena couldn't hear. "Will you find out?"

Carena felt suddenly tired. "Yes," she said at last. "Yes, I will."

"Carrie?"

"What?"

"It's a pretty name, isn't it, Lynnelle?"

"Yes, Caitlin. Yes, it is."

After she hung up, Carena put on her heavy robe and dry socks and fixed a cup of peppermint tea, which she carried out to the screened porch off the kitchen. Sitting in the dark in a white wicker chair, she listened to the rain patter against the roof and breathed in the aroma of the tea. She thought about that awful hot summer twenty-one years ago. Was it all going to come out now? Somewhere, an owl cried and a bit of Shakespeare came to mind.

> *A falcon, towering in her pride of place,*
> *Was by a mousing owl hawked at and killed.*

She shivered, took one sip of scalding tea, then got up, left the cup on the kitchen cabinet and went to put on her shoes and coat and find her car keys.

Lynnelle tossed the few pieces of dry wood she'd been able to find—on top of everything else the furnace had conked out—into the Franklin stove and then sat cross-legged on the small white rug in front of it. She picked up the guitar and strummed softly. Thunder rumbled, muted and distant, and the big white Samoyed stretched on the floor beside her raised head from paws and gave her an anxious look.

"Stupid, sentimental shit," Lynnelle told the dog. "Believing in fairy tales. And they all lived happily ever after."

The floor lamp next to the gold plush chair threw a circle of light on the ceiling. Rain leaked from one corner with a steady plink, plink, plink into a coffee can.

"She didn't even want to see me. Boy, didn't she even want to see me. Sat there looking like I'd punched her in the stomach."

Bending her head, Lynnelle brushed a strand of hair behind her ear and sang harshly.

> *"She's tied it in her apron*
> *and she's thrown it in the sea;*
> *Says, 'Sink ye, swim ye, bonny wee babe.*
> *You'll ne'er get mair o' me.'*

"I *cried,*" she ground out through clenched teeth. The tears made her madder than anything. Weak, pathetic little shit.

She dropped the guitar back in its case, uncrossed her legs to get to her knees and buried her fingers in the dog's thick fur. "Alexa, it's just you and me, baby. A couple of rejects. We don't care, do we? We don't need anybody else."

Her fingers tightened on the dog's fur as she pictured Carena Egersund's shocked face. Alexa yelped. "I did it all wrong. Just blurted it out. I should have worked up to it. I meant to. It just—"

Suddenly, the house felt suffocating. Air, she had to have some air. She rose in one quick movement and padded in stockinged feet to the kitchen. The dog scrambled up and followed. Heavy boots sat drying on a newspaper by the door and Lynnelle pulled them on, snatched the poncho from its hook, whirled it around and over her head. While she rummaged in a drawer for the flashlight, Alexa waited eagerly by the door.

18

"I like to walk in the rain," Lynnelle told her. "You don't."

Alexa waved her plumy tail and dashed out when the door was opened. She started down the steps, stopped and gave Lynnelle a reproachful look.

"I told you so."

Alexa backed up, tucked herself well in under the overhang and collapsed with a sigh. Lynnelle laughed, stooped to ruffle the hair on both sides of the dog's neck, then snicked on the flashlight and set off along the irregular stones on the muddy ground under the big oak tree. An old rope swing hung from one branch; she gave it a push as she went by and headed across the open field to the woods.

Lightning flickered and thunder rumbled. The trees were thick overhead. In the three months since she'd moved in here, she'd spent a lot of time walking these woods and sitting by the creek watching the water gurgle past. There was an old cottonwood she liked to sit under with branches that reached up over the water.

The night was full of sounds; the spatter of rain, the moans of the wind, the squish of undergrowth beneath her feet, a rustling that suddenly stopped, then a long haunting note that sent nerves crawling along her spine.

It's only an owl.

A twig snapped, louder rustling, then the owl spoke again. Hair seemed to rise on her neck and she thought of all those old movies, Indians gliding from tree to tree, alerting each other with the voice of the owl, stalking the unwary. She stopped, shined the light behind her; trees and shadows and tangled growth on the ground. The air smelled like damp and dead vegetation.

She shook her head irritably. Afraid of the dark too? There's nothing here but trees and low, tangled vines and dead leaves and small furry things like squirrels and mice. She plodded on.

19

Lightning splintered the darkness. For an instant, she saw, clear as day, a dark figure against a tree trunk.

She froze. Her breath caught, her heart thudded.

The figure came toward her.

"Oh." Lynnelle pulled in a deep breath. "You scared me to death. What are you doing here?"

They walked through the dripping trees and, shaky with relief, Lynnelle babbled on and on. God, I sound like a dreep. "Do you ever think that life's just a cheat? All promises that never come true? I mean, good things are supposed to happen, aren't they? Sometimes? How come they never do? How come you plan and you look forward to, and you hope and then it's finally there and then—" She raised her head and let the rain run down her face. "You end up crying over a broken pumpkin."

A crackle of lightning lit up the sky just as they reached the creek. Recent rains had swelled the usual trickle into a rush that fountained up over rocks and fallen branches.

She sensed movement behind her and felt a moment of fear. Before she could turn, a blow smashed against the back of her head. Intense white pain zigzagged through her mind and the owl cried again just as she felt herself falling.

3

Hunched over the steering wheel, Carena tried to see through the windshield as the wipers struggled courageously against the rain. When she pulled into the dark garage, she relaxed and turned off the headlights and motor. She rattled down the overhead garage door and, head bent, sloshed through the driving rain toward the house. From the corner of her eye, she caught movement inside the lighted screened porch but before she could gather her wits, the screen door opened and a man in a ski jacket trotted, loose-jointed, down the steps. In the dark, he looked huge.

"Michael?" She was taken by surprise that this large person was her son. When had he gotten so adult?

"Where have you been? I'm going to have to speak to you about staying out so late. Irresponsible parent. Now you listen to me. There's no reason why you can't let me know—"

She hugged him and he squeezed her tightly, lifting her off her feet.

"And furthermore—"

Vigorously, she rubbed the top of his blond curls with her knuckles. He released her and, one arm over her shoulder, shepherded her inside.

"When did you get here?"

"An hour ago." Shrugging off his jacket, he tossed it over the back of a chair.

She picked it up and hung it along with her own on hangers over the bathtub, then replaced her wet shoes with down booties and went back to the kitchen. "How's everything in Boulder? Classes okay?"

"Great." Michael, in white sweatshirt with University of Colorado printed on it, sprawled in a chair, stretched his long blue-jean-clad legs halfway under the table. "Anything to eat? I'm starving."

Of course, starving; some things never change. "That could be a problem." Opening the refrigerator door, she peered at almost bare shelves; block of cheese, half a loaf of stale bread, several limp carrots, eggs, orange juice, a jar with one dill pickle, a carton of milk.

She lifted the carton and shook it to judge how much was left. "Scrambled eggs?"

"Yeah." He chose an apple from the bowl on the table and bit into it with a juicy crunch. "Where you been?"

"Driving around." She turned the burner on under the skillet and cracked eggs into a bowl.

"It's after midnight."

"I had some thinking to do." With a fork, she whipped the eggs, crumbled in some cheese and added a dash of milk.

"Want to tell me about it? Now that I've had Psych One I know all about that stuff."

"Thanks, but I'll just muddle through on my own. What are you doing here?" She got out toaster and bread and poured eggs into the hot skillet.

"My roommate—Rich, you remember Rich? He has this girl in Kansas City and he was overcome with love and longing. Since he doesn't have a car, he offered to pay for gas if I'd drive."

"Why didn't you let me know you were coming?"

"Spur of the moment. When love strikes, you can't wait around. Besides, I thought I'd surprise you."

"It's a lovely surprise." She set a steaming mound of scrambled eggs in front of him and kissed his forehead, this large blond son, then sat across from him and sipped reheated peppermint tea. "So, tell me what you've been up to."

He bit off a corner of toast, chewed and swallowed. "Well, I met this weird chick."

"Michael! Young women are not chicks."

He grinned. "Just checking to see if you're paying attention. Anyway, this *young woman* is weird. Kind of intense. She asked all these questions."

"What about?"

"Me. You. The family." He waved his fork. "Just questions."

"Maybe she likes you."

"Natch." He gave her a cocky look from under lowered lashes, and chased the last of the eggs around on the plate and scooped them up. "She has an attitude." He chewed and swallowed. "Like she knows something I don't. You know, the way you might if you knew what somebody was getting for a birthday present and he didn't."

Oh no. No. Couldn't be. Carena sipped tea. "What's her name?"

"Lynnelle."

Carena choked and coughed.

He whacked her, almost fatally, on the back. "You all right?"

"Fine," she wheezed. "Where did you meet her?"

He shrugged. "Around. You know, on campus. In the book store. Once at a party. In the Union. Seemed like everywhere I went, there she was."

He pushed himself upright and ambled to the refrigerator, refilled his glass with orange juice and stuck bread in the toaster. "After a while she disappeared and then I got letters. I mean, I barely know her and there's these letters. Can you believe it?"

He flopped into the chair and hooked an elbow over the back. "Turns out she's living here. Isn't that weird?"

Not weird. It explained how Lynnelle had found her. How had she found Michael?

"You ever meet her?" The toast popped and he leaped up to snatch it and slather on butter, giving her a moment of reprieve.

Even though she didn't believe in keeping secrets from her child, always felt he had a right to know what was happening in his world, she'd kept this one. Her own parents had operated under the attitude the less the children knew, the better; that way led to confusion, anxiety and unwarranted guilt. For a moment, she was tempted to explain, then put the thought out of her mind. Too soon, too many random variables. "What did the letters say?"

"Oh, you know. Stuff." He brought the plate back to the table and sat down. "About this job. Boring, but it's money. About this place. Small town, different. Finding out stuff about people." He washed down toast with a slug of orange juice. "I think she likes knowing things about people. Makes her feel important or something. And something about somebody she was scared of."

"Who?"

He shrugged. "Who knows. Like I said, she's kinda weird and— I don't know, something about her interests me."

Oh dear Lord. "You plan to look her up?"

"I already tried. Since you weren't home." He eyed her with mock reproach. "Thought I'd never find the place. It's way out somewhere. Shacky house. Woods. Hansel and Gretel stuff."

"You saw her?"

"Nah. A car was there, yellow VW, and a big dog I thought would probably tear my leg off, but she wasn't. At least, she didn't answer the door." He pushed empty plates aside and leaned back.

"You plan to see her tomorrow?" Today really, it was already Sunday.

"No time. We have to head back for Boulder pretty early. I got a German exam on Monday. Next time I come."

Oh thank you, God, a little time anyway.

After too few hours of sleep, she was again scrambling eggs and, with a brief thought for cholesterol, feeding her ravenous child. When he finished, he stuck two apples in his jacket pocket and she walked with him out to his car. Only youth would drive over five hundred and fifty miles from Boulder, Colorado, to Hampstead, Kansas, to spend a few hours with a girl. The rain had stopped, the clouds had thinned and it looked as though sunshine might be a possibility.

"Michael—" She was trying to think of some way to tell him he shouldn't necessarily believe everything Lynnelle had said.

He looked at her, waited and grinned. "Again with the advice, Mom?"

She scowled at him. "You're setting off on a journey. This is when mothers are supposed to give advice."

"You already did that. When I left for school." He drew himself up and spoke pompously. " 'Study hard, my son. Virtue is its own reward. Beware the dangers of bad companions and loose women, and don't take any wooden nickels.' "

She smiled and patted his cheek rather sharply. "You know, I'd like you a lot better if you weren't such a smartass. Wooden nickels, indeed."

"You might as well forget it, Mom. Advice isn't really your style."

Probably not. She hugged him. "Take care of yourself, love."

Drive carefully, she added to herself as she watched the car pull away. And don't take any wooden nickels.

In the kitchen, she poured herself a fresh cup of coffee and sat down to drink it. Maybe the caffeine would help her figure out what to do when she went out to the Creighton place.

25

4

SUSAN STOOD ON tiptoe, struggling to release the bird feeder from a hook on the elm tree while a blue jay hopped from branch to branch and made raucous complaints of impatience. Daniel had put the feeder up long before she knew him; he'd been six-foot three. With her five-eight, the thing was just enough too high that she never bothered with a stepping block, only swore. She opened the bag, poured in seed, and teetered on her toes to catch the wire back over the hook.

Inside, at the kitchen window, she watched the jay dive-bomb at sparrows to chase them away. She lit a cigarette and inhaled deeply. February already, the thirteenth. A year, over a year since Daniel's death. She'd had his job longer than she'd been his wife.

She exhaled a stream of smoke. Everybody said she'd be okay after a year. Everybody was wrong. Sparrows fluttered like brown leaves blown in a sky covered with thin gray clouds. I have to do it, I have to go upstairs and open that closet door and box up all those clothes.

Daniel isn't there; nothing's there but pants and shirts and jackets. Right. And ghosts. Ghosts that will rise up as soon as the door is opened.

The doorbell rang and she looked down at her jeans, long past their prime, a disreputable red sweatshirt that had been Daniel's and sneakers with holes in the toes. She stubbed out the cigarette, raked fingers through her shoulder-length dark hair and took her time getting to the door, hoping whoever it was would decide she wasn't home.

The bell sounded again and she thought it might be the kid up the street. Jen had taken to dropping in at odd moments when life got too much for her, which it did a lot lately. The living room didn't look so hot either; newspapers everywhere, books, filled ashtrays and dirty coffee mugs, dust on the oak tables. Maybe she should consider a cleaning woman.

A white box—ordinary shoe box, size six and a half B, tied with string—sat all by itself on the porch. As she eyed it, an ominous awareness surfaced. Oh no. Moving fast, she jumped over it and hit the steps, looked up and down the street—wide tree-lined street with bare branches meeting overhead, neat middle-aged homes, some brick, some woodframe. Halfway down the block an elderly white Chevy tore off with a squeal of tires.

Oh no, Sophie, no you don't. Hands on her hips, she watched the car disappear, then trudged up the steps and picked up the box. Inside, she gingerly placed it on the coffee table. Ha, am I going to feel stupid if there's a bomb in here. She untied the string and lifted the lid. A tiny beige kitten with a chocolate-brown face popped its head up and regarded her with unblinking blue eyes.

"Ahh." A silly smile spread itself over her face. The little thing was about as substantial as a feather. Only a baby. She and Daniel'd had plans for a baby. Didn't happen. Won't happen now. Nobody for a father and there's all that biological clock stuff.

"Sorry, baby. You have to go right back to Sophie." Sophie was a nutty old woman devoted to cats, and she was constantly searching out homes among the unwary. Clapping the lid back, Susan tried to hold it down while she fumbled for the string. The kitten spurted out one end, skittered across the coffee table and somersaulted to the floor.

Just as Susan made a dive for it—and missed—the phone rang. She hustled into the kitchen and answered sharply.

"Sorry to spoil your Sunday," Hazel said, "but a body's been found at the old Creighton place."

"Whose body?" She had a bad feeling.

"A young woman. Her name is Lynnelle Hames."

Damn, damn. Leaning an elbow on the countertop, Susan rested her forehead on her fingertips and remembered Lynnelle standing in the doorway of that grim little house. "Has Dr. Fisher been notified?"

"Yes. And Ben's out there with Osey."

Upstairs in the bedroom, she shed her jeans and sweatshirt, selected a pair of navy-blue wool pants, a bulky blue sweater and pulled on black ankle boots. She ran a brush through her hair; makeup, she didn't bother with—she seldom did unless she was feeling vulnerable—and checked the gun in her shoulder bag. As she slipped on her charcoal trenchcoat with its wool lining, she glanced at the other closet door, the one with Daniel's clothes inside, then trotted down the stairs.

It was just after eleven when she headed the pickup crosstown on Rockridge and cut north. Fifteen minutes later, she turned into the long driveway, all the potholes now filled with rain water, and angled the pickup nose in to the shrubbery at the end of a line of cars, patrol cars and emergency vehicle. The local radio station van was also there, she noted; not surprised, but not pleased either.

Ben Parkhurst, in black pants and gray wool jacket with the collar turned up, crunched down the driveway toward her. He was a compact man about five-ten with dark hair, intense dark eyes, and olive skin. During the year she'd been chief, they'd

28

moved from hostility and distrust to grudging respect and finally, like two suspicious dogs sharing the same territory, had worked out an uneasy truce. In the past few weeks he'd regressed to icy arrogance and she'd wondered what that was all about. "Where is she?"

"This way." With a jerk of his head, he started back up the driveway.

When they came around the rear of the house she saw, with surprise, David McKinnon standing under an oak tree that spread out overhead like a giant umbrella. David, an attorney, was a friend; she wondered what he was doing here. The woman with him had Lynnelle's dog, who lunged at them, barking wildly, and was brought up short by the leash. Susan hoped it would hold.

Officer White, spruce in his uniform and keeping a discreet eye on them, stiffened when she glanced at him. He was the youngest and most recent of her officers and didn't quite know how to handle himself in her presence, so he opted for military correctness.

"Susan." David took a step toward them. He looked tired; a handsome man, late thirties, blond curly hair, but fatigue lined his fine-chiseled face and his sharp blue eyes had dark circles. He wore a tan leather jacket, brown turtleneck sweater and brown pants dripping wet, expensive boots soaked.

He turned and touched his companion's arm. "This is Carena Egersund."

Susan knew the woman by sight; math professor at Emerson. Egersund's pale skin stretched tight over sharp cheekbones, green eyes shadowed with shock, rigid stance suggested a hard rein on her emotions. A breeze ruffled her short blond hair and she clutched her tweed jacket together at the throat.

"I'll need to talk with both of you," Susan said. "I hope you won't mind waiting. It'll be just a few minutes." If David was irritated by her official manner, he didn't show it.

Irregular stepping stones led across the muddy ground to an open field of winter-dead weeds. Fifty yards further was a thick stand of trees.

"Those two found her," Parkhurst said when they were out of earshot and headed for the woods.

Moldering leaves squelched and slid underfoot as they tromped through the trees. "The dog led them to her, some kind of Lassie bit." He grunted. "Your friend McKinnon moved the body."

At the edge of the creek, the photographer was packing up his gear, the ambulance attendants were waiting patiently with a stretcher, Dr. Fisher was kneeling by the body. Water from sodden jeans and black poncho puddled over the plastic sheet under it.

Parkhurst went off to check with the officers he had searching the area. Susan looked down at Lynnelle, made even smaller by death, her pale skin almost colorless except for the bruised-looking patches of lividity, her matted blond hair pasted to the skull, mouth hanging loose, eyes open and staring. The wind plucked forlornly at a clump of curls.

The creek bank showed marks in the mud where the body had landed and tumbled down. They were crisscrossed with paw prints. To one side, sliding footprints gouged the mud, made by somebody climbing down in a hurry. Probably David. They, obviously, were made after the rain had stopped.

"Owen?" She looked at Dr. Fisher, a large solid man, stocky and slightly overweight, square fleshy face and heavy dark eyebrows that contrasted sharply with an abundance of white hair. Latex gloves covered his long-fingered hands; hands that looked borrowed from a much thinner, more delicate man.

"She probably drowned."

"Accident?" Susan had a great deal of respect for him, he was thorough and precise and tackled each task with unending patience and enthusiasm. Being a gentleman of the old school, he disapproved of female cops and especially female police chiefs, but he was a gentleman and never let his disapproval show. She also appreciated the fact that he didn't indulge in crude humor like some pathologists she had known.

"She took a nasty blow to the occipital region. It's hard to see how that could happen accidentally and have her end up face down in the water."

He turned the girl's head to one side and tenderly eased his fingers through the dripping hair. "Rain and creek water washed the blood away. It doesn't feel like more than one hit. I won't know till I get her on the table. Then I'll tell you if that blow could have killed her if she hadn't drowned." He rose, brushed at the damp spots on his dark blue trousers and peeled off the latex gloves, fussily wiped his hands with a white towel.

As she studied the dead face, a monumental sense of rage coiled up deep inside her and burned in her chest. She clenched her teeth and shoved her hands deep in the pockets of her trenchcoat so he wouldn't see them shaking. "How long has she been dead?"

"I might know after the autopsy." He replaced instruments in his bag and snapped it shut with a final click.

"Some rough guidelines would be helpful."

He gave her an irritated look. "That water's cold. It's going to complicate things."

She waited.

He frowned. "Maybe ten to twelve hours. Rigor still evident. A guess," he added. "A very rough guess." He nodded curtly and began to pick his way, fastidious as a cat, across the wet ground.

She struggled with a hideous thought. Did I let this happen by being in too much of a hurry? If I'd gone back yesterday, asked the right questions, found out why she came here, could I have prevented this?

She felt the helplessness that was always her response to a

violent death. The awful finality. Lynnelle was so young, she should have a lifetime ahead; career, marriage, children, all of it.

I'll find who did this, Susan promised her silently, for whatever that's worth.

When Parkhurst returned, she left him to examine the surround and see to the removal of the body. As she walked back through the trees, skirting a boarded-over well, she caught glimpses of the men searching for evidence and hoped they would find something. With the size of the area and the various layers of rotting vegetation, any success would be mainly a matter of luck.

Egersund and David sat side by side on the wooden step by the back door, the dog lay on the ground with her head across Egersund's feet. All three rose as Susan approached.

"I'm sorry to keep you waiting. I just need to get a few things clear and then you can go." Osey Pickett was still inside the house gathering fingerprints and she wanted to get David out of the cold air. From all that standing around in wet clothing, his lips had turned decidedly blue. She shouldn't have kept him waiting.

"Dr. Egersund, perhaps you'd like to wait in a squad car with Officer White. Out of the wind."

Egersund shook her head. "The dog will be less upset if we just wait here."

Susan nodded. "I won't be long. David, would you mind?" She led him along the driveway, intending to question him in her pickup.

When he realized where they were headed, he suggested his own car, a snappy little black Mercedes with soft leather interior. He started the motor and switched on the heater. "Was it really necessary to have your storm trooper standing guard?"

"White? A storm trooper?" White was an apple-cheeked kid who looked more like a boy scout than a police officer.

David smiled a wry acknowledgement. He had the half-angry expression that comes with "if only," the constant replay so it all comes out right.

"All right, David, why did you move the body?"

"My God, Susan, she was facedown in the water. I didn't know she was dead." He took in a breath and spoke in a calmer voice. "Sorry. I just feel some blame here. I never should have let her stay."

"What do you mean?"

He gestured with a thumb over his shoulder. "I own the place. And the woods, however many acres. You can see the house has been abandoned for years. She liked it. She wanted to live in it."

Susan turned to look through the rear window at the dilapidated house. "You rented that?"

"Yes, well, in love as in literature it's often difficult to understand someone else's choice. She wouldn't give up. She needed a place to live. It was empty. Why not? She loved the woods. Oh hell." Resting an elbow on the steering wheel, he pinched the area between his eyebrows as though he had a headache.

"How could anybody in all good conscience collect rent for that?"

"I didn't go that far. She would live there and make this and that repair."

The bright red paint on the front door must have been an attempt to impose some cheer on the squalor. "I'm surprised you weren't concerned about liability."

"Believe me, I thought of that. Ordinarily, I wouldn't have allowed anyone in there."

"But?"

"There was something so angry and needy about her that I felt sorry for her. She was a young lady battering at walls. She seemed totally guileless and trustworthy. I waived my better judgment. Based on my assessment of her, and let me remind you I've had a few years of judging character, and based on the strength of her desire to live here, and based on her financial position—" He stopped speaking as though he were addressing a jury. "She wanted a place where she could keep the dog. She couldn't find one. You think I could say no? I did have a contractor check it first. It's not as bad as it looks. At least, the structure's sound."

"How long did she live here?"

"About three months."

"Tell me what you know about her." The heater hummed softly, sending out warm air. It certainly worked well; maybe there was something to all this luxury stuff. She unbuttoned her trenchcoat.

"Only her name."

"David—"

"Oh yes, I asked. She'd recently arrived in Hampstead; she wouldn't say from where. She wouldn't tell me anything at all about herself. She was—" He put both hands high on the steering wheel. "Worried, troubled, apprehensive—" He lifted his shoulders. "I don't know. I tried to keep an eye on her."

"How often did you see her?"

"Not as often as that question seems to imply," he said dryly. "Half a dozen times, maybe."

"What time did you get here this morning?"

"Ten."

"Why did you come?"

"The furnace quit working. She phoned about it yesterday evening."

"You fix furnaces too?"

"Of course not. I was going to look at it intelligently, kick it a few times and call somebody to fix it."

"Why wait until this morning?"

"Her choice. She said she was busy, plans for the evening."

"What plans?"

34

He hesitated a moment before answering. "She didn't say."

"Did you ask?"

He sighed. "No."

A flock of small birds swooped to the shrubbery in front of the car, hopped around twittering, and then took off again, dark spots against a cold gray sky.

"You came out with Dr. Egersund?"

He slouched back in the seat. "She came while I was waiting for Lynnelle."

"You going to tell me what happened? Or make me get it question by question."

"We're not friends here, is that it? You're just a cop doing a job."

She shrugged, smiled, and nodded mildly. What kind of half-assed remark was that? He seemed to imply something that she didn't catch. The hell with it. She was a cop and this was her job. "What happened after Dr. Egersund arrived?"

He slouched further, letting his head rest on the seatback. "We stood around a while. The dog kept nudging us. She'd bound off, then trot back. Finally, we followed her."

"Whose idea was that?"

He looked at her. "Dr. Egersund's."

Susan waited.

He turned to look through the windshield. "The dog jumped in the creek. Pawed at Lynnelle, tugged at her. I got her face out of the water." He paused. "It was obvious she was dead."

"Did you touch anything in the house?"

"Only the telephone." He rubbed a hand over his face. "And the leash. The damn dog didn't want to leave her."

"Egersund go in the house?"

"No."

"How well do you know her?"

"We just met."

Susan buttoned up her trenchcoat and reached for the door handle. "Just for the record, where were you last night?"

He snapped alert. "It wasn't an accident?"

"Doesn't look that way."

"I'm a suspect," he said tightly.

"Come on, David, you're an attorney. You know how this works."

"I see. What times are we talking about?"

"From around eight to eleven."

"Home. Alone."

She nodded, opened the door and slid out. "You better go and change into dry clothes."

"If it's all the same with you, I'll wait till after you've wrung out Dr. Egersund."

This concern seemed a little odd, if they'd just met.

Egersund looked as though she hadn't moved the entire time Susan was with David. She still stood by the back step, one hand bunching her jacket at the throat, dog at her feet. In response to some imperceptible stiffening, the dog sat up and shifted nervously. Egersund reached down to pat her and her fingers twisted the thick fur.

Mistake, Susan thought. I should have questioned her first. Now she's had time to think about the answers. "How long have you known Lynnelle Hames?"

"I didn't know her." The words were barely audible, spoken through a thick gumbo of emotions.

What's this? "When did you meet her?"

Egersund blinked and seemed to bring her mind back from far away. "She came to my house last night and—"

"What time?" Susan deliberately interrupted. Rattle the woman a little, maybe shake her faith in her predetermined answers.

"About eight," Egersund said and waited.

Susan also waited a beat, then asked, "Why?"

"I think she wanted to ask about math classes."

The woman was lying, Susan thought, and not at all comfortable with it. Basically honest people don't make good liars. "You think?"

"I only assume that. She didn't stay long, simply said she'd changed her mind and then she left."

"You didn't know her. She came to your house at eight o'clock at night. She didn't say why she came. The only thing she said was she changed her mind?"

Egersund didn't respond.

"I don't understand, Dr. Egersund, since you didn't know her, saw her so briefly, why you came out here this morning."

She'd prepared herself for that one and had the answer ready. "Her coat." Egersund nodded at the blue down jacket lying across the board on the rope swing. "She forgot her coat."

Forgot her coat. Uh-huh. It was cold; it was raining. Lynnelle wouldn't have forgotten her coat unless she was greatly upset. Now, just what might she be upset about? And why hasn't Egersund mentioned it?

The medics came out of the woods carrying a stretcher with a black body bag. The dog trembled and whimpered as they stumbled along over the stepping stones, passed under the oak tree and turned to go up the drive. They loaded the stretcher, slammed the doors, and tramped around to the front of the ambulance. When they pulled away, the dog yelped and lunged, twisting and straining. She managed to slip her collar and tore after it, barking frantically in a high-pitched bark. She charged down the driveway and along the road.

When the ambulance disappeared, she padded back slowly, head down, tail drooping, sides heaving. She flopped to the gravel and dropped her head to her paws.

5

"BE IT EVER so humble." Susan, hands in her trenchcoat pockets, hunched her shoulders and shivered. The grim little house was so cold inside, her breath was visible.

"In a corner of hell called home," Parkhurst said dryly, as he glanced around the kitchen.

She raised an eyebrow; he had a greater capacity for concealment than anybody she'd ever known, and this kind of offhand comment made her curious.

They did one quick pass through the house; living room, two bedrooms, old-fashioned bathroom with ancient, stained claw tub. Fingerprint powder was everywhere. No need to worry whether Osey had missed anything; he loved to lift prints, and checked every surface available to touch and many that were not. The clouds and narrow windows kept out much of the daylight, making the house dim and gloomy; it smelled of damp wood and mildew.

Parkhurst prowled beside her with a tighter than usual control on the taut, economical way he moved. That extra edge bothered her, made him distant, as though he had something on his mind. They weren't exactly friends, but she'd come to rely on him and they'd developed bonds of respect, even affection, from working closely together.

Back in the kitchen, they started a thorough search. Lynnelle had attempted to jolly the place up with patches of vivid color; pink-flowered curtains at the window, oranges in a pottery bowl with a deep blue glaze on the rickety table. Susan snagged one of two mismatched wooden chairs, climbed up and peered into cabinets, half her mind occupied at feeling into dark corners behind dishes and the other half trying to contend with the startling idea that bedrock Parkhurst could change to shifting sand. Personal problems? For Christ's sake, he had no right to be anything but a Herculean tower of strength.

"Considerate landlord," he muttered.

She turned and looked down at him. "David?"

Parkhurst closed the door onto a closet space that housed the nonfunctioning furnace. "Who needs heat?"

"He offered to look at it." Why did she feel pushed into defending David? "Lynnelle was the one who said it could wait until morning. She had plans. What could be more important than heat?"

Parkhurst grunted, his face impassive, but a small muscle ticked at the corner of his jaw, the way it did when he was angry. He crouched to sort through cleaning supplies under the sink.

"You get anything from those two?" she asked, meaning David and Egersund. She wanted to check Parkhurst's reactions against her own.

"Our lady math teacher was flat-out lying and making a poor job of it. McKinnon was smoother."

"Smoother? You think David was lying?"

"At least withholding."

She trusted Parkhurst's instincts and agreed with him about Egersund, but wasn't so certain he was right about David. For some reason, he'd taken a dislike to David.

She jumped down, moved the chair aside and knelt in front of the lower cabinet. Stacking canned goods, mostly dog food, on the floor, she made a mental note to pick up some cat food.

Milk and salami probably wasn't an adequate diet. She didn't want the damn kitten to develop scurvy before she could get it back to Sophie.

One bedroom was completely empty except for a sleeping bag. The other also had a sleeping bag, a table lamp on the floor beside it, clothes hanging in the closet and, in the absence of a chest, cardboard cartons with socks, sweaters and underwear. A row of paperback books was lined up against the wall below the window. All the personal possessions in the whole house wouldn't amount to more than about one carload for the yellow VW.

"Why two sleeping bags?" she said.

"Guest room?"

"For someone who travels so light, it's odd she'd have two sleeping bags."

"Dog has her own room?"

"The dog slept with her." The blue bag was covered with white hairs. "Probably for companionship in this isolated place."

Parkhurst, squatting on the balls of his feet, riffled through the books. She examined the clothes in the closet with a faint flavor of apology. Any death did away with privacy, leaving no chance to take care of jumbled drawers or messy closets, throw away the useless or embarrassing, or protect secrets. A violent death meant strangers picking through all the personal possessions.

After her first homicide investigation, she'd tossed out every nonessential in her apartment, but she had kept things that were important, pictures—even photos of numerous cousins she barely knew in her father's large Catholic family—and other things of no value, but that had meaning to her; the locket Aunt Frannyvan had given her for her eighth birthday, shawls knitted by her Grandmother Donovan, addresses of long-gone friends. There was nothing like that here, no hints to secrets, nothing that indicated who Lynnelle was, what she was like.

"Where did she come from?" Susan closed the closet door, leaned against it and crossed her arms. "Why was she here? Why isn't there anything to go on? No snapshots, no letters from friends, no phone numbers, address book. Nothing."

"Runaway, maybe."

"She's a little past the age for that."

"Maybe running away from something."

"Uh-huh." Susan knelt, unzipped the sleeping bag, turned it inside out, checked beneath it. "This isn't right. She's got a phone." Susan lifted the receiver and listened to the dial tone. "Where are the phone bills? Gas bills? She had gas, electricity." Susan switched on the lamp, then rose, took two steps to the corner by the small window and looked out.

A red squirrel skittered along the tree branches outside. "She had a job, that means a paycheck. No checking account? And if she used cash, where is it? She had $9.47 in her wallet. No credit cards. Okay, she might not have any credit cards, but where's all this other stuff?"

"McKinnon, maybe?" Parkhurst rocked forward, got to his feet and handed her a hardbound book, cover open. "Julie Kalazar" was written on the flyleaf.

"Ah, our vice-chancellor's daughter." Susan closed the cover and read the title. *Theory of Probability.*

"Egersund teaches the class, if that means anything," Parkhurst said.

In the living room, he studied the brightly colored posters thumbtacked to walls splotched with damp spots. Behind the shabby gold chair, a coffee can brimmed with rainwater from a leak in the roof.

Susan couldn't see anything liveable about this house; even a working furnace, welcome as that would be, wouldn't do a whole lot. A guitar case lay by the Franklin stove and she knelt to open it. Guitar inside. Big surprise. She lifted it out and found a snapshot, facedown. She flipped the snapshot, then picked it up. "Well."

"What?"

She handed it to him. "Somebody we know?"

He grinned. "I do believe we have here a picture of Dr. Carena Egersund. Didn't she tell us she barely knew Lynnelle Hames?" He tapped the photo gently with a fingernail. "Taken some years back. I wonder who the kid is."

"Why would Lynnelle have a cozy picture of Egersund and kid tucked in with her guitar?"

Parkhurst looked at the snapshot like a hawk thoughtfully taking notice of a chicken wandering into view. "I will ask."

"Rouse somebody in personnel at Emerson and look at Lynnelle's file. Damn, it's Sunday. That's going to slow everything down. We've got nowhere to go here."

Irritated, she picked up the full coffee can, dumped it in the kitchen sink and set it back in its original place. "What have we got? Driver's license issued in Oklahoma. License plates on the car, ditto."

With both hands, she brushed hair back from her face. "Nothing we can do with that until tomorrow. First thing in the morning get a registration check from Department of Motor Vehicles and put through an inquiry to Department of Licensing. In the meantime, check Missing Persons. Maybe something will turn up there. And get started on the paperwork. We'll need to see phone company records, Kansas Power and Light, talk to somebody at the post office and find out if she's got a bank account."

He waited impassively. She didn't need to tell him all this; he knew it.

"I'll look at her personnel files right away," he said.

"You'll need a subpoena." That required a signature from the county district attorney. And that took time.

Parkhurst shook his head. "Oh, I don't think so. I'll get along to Mildred Makem. She's worked personnel at Emerson since the first brick was laid. She'll be delighted."

Susan stared at him. Once again, she was learning small towns were different. In San Francisco, she'd be cooling her heels until all the right papers, duly signed, were in her hands. She'd known cops who did a search first, and if they found anything, then applied for a search warrant and went through it all again. She liked to keep investigations clean; it avoided problems when it came to arrest and trial.

"It ought to show next of kin," he said. "Previous employment. And social security number."

"Yeah," she said. Although Social Security was notoriously slow and difficult to get information from. All those privacy laws. "Let me know what you find." She stuck the math textbook in her shoulder bag and set off for the Kalazar residence.

And it was a residence, as opposed to simply a house.

She knew Audrey Kalazar only in the way a good police chief knows the important people in town, and the vice-chancellor was never a woman to underestimate her importance. In other words, a certain amount of kowtowing was necessary. Keith Kalazar, a writer of some note, received celebrity status. Hampstead didn't have many celebrities. His books were of the life-is-grim, human-relationships-are-destructive variety; quite good books, actually.

The house was a two-story red brick with a row of white columns across the front, terraced grounds and flower beds waiting for spring flowers. She trudged up steps lined with cement urns and poked the doorbell. Chimes echoed away inside.

Keith Kalazar answered the door; a man straight out of central casting. Send us a writer. Late forties, brown hair and well-trimmed beard with a tasteful touch of gray, fawn jacket with leather elbow patches, pipe in hand. He looked distracted, as though she'd interrupted him in the midst of creation; maybe writers—like cops—worked on Sundays.

"Chief Wren. Is something wrong?"

She was a little surprised he knew her. She'd met him once or twice at town functions where Audrey was involved and he was always in the background; soft-spoken, rather vague and seemed a spectator in life rather than a participant. He must be more observant than she thought. "I'm sorry to interrupt you. I won't take long."

"When it's not going right, writers seize any chance at interruption." He led her into a large living room so immaculate it was intimidating; dark walnut floors, walnut tables, ivory rugs with beige borders. She perched on an ivory couch and hoped she wouldn't leave a crease, or, God forbid, a smudge.

"Can I offer you a drink?"

"No, thank you."

"If you've come to see Audrey, you're out of luck, I'm afraid. She's off to some conference." He stood with his back to French doors that opened onto a wide porch and an expanse of winter-brown grass with a pedestal birdbath in the exact center.

"It's Julie I need to see."

"Why?" His attention sharpened.

"A young woman has been killed—"

"Who?" He left his spot by the door and dropped into a wingbacked chair.

"Lynnelle Hames. Did you know her?"

He shook his head as he searched through pockets, found a book of matches, struck one and took a long time puffing on the pipe with the lit match held over the bowl. "What happened to her?"

"We don't know yet. Where can I find Julie?"

"Why Julie?" The words were heavy with worry.

"Just a few questions," she said calmly. "Lynnelle was a friend. I'm surprised you didn't know her."

"I may have met her. Kids seem to be in and out all the time. Sometimes I lose track."

Susan, nodding understandingly, wondered why he was reluctant to tell her where his daughter was. Parental protectiveness or something more? "Where is Julie?" she repeated smoothly, as if she were prepared to go on asking, all day if that's what it took. She watched him hesitate.

He puffed on the pipe, then said, "On campus. Studying. At the library."

As she opened the door of the pickup, she glanced up at the house and saw a curtain flick in a second-floor window. Making sure she left? She dropped down to Ridgefield and set off for campus. As she drove past Erle's Market, she spotted Sophie nipping inside. Susan made a left, parked the pickup in the lot and entered the store from the rear, wandered up and down aisles looking for Sophie.

"Chief Wren." The mayor's wife pinched an anemic-looking tomato and put it back. "We're not at all pleased."

I'm not at all surprised. Murder usually doesn't please anyone. Except the perpetrator.

Mrs. Bakover, a thin woman with artfully applied makeup and a sculptured hairdo that looked ten minutes old, waited for a reply. Susan complied. "I'm sorry to hear that."

"Those college girls came to see me yesterday with another application."

Oh. That. Mrs. Mayor obviously hadn't been listening to the local radio station.

"They claimed you told them they were entitled to a booth at the fair."

"It's to raise money for the Helping Hand Fund, right? They simply want to help."

"They'd better have something *hand*made, I can tell you that." Mrs. Bakover fingered the strand of pearls resting on her

45

beige sweater. "I hope you're prepared for trouble because trouble there's bound to be."

"What kind of trouble?"

"You mark my words. Information on AIDS." She looked highly indignant. "At the fair!"

"It could prevent someone from contracting the disease and the Helping Hand could then help someone else."

Mrs. Bakover sniffed and went back to selecting tomatoes. Not finding Sophie anywhere, Susan bought two slightly green bananas—not because ripe ones weren't available but because she only liked them green—and ate them while she drove to the campus.

Emerson College, with its mixture of modern glass and steel and old creamy limestone buildings, sprawled over and around small hills thick with trees and crisscrossed with pathways. On a knoll overlooking Pauffer Lake, a bronze statue of Josiah Hampstead gazed benignly into the distance. He'd come here in 1856 when Kansas was still a territory, laid claim to all the land he could see and built the gristmills that made him wealthy; mills famous for their ability to grind fifteen bushels of corn per hour. A free-stater, he was engaged in the bloody conflicts with pro-slavery men. The town was named after him, and he'd donated the land for the college.

She parked in the faculty lot, almost empty on Sunday afternoon. Heavy black clouds roiled overhead and one or two fat raindrops splotched across the windshield. The campanile bells chimed the hour and then struck four times. No wonder she was starving.

Turning up the collar of her trenchcoat, she strode along a path in the direction of the library. A student, huddled inside a hooded blue sweatshirt emblazoned with the glittery snarling wildcat, came toward her, muttering grimly to himself. "A equals F over M equals Wt minus R over M. *Remember* if R equals Wt then A equals O."

Right. I'll try to remember that. For all she knew he might be reciting the formula for a bomb. She trotted up the black marble steps of Keller Library, entered the hushed atmosphere of higher learning and scouted around for Julie. The long wooden tables were clotted with students, heads bent over books, scribbling away in notebooks. One young man lifted his head, stared at her, then darted a guilty look at his backpack. Oh ho, carrying around an illegal substance? It wasn't until she reached the top floor that she spotted Julie in the stacks.

"We can't," Julie, in blue jeans and a man's white shirt with the shirttail hanging almost to her knees, was whispering fiercely to a young Hispanic male in an Emerson sweatshirt.

"Why?" He had his hands in his back pockets and a scowl on his handsome face.

"Because." She put an imploring hand on his wrist.

He shrugged it off and brushed past her, stalking around Susan without a glance.

"Nick—" Julie turned and spotted Susan. "Oh— Chief Wren—" Surprise and dismay flickered in her hazel eyes.

"I'd like to speak with you for a few minutes, Julie."

"Oh. Well." She looked at Susan a shade frantically. "Sure. I guess." She shoved hair behind one ear, rapidly blinking back tears.

"Let's go across to the student union. I'll buy you some coffee."

Sprinkles of rain fell as they headed up the path to the union, one of the newer buildings, a row of glass doors along the front. They went down a flight of stairs to the coffee shop, rather cutely called the Cat's Cradle, in the basement. A snarling gold-painted cat, two feet high, crouched just inside the door.

The place was crowded with students; the babble of voices and clatter of crockery made the noise level just beyond bearable. This may not have been the best choice, Susan thought. Blue banners picturing the snarling cat hung on the red brick walls. The air felt steamy with the odor of brewed coffee and damp wool and frying grease. The almost palpable energy emanating from all these kids made her want to sigh. Had she ever been this young and fresh-faced? She bought coffee for herself, cinnamon tea for Julie, and they worked around to a far corner where they managed to snag a table.

"Who were you talking to?" She asked Julie when they were seated.

"Nick. Nick Salvatierra. A friend."

Uh-huh, Susan thought.

Julie hunched her shoulders and busied herself dunking the tea bag in the mug of hot water. "He's in my calculus class."

Susan took a sip of bitter coffee and studied the girl's bent head. She was attractive, with a wholesome, scrubbed appearance, and at the moment very worried about something.

Julie glanced up, caught Susan's gaze and sat straight. "So. What did you want to ask me?"

Susan pulled the textbook from her bag and slid it across the table.

Julie grabbed it and dropped it in her lap. "Where'd you find it?"

"Lynnelle's house."

A deep flush spread across Julie's cheeks, tears welled in her eyes. "I heard about that. What happened?"

"I don't know yet. How did your textbook get out there?"

Julie rubbed the back of a finger across her eyes, then fiddled with the spoon, smoothing the ball of her thumb in the bowl. "We were friends."

"She wasn't a student."

"That doesn't mean we couldn't be friends," Julie retorted.

"Of course not." Nevertheless, it was unusual. Students made friendships among themselves and seldom went outside their own circle. "Has somebody suggested otherwise? Nick maybe?"

"No. Why would he?"

"Did he know her?"

Julie shrugged. "Sure."

Something was going on here that Susan didn't understand. Handsome Nick might deserve some attention. She fished in her bag for cigarettes and lit one. Julie, with a tiny frown of disapproval, lifted the mug with both hands and took a cautious sip. Susan turned her head to exhale.

"Probability stinks," a young male at the next table said to his friend. "I miss one lousy question and Egersund gives me a *B.*"

"Well shit, man. She gave me a *C.*"

"Yeah? What'd you miss?"

Susan turned back to Julie. "Did Lynnelle ever talk about her family?"

"Not a lot. She was kind of secretive, but I don't think she liked them very much. She said one time that you can't trust anybody. Not even your own parents." Julie gave her a wry smile. "Sometimes I can sort of understand that. Not that I don't trust my parents, but sometimes they can be too much."

"Did she ever seem worried about anything? Or frightened?"

"She did, kind of," Julie said slowly, as though she was thinking back. "She never said much. I might of been worried living out there all by myself, but that didn't seem to bother her. Well, she had the dog. Not that Lexi'd be much good. I told her that dog couldn't even protect her from the ghost."

"Ghost?"

Julie pushed hair behind her ear and twisted a strand. "You know, old man Creighton. He died years and years ago and he had pots and pots of money. When I was a kid, we were scared to go near the place because old Creighton's ghost was supposed to be hovering around protecting the money."

"Did she say why she came here?"

"She was looking for her past."

How much past could a twenty-one-year-old girl have? "What did she mean?"

"I never figured that out. It's probably in her notebook though."

"Notebook?" There had been no notebook in the house.

"She was always writing in it. A three-ring binder, blue."

"Who were her friends?"

Julie lifted the mug and held it between both hands. "Well, Edie."

"Edie Vogel? Your mother's secretary? Anybody else? What about boyfriends?"

Julie shook her head, lowered the mug and sat peering into it.

Susan could tell she was concealing something; it sat oddly on her fresh-scrubbed face, but Susan felt no further progress was possible until she learned more. Julie looked back up and her eyes were shiny with tears.

"Call me," Susan said, "if you think of anything else that might help."

With a nod, Julie rose, clutched the textbook to her chest and edged around crowded tables toward the door.

Susan spent forty minutes looking for Nick Salvatierra. He was no longer at the library; he wasn't in his room at the dorm; nobody she asked knew where he was. She gave it up and walked through the fading daylight and light rain back to the parking lot.

A couple, oblivious of the rain, stood nose to nose in front of the pickup. "Jerk!" the young woman spat. "You'd probably understand me better if I was a football."

The young man, looking bewildered and guilty and contrite, scooped her into an embrace. Over her shoulder, he glanced at Susan and crossed his eyes. Smiling, Susan aimed a finger at the center of his forehead and climbed in the pickup.

6

THE RADIO CRACKLED and Susan picked up the mike.

"Ben's trying to get hold of you," Hazel said.

"Patch him through."

Parkhurst's voice came over, distorted by interference. "In regard Lynnelle's job application. No next of kin listed. Previous address in Boulder, Colorado. Previous employment, ticket seller at a movie theater in Oklahoma City, receptionist for electronics firm, also Oklahoma City. Social security number."

"No home address or permanent address?"

"Negative."

Damn. "All right. Get on to Boulder PD. See what they can give us. Contact previous places of employment. Although that'll probably have to wait until Monday. Lynnelle is not Jane Smith. It can't be that hard to track down."

"Right. And I'll have another shot at Egersund and McKinnon."

"Be polite."

It was five-thirty when Susan parked in front of the small white frame with brick trim where Edie Vogel lived. A street light sparkled through drizzle, and moisture dripped disconsolately from the bare-limbed tree in a deep front yard full of dead weeds which straggled across the walk. She tapped on the aluminum storm door; the front door had a heavy glass panel covered by a sheer curtain stretched between two rods. A porch light went on. Edie pulled the curtain aside and peered out, then slid back the curtain; a second or two went by before she opened the door.

"You've come about Lynnelle," Edie said in a flat voice.

Although light spilled from the kitchen, the living room was in darkness and Edie, moving heavily, switched on lamps. She was a sturdy young woman of twenty-two with broad shoulders and brown hair cut into points around what should be a pert little face, but her face was pale and slack with a shadow of despair behind her brown eyes, and the eyes were red and puffy.

Last November, her ex-husband had picked up their two-year-old daughter for the Thanksgiving weekend and never brought her back. After several days of frantic phone calls trying to find them, she came to the police. Susan hated any domestic disturbance—all cops did, too potentially explosive—but snatching a kid made her savagely furious. She'd explained the legalities and Edie obtained a court order stipulating the ex-husband had violated the custody agreement. With that, Susan could put out his description, photo and a pickup alert. She'd also suggested a private investigator. Edie had clutched at that like a drowning woman. Each time Susan saw her she seemed a little thinner, a little more bleak.

A tea kettle whistled in the kitchen and Edie jumped. "I'll just turn off the stove," she said.

Susan sat in an armchair upholstered with a fuzzy fabric of large pink flowers and green leaves. On the matching couch lay a dog-eared teddy bear and two tattered children's books. A ceramic vase of a sleeping puppy with plastic flowers sat on the coffee table. A child's square wooden stepping block was pulled up close to the coffee table, across the seat was a verse: *This is my stool for watching TV. For brushing my teeth. Or doing a job that's bigger than me.*

From the kitchen came the sound of running water and a moment later Edie reappeared. She settled on the couch, feet close together on the floor like a schoolgirl, and arranged the tan plaid skirt over her knees.

"When did you last see Lynnelle?"

"Friday after work we walked to the parking lot."

"She had plans for Saturday evening, something that was important. Did she mention them?"

Edie stared at her hands, picked at a Band-Aid on one finger, and shook her head.

"What did she say?"

"Nothing really. We just talked. I told her about Dr. Egersund."

"What about Dr. Egersund?" Finding the body automatically made Egersund a suspect, but Susan was beginning to think they should take a real serious look at the woman.

"Dr. Kalazar was furious with her. She called her into her office, Dr. Kalazar's, I mean, and I heard them through the door."

"Arguing?"

"More like Dr. Kalazar was reading her out. In this loud voice. Not shouting, but mean and threatening."

"What did she say?"

"I couldn't hear it all." Edie hunched her shoulders. " 'How dare you interfere.' And 'I know what's best for my daughter.' And she said, 'You better stick to teaching or I'll see to it you won't teach here.' "

"What had Dr. Egersund done?"

"I couldn't hear that part. She came out all mad, Dr. Egersund, with her face all tight and walked real soft right by me without saying anything." Edie paused. "She better be careful because Dr. Kalazar gets real irritated when things aren't the way she wants and she doesn't give anybody a second chance."

Grabbing the teddy bear, Edie held it in the crook of her arm and caressed its grimy head. "She didn't like Lynnelle."

"Dr. Egersund?"

"Dr. Kalazar."

"Why not?"

Edie gave a quick grin and for a brief moment she was the impudent farm girl with a sly sense of humor. "Lynnelle told Julie she was old enough to make her own decisions."

Susan could well believe Audrey didn't like that. Audrey kept firm control over everything that was hers, and wouldn't put up with any sort of palace revolution.

The flash of animation disappeared. "It's not right. Lynnelle was a friend. She helped me. Told me I had to keep going." Edie stared unseeing at the stepstool by the coffee table, her face so sad Susan wanted to track down the ex-husband and string him up by the balls. Jesus, how could a parent damage a child like that?

Tears trickled down Edie's face; she wiped at them with a tissue and blew her nose. "I'm sorry. I can't seem to help it."

Susan got the impression Edie had said that a good many times recently. "Did Lynnelle ever mention her family?"

Edie took a moment before answering. "Not much. I got the feeling she was mad at them about something, but she never said. She did talk about Rose dying though."

"Rose?"

"Her mother. She had cancer."

Edie started crying again, head bent over the teddy bear. Susan waited, feeling helpless.

"Why did it have to happen?" Edie's words were barely audible.

"I don't know, Edie," Susan said in a voice almost as soft.

Edie took in a deep shuddery breath. "I think she was afraid of somebody."

Susan's ears twitched at that. "Who?"

"She got a phone call and she went all stiff like she was mad and scared at the same time. She said 'no' two or three times. Not right together, but no and then she would listen and no again. Then she said, you'll be sorry and she hung up real hard."

Caller threatening Lynnelle? Lynnelle threatening caller? "Who was she talking with?"

Edie blew her nose again. "I asked her. She said she couldn't talk about it."

"Where were you?"

"At her house."

"What time was it?"

"Evening. We were going to a movie and the phone rang. She was real quiet after that. We saw the movie and all, but she didn't say much after."

"What day was this?"

Edie took a slow breath. "Two Saturdays ago."

"What made you think she was afraid?"

"I don't know exactly. She just seemed kind of scared-like."

"Thank you, Edie," Susan said as she stood up to leave. "You've been very helpful."

Even the drizzle had given up when Susan headed for the station. She needed to talk with George. As late as it was, he'd probably gone home, but she'd leave him a note to see her in the morning.

The police department, a square red-brick building adjacent to city hall, was located near the heart of town on a side street lined with bare-limbed maple trees. George, seated at his desk, raised his head when she ambled in and his glasses flashed from the harsh glare of the fluorescent ceiling fixture.

"You're still here." She slid up a chair, plopped down and fumbled for her cigarettes.

"Catching up on a few things." He gave her a long look, then with a sigh dumped the paper clips from the ashtray. "You smoke too much." A man in his early sixties, wearing a gray suit, white shirt and tie, he was everybody's idea of the kindly grandfather; gentle face with a touch of wry humor, mild blue eyes behind rimless glasses, gray hair bald spot in back. He looked all set to entertain the kiddies with magic tricks. None of this meant he wasn't very sharp. He was a lot smarter than most and his memory was phenomenal. He'd spent his entire life in Hampstead and a big portion of it as a cop. He knew more about the residents then they probably knew about themselves.

"Lynnelle Hames." Susan clicked her lighter, lit a cigarette, and blew smoke at the ceiling. "According to Julie Kalazar, Lynnelle came here looking for her past."

"Past meaning relatives here?" He picked up a pen and tapped it thoughtfully against the desk.

"Her mother's name was Rose. She died of cancer."

George shook his head. "I can think of half a dozen name of Rose, but to my knowledge there's never been a Hames. It's possible she's related to somebody who lived here at one time, now long moved away. Or the Hames could have been married into. If she has relatives here, why haven't they come right out and said so?"

"Maybe they didn't know she was related. Or maybe they— he, she, whoever—killed her."

"Well now, that's a possibility, I suppose. You got any ideas why anybody'd do such a thing?"

"No."

"Well then, while you're thinking up fancy plots, I'll see what I can find out about unknown relatives. Any leads to the killer?"

She stubbed out the cigarette and rose. "Not unless a ghost did it."

"You heard about the ghost, did you?"

She slung the strap of her bag over her shoulder. "Let me know what you find."

"You don't want to hear about Howie's ghost? Now, Susan,

56

we'll never make a small-town cop out of you, if you don't learn all this local history."

"Is this a long story, George? Because I'm tired and I'm hungry and I need to stop at the market before I can go home."

"Hardly take any time at all. Sit yourself."

Settling back with a squeak of the chair, he rested his elbows on the arms. "Howard Creighton died eight years ago at the age of eighty-four. For thirteen years prior he was a recluse, closed himself up in that house and fired a shotgun at anybody who set foot on the land."

"Anybody killed?"

"Nope, salt pellets. Left a few kids with sore behinds. Everybody knew he was crazy, but he was one of ours, so we made room for him, like happens in small towns. His folks were farmers and when they died, he got the farm, which turned out to have oil under it, and he already had a going tractor business."

"You saying he was rich? Then why did he live in that shacky house?"

"I'm getting there, just be patient. The man was a genius with machinery, invented some kind of carburetor for tractors. He married and had one son late in life who was supposed to be big and strong and carry on the business. Except the son—Lowell, his name was, after his mother's father—wasn't much good with machinery. He wanted to play the violin."

"You're making this up."

"God's truth. Old Howard was blustery and gruff, and didn't see eye to eye with Lowell about most things. Lowell's mother left him some money when she died—some kind of female troubles—and Lowell was the one who bought that house so he could get away from Howie. Besides the trouble with his father, he was having a love affair with his music teacher and folks were beginning to talk."

Susan snorted. "Was she the church organist or something?"

"Close." George hooked a finger over his glasses, slid them down and looked at her over the top. "Mr. Spenski was the choir director."

"Oh."

"You can imagine the kind of scandal that caused. Lowell's life was made miserable. One Halloween night he up and hanged himself in that little house."

"That's a ghastly story, George. I assume the ghost is going to turn up here soon."

"After his son's suicide, Howie started getting peculiar. He sold out everything and moved himself into that house. Rumor was he hid all the money out there somewhere. When he died, nothing was found. That's when the ghost stories started, eerie noises and strange lights flickering. The idea was that old Howie's spirit was guarding the money."

George leaned forward with another squeal of the chair and rested his forearms on the edge of the desk. "The reality of it was treasure hunters, creeping around trying to find buried gold. Nobody ever did and after a time it all faded away, including Howie's ghost."

"Does any of this have anything to do with Lynnelle's death?"

"Well maybe not, unless she stumbled across the gold and somebody killed her for it, which does sound like a heap of nonsense, doesn't it?"

"Did Creighton have any relatives?"

"Well now, there's something a mite interesting maybe. One nephew, his wife's sister's son, who lived in Boston at that time."

"What's his name?"

George smiled. "I wondered if you'd get around to that." He leaned back and crossed his arms. "Attorney by the name of David McKinnon."

At ten past seven she set off for home, thinking about David McKinnon. She couldn't believe in buried treasure and strongly doubted, even if it existed, that it had anything to do with Lynnelle's death. David had found the body, and he had moved it; that always roused suspicion and, as an attorney, he knew better, but his reason was tenable. He'd inherited the land and hadn't bothered to mention it, but he may have thought she already knew about Uncle Howard.

As she waited at a red light, she rubbed her eyes and told herself it was too early to speculate. She'd only just begun. She didn't even know anything about the victim yet. What past did this child have? Where did she come from? What happened in her short life that led to murder?

The light turned green and after a moment of unawareness, Susan drove on. Much of her fatigue came from a sticky feeling of negligence.

Let's not get carried away. That instant bond she'd felt with Lynnelle, sensing they shared feelings of abandonment and loneliness and isolation were all in her own mind. Maybe it had been nothing but projection.

Halfway home, she remembered the cat and with an irritated sigh backtracked to Erle's market for kitty munchies and flat cans of liver and fish.

Twenty minutes later, she pulled the pickup into the garage, grabbed the grocery bag and hurried to the house, hoping the damn kitten was all right; she'd been gone a long time. Snapping on the kitchen light, she plunked the bag on the table. "Cat? Where are you?"

In the doorway to the living room, she looked around with appalled disbelief. Ashes had been excavated from the fireplace and spread across the silver-blue carpet. Smudged paw prints covered the blue flowered couch and oak tables. The kitten, black as a coal miner, high-stepped toward her with its tail erect, nattering delight at her arrival.

"Ooh," she muttered darkly, "your days are numbered."

7

GRILLED, CARENA THOUGHT, closing the door after Lieutenant Parkhurst's retreating back. Roasted over the coals on one side, then flipped and roasted on the other. She'd felt he never would leave; just sit forever on her couch asking question after question, and making it obvious he didn't believe anything she said. And why should he? It was riddled with lies.

Scary man, this Parkhurst. He made her think of Jehovah, the angry God her father knew so well. Thou shalt not tell a lie. Bear false witness, a voice in her head pointed out with pedantic accuracy. How damnable was that one? Probably right up there between Thou shalt not commit adultery and Thou shalt not kill.

Alexa nudged her knee and looked up anxiously. Carena ran a hand over the dog's furry head. And that was a stupid thing to do too, offer to keep Lynnelle's dog until her family was located. She'd known it even as she opened her mouth, but couldn't stop herself. She'd felt guilty, or angry, or resentful. Or something.

The tape in her mind constantly replayed itself; the trees and the creek and the body in the water, like a bundle of old clothes, soaked and moving slightly with the current.

In the bedroom, she punched in a phone number. Phil answered. Damn. She couldn't talk to Caitlin while her husband was there. She asked for Caitlin, thinking she'd tell her to call back when he was away.

"I thought she was with you," he said.

"What do you mean with me?"

"She said you called."

"Yes." She tried not to bristle at the implied accusation. She and Phil had never liked each other but there was no point in antagonizing him.

"She left a note." Papers rustled in the background and she pictured him at his very organized desk flipping through a file labeled Problems, Domestic. "Don't worry, I'm fine. Something came up. I'll call."

"Has she called?"

"Not yet."

"Well, when she does would you tell her to call me?"

"Sure," he said and hung up.

Carena wasn't so sure he would.

Sleep was a long time coming that night. Her mind was remembering the awful summer twenty-one years ago. The heat—sticky, oppressive heat—the scared feelings of inadequacy, and the worry, lying awake at night with worry. All the lies and agonizing over whether she was doing the right thing. And then time running out, summer coming to an end and the panic increasing as each day went by and the baby still didn't arrive and it was one more day closer to the beginning of school.

Let it go, she told herself, rolled over in bed, bunched the pillow under her head and looked at the clock. Two A.M. Get to sleep. She rolled the other way, turning her back to the clock. If she didn't watch the time, maybe her body wouldn't realize how little sleep it would get.

As soon as she closed her eyes, she saw Lynnelle again, face down in the water, blond curls moving lazily with the current.

Oh no, a voice said. Let's not do that again. We've been over it and over it too many times already.

When she finally went to sleep, she dozed fitfully and woke at six on Monday morning with a headache. The picture of Lynnelle in vivid color popped immediately to mind and she tried to erase it with aspirin and a shower. She still had to teach and she'd better start thinking about today's classes. Even before Lynnelle, this school year had been hard-going. In all her years of teaching, she'd never had one so difficult. Of course, she'd never taught after a divorce before. It did powerful things to the concentration, like giving it a tendency to sit in one groove and snivel. Embarrassing too. When your wonderful husband suddenly decided to run away from home to find himself and took along a grad student, presumably to help him do it, you tended to be mightily embarrassed, and wonder what a nice person like you was doing in a cliché like this. And now there was Lynnelle. Why hadn't Caitlin called?

"Have you seen this?" Hazel sat a mug of coffee on Susan's desk and handed her the *Herald,* tapping a finger on the front page article about Lynnelle's murder. No picture. Probably couldn't find one.

Susan nodded. The paper, more accustomed to lost dogs, local sports events and articles on Mrs. Whatsit took first prize in the raspberry strudel competition and Mr. Whoever caught a so-many-pound catfish at Potter's Point, would play it for all it was worth. If she didn't kick into second gear here, the good citizens would be cowering behind locked doors and acquiring Dobermans who would eat the neighbor's children.

She dropped the newspaper on the budget, which was still blank. And blank was what they still were on Lynnelle's background. Missing Persons turned up nothing; routine check of police records turned up nothing. Department of Licensing in Oklahoma had come through with a confirmation of driver's license issued to Lynnelle Hames with not so much as a speeding ticket against it. Department of Motor Vehicles had the yellow VW as registered to William Radler in Oklahoma City. No stolen vehicle report. No word yet on this Radler.

"Dr. Fisher's office called," Hazel said. "He's finished the autopsy and you can stop by the pathology department and pick up the preliminary results if you want."

"Tell him I'm on the way."

The pathology department was located in the basement of Brookvale Hospital in the middle of a warren of offices connected by corridors leading to the various nonmedical departments required to keep the place running; generators, laundry, housekeeping, maintenance, engineering.

Upstairs, all was light, and pleasantly decorated; down here was strictly utilitarian, brown vinyl floors and scuffed white walls. She sensed, rather than heard, the hum of huge machinery and caught glimpses through open doorways of electrical ducts large enough to crawl through. Hospital personnel, busy and purposeful, constantly bustled along from place to place.

She passed the lab, brilliantly lit, with technicians working on the specimens of blood, urine and tissue from the patients above. Computerized equipment softly muttered to itself as it churned out the results of the information fed into it. Detective work of a different kind, she thought, tracking down perpetrators of pain and illness; after death, pursuing the killer.

Owen Fisher's office was small, lined with bookshelves, framed anatomical illustrations on the walls. Wearing surgical greens, including booties, he sat at his desk, littered with what looked like exotic insects, deftly twisting string around little bits of fluff. He finished the one he was working on and put it in line with its fellows.

"Fishing lures," he said, noticing her glance. "I'm donating them to the fair." He pushed a file across the desk toward her.

She paged through it, scanning rapidly. "Death by drowning."

"Just like I thought. The blow was enough to cause loss of consciousness, but not severe enough to be fatal. If she hadn't had her face underwater."

"What kind of weapon are we looking for?"

"A hammer, something like that."

"Time of death?"

"Ten Saturday night, an hour either way." He picked up something vaguely green and, almost too quickly to see, his long slender fingers created a dragonfly.

"Identifying marks?"

"Nothing out of the way. Small scar on her knee, superficial cut that should have been stitched. Some dental work. Two small fillings in back molars. Last meal maybe five hours earlier. I'm working on stomach contents. I'll let you know."

"Drugs?"

He shook his head, frowned at the dragonfly, apparently found it lacking and tossed it in the wastepaper basket. "Healthy young female. Five-foot one, a hundred and three pounds."

"Trace elements?"

He looked at her. "She was in the creek with water rushing over her in pouring-down rain. What do you think?"

Susan nodded. "Is there anything else?"

"One thing." He started twisting together another dragonfly. "She had a splinter embedded in her left palm. Half-inch long. Happened shortly before death. I've sent it to the lab."

"Where'd it come from? The weapon?"

"Maybe. Could have tried to grab at it, protect herself. Not my department. Could have tried to grab at her assailant and he had wood slivers on his clothing. Any fibers, if there were any, got washed away."

When she got back to her office, she mentioned the splinter

to Parkhurst. "Keep an eye out for any place it might have come from."

"Right," he said and started to leave.

"Parkhurst, did Egersund tell you anything yesterday evening?"

Parkhurst, in black pants and black turtleneck sweater, turned back and paced across to the window. "No," he said with a half-admiring shake of his head. "She's worried, and a couple of times I thought I had her, but she just got more tight-lipped and stuck to denials. Her stock answer was, I don't know, occasionally varied with, I have no idea. I asked her about the snap of her and the kid. She said the kid was her son. What was Lynnelle doing with it? She had no idea." He rubbed the back of his neck. "I haven't yet found anybody who ever saw the two of them together."

Susan thought Egersund must be pretty strong to stand firm against Parkhurst's questioning. "What have we got on her?"

"Osey's working on it." He paced back across the room, reversed direction, took six strides to the desk and stopped. "What happened to your hands?"

"Nothing." She slid her hands, crisscrossed with scratches, from the desktop to her lap. Giving the kitten a bath hadn't been one of her brighter ideas. "If you see Sophie anywhere, let me know. I want to talk with her."

He took six strides to the window, paused to stare through the blind slats. "I just came from your hotshot attorney."

"Mine?"

"McKinnon's one of the new breed." Parkhurst turned. "Sensitive, probably has emotions. The kind recommended in how-to-choose-a-mate books written by women."

"Ha. In other words, a nice man. Never having had that quality yourself, you simply didn't recognize it."

Parkhurst grinned. "Never trust a man who doesn't hit you when you call him a liar."

"You called David McKinnon a liar?"

"The merest of suggestions." He resumed pacing.

"What did you merely suggest he was lying about?"

"The reason he let the kid stay there. He said she needed a place to live, the house was empty."

"You have a quarrel with that?"

"I pushed on it a little, *merely suggesting* there might be more to it." Parkhurst picked up a glass paperweight from the desk on his next pass and tossed it into the air. "In a manly cringe of embarrassment, he admitted that was true. What else, I asked. Guilt, he said."

"I assume you followed up on that?"

"You can believe it. That's when we descended into pop psychology. Turned out we weren't talking guilt about murder, but Guilt with a capital *G*. Vague concerns of neglecting—unfortunate result of divorce—his own daughter who is only a few years younger." Parkhurst held up the paperweight and stared broodily into it. "I prefer simple motives like lust or greed."

"What are you getting at?"

"Lust is fairly self-explanatory. Greed, maybe that doesn't apply. Unless it came from the other side." He tossed the paperweight, caught it and set it back on the desk. "Maybe Lynnelle had some leverage to convince him to let her stay there."

"Blackmail?" Susan thought of the phone call Edie had over-heard. *You'll be sorry.*

"It's another simple motive, self-preservation."

"Any evidence?"

"No." He paced to the window.

"Parkhurst, sit down! You're making me dizzy."

Hazel stuck a worried face around the doorway. She'd been dispatcher here for more work years than Susan's and Park-hurst's combined and took care of everybody with little clucks of concern. The friction between the two of them bothered her motherly soul.

Parkhurst leaned back, propped his shoulders and one foot against the wall and raised an eyebrow. Susan put an enquiring look on her face. Hazel gave them each a frown of exasperation, the adult who is about to say, if you two can't get along, go to your rooms. When she withdrew, Parkhurst hooked an ankle around the chair leg, pulled it closer and sat low on his spine.

Susan told him about Julie Kalazar's mention of a notebook and her defensiveness about Nick Salvatierra. "Check again for that notebook. I know—" She raised a hand. "We couldn't have missed it. Just check. And get a read on this kid. Julie's afraid for him, and I want to know why."

Parkhurst rose.

"And Parkhurst, don't be rough with this kid. Understand?"

"I'll use my fatherly manner."

"You don't have a fatherly manner."

He smiled. "Depends on what kind of father you had."

At one, Susan walked the three blocks over to Second Street, headed for the Coffee Cup Café. Whenever she passed two or more people together, she heard Lynnelle's name mentioned. Six times in the five minutes it took her to get there. People were nervous. Take heed, she told herself, raise the department's visibility.

Above the café, a sign showed happy donuts and sandwiches dancing on the steam rising from a huge cup of mud-colored liquid. Inside, it smelled of frying hamburger and fresh-cut onions. The place was crowded, noisy with chatter and the clatter of crockery; all the booths along the front windows were full and most of the stools at the counter.

Bess Greely presided at the cash register and greeted her with a big smile. "What can I get for you?" Large-boned and stout, short brownish hair, round face with a short upper lip, her greatest pleasure in life was feeding people. She wore a loose-fitting dress in a loud print, red and orange poppies.

"It's terrible about that young one," she said as she packaged the turkey sandwich Susan had requested.

Big-city crime was anonymous, small-town crime touched everybody.

The two brawny males in Levi's and plaid shirts sitting on the nearest stools stopped arguing politics and looked at her. "Just let me alone with him in a dark alley for ten minutes," one of them said. "I'd show him how we feel around here about murdering girls."

Oh great, Susan thought. Just what we need.

Bess nodded agreement at the vigilante, turned back to Susan and handed her the sandwich. "What else would you like?"

"That'll do it."

"Now you have to have more than that. That's not enough to keep a bird alive. How 'bout a nice piece of apple pie? Fresh-baked."

It was easier to agree than to argue and Susan left with sandwich and pie before Bess could suggest ice cream to go along with it.

Back at her desk, she spread out a napkin, opened the wrapper and was all set to take a hefty bite when Detective Osey Pickett ambled in.

"Just got off the phone with Austin, Texas." He collapsed into the armchair. "About this Radler guy. Owned the VW?"

Osey, twenty-nine years old with straw-colored hair, was thin and lanky, and had large hands and feet that always seemed to get in his way. His speech was a lot slower than his thoughts, and he had a bashful, aw-shucks sense of humor. In dealing with the public, he was affable and low-keyed. Unlike Parkhurst, who could put the fear of God into people, Osey went out of his way to be generous and considerate. People tended to like Osey.

"Said he traded it in for a new Ford Taurus six months ago. I got Oklahoma City putting an eyeball on the dealer's invoices."

"Anything else?"

"Well, not really. Mail carrier remembers letters from somebody in Kansas City. First name is Shelley. He remembers it because his little girl's got the same name. Can't remember the last name. Thought it was something like Shoehorn. Near as I can find out, there's nobody name of Shoehorn in Kansas City."

"What about the telephone records?"

"I'm just about to go over there right now." In a series of uncoordinated jerks, he got to his feet.

"Let's hope she called home once a week."

"Or even somewhere with a toll." He sketched a salute.

She picked up the sandwich, but hadn't even gotten her mouth open when the phone buzzed.

"Mayor Bakover on the line," Hazel said.

Briefly, Susan considered saying she was out. "Put him through."

"Where are you on this hippie's murder?"

"We are proceeding with the investigation."

"I hope you're proceeding in a hurry. I told you to get her out of there. If you had, this wouldn't have happened."

That was so unjust, she didn't even bother to respond to it.

"Concerned citizens are wondering if we should set up a curfew."

"That might be a little precipitate." She could just imagine how the college students would react to that.

The mayor made a disgruntled sound. "Keep me informed."

"Yes sir, I'll do that."

When she finally got to her sandwich, the bread was slightly dried around the edges.

* * *

Carena was short-tempered with the denseness of young minds that weren't grasping the elements of statistical test of hypothesis. She labored to get across null hypothesis, alternative hypothesis, test statistic and rejection region. With forced patience, she attempted to explain that the specification of those elements defined a particular test and changing one or more created a new test. By last period the pounding in her head was so great her teeth hurt and when the class finally ground to an end the skin on her face felt too tight.

Most of the students scooped up their belongings and clattered out, but a handful clustered around her desk. Standing behind it like it was a barricade, she forced a smile and murmured as she packed her briefcase that questions would have to wait, she didn't have time this afternoon. With good-natured grumbling they scattered, all except Julie Kalazar, who hesitated, hands in the pockets of a full khaki skirt. She wore a long yellow sweater over it with a print scarf tied around her waist.

"Dr. Egersund, I wonder—"

Carena shoved papers into her briefcase and snapped it shut with a loud click.

"Could I talk to you for a minute?"

Carena clenched her teeth against a sharp response; she'd reached the end of her reserve and couldn't cope with one more problem. "I'm sorry, Julie, I really must go. Could it wait until tomorrow?"

"I just wondered if the police were, you know, guarding the place."

"I have no idea, Julie. Why do you ask?"

"No reason," Julie said too quickly.

With an effort, something like separating velcro, Carena pulled her mind from her own worry and really looked at Julie. Her young wholesome face, framed by straight brown hair, looked sallow above the yellow sweater, and the skin slack with worry.

Carena regretted her shortness. Poor kid. Her well-structured life had suddenly developed cracks in the walls and she could glimpse the monsters outside.

"Well, thanks—" Julie started to leave.

"Julie?"

She turned.

"I doubt the police are still out there, but I don't know. Is there something there you wanted?"

"No. I just, you know, wondered."

"Can I help—?"

Julie shook her head, and Carena got the impression she was sorry she'd opened her mouth. She's afraid, Carena realized, scared stiff the police will find something out there. Wondering if it's safe to go and get it.

Clutching her briefcase, Carena walked slowly and carefully to avoid jarring her pounding head.

In the parking lot, she had to set the briefcase on the ground before she could unlock the car door. Resting her forehead against the steering wheel, she thought, if the old Volvo doesn't start, I'm going to shriek. Cantankerous at the best of times, it invariably picked last straw moments to refuse to budge.

She straightened, stuck the key in the ignition and turned it. The motor ground slowly and she fed it a little gas—too much and she'd flood it, then it wouldn't start for God knew how long. The motor coughed and sputtered, she coaxed it gently, and remembered Lynnelle's dog. The poor thing was probably in dire need.

Alexa heard her drive into the garage and barked with short, staccato yips. When the kitchen door opened, the dog threw itself on her with joyous delirium. Dodging wet kisses, she knelt and hugged the big furry dog. "Never before has my mere appearance made anybody so happy."

When Alexa calmed a bit, Carena let her out in the backyard and stood in the screened porch while the dog trotted around investigating interesting scents and taking care of needs. The yard was fenced across the back and along one side; the only unfenced area was the space between the garage and the house.

The dog, glancing up at Carena every now and again with a wave of her tail, worked her way toward the garage. Then with a final glance, she took off, bounding down the driveway.

"Alexa!" Carena hit the screen door with her palm and dashed down the steps. At the end of the driveway, she saw the dog streak around the corner.

"Lexi!" She raced to the corner, circled the block, then dashed in for her car keys and drove through the neighborhood, making wider and wider circles. "Should have known better than to let the damn dog out without a leash."

She doesn't even belong to me. Oh gee, I'm sorry, Lieutenant, but you see I let her out. She had to go out, you know, and then she ran away and then this great big truck came along and squashed her flat.

Oh hell, bloody hell.

Don't panic. *Nicht panikan,* as Father says. Maybe the dog is headed for Lynnelle's; it is the only home the poor thing knows.

Carena searched both sides of the streets, horribly afraid of coming upon a furry white carcass in the gutter. By the time she reached the Creighton place it was almost four-thirty and beginning to get dark. The temperature had dropped and she shivered as she got out of the car. Pigeons or something nested under the eaves and she heard ghostly stirrings. The wind blew, stinging her face. She shoved her hands into the pockets of her tweed coat.

"Alexa? Lexi!" Her breath made little frosty clouds in the cold air. She waited, called again and then heard a responding bark. The dog was somewhere in the woods.

"Lexi!" She set off across the irregular stones under the oak tree with the rope swing, and traipsed through winter-dead grass.

It was darker under the trees, a shadowy dark that lent imagined form to shapes just behind the next tree trunk. She wasn't dressed for hiking through the wilderness and her heels sank into damp, rotting vegetation. There goes a perfectly good pair of black pumps.

She heard squishy sounds of footsteps on wet leaves and stopped to look behind her, expecting to see someone. Trees and low undergrowth, not even a squirrel scampered along the ground. Letting her imagination get away from her.

"Lexi? Come here, you dumb dog." She forged on and heard more squishy sounds. Hair prickled on the back of her neck. She spun around and thought she saw a shadow melt behind a tree. She waited, but there was no movement. The wind, she told herself. "Lexi?"

She felt someone watching her, the sensation was so strong a chill shivered through her. She turned again and saw nothing. Angrily, she marched ahead and found a bicycle propped against a tree trunk. Nothing sinister about a bicycle. Oh yes? What is it doing here? And where is whoever belongs with it?

"Alexa!" Yelling didn't seem such a good idea. Creeping away seemed a good idea.

She heard thrashing sounds and started to run. Her foot got tangled in undergrowth and she stumbled, struggled to regain her balance, then fell. The thrashing grew louder. She covered her head with her arms.

Alexa leaped over her, skidded to a halt, then wheeled, and crouched. She dropped something and woofed. A new game? She was ready to play.

Oh Lexi, you haven't killed some small animal. Carena grabbed her and snapped on the leash, then scattered through dead leaves. Ohh, a bird. She picked up a soggy clump of blue feathers. It wasn't a bird, only feathers attached to a short chain, part of a key ring. She pitched it and Alexa dived after it.

"Drop it, you stupid dog." She pried feathers from the dog's mouth and started to throw it again. Alexa watched eagerly, all set to go after it. Carena stuck the wet mess in her pocket.

"We're getting out of here. If anything happens I'm counting on you to protect me."

8

WHILE PARKHURST PERUSED Lynnelle's checking account records at Hampstead Federal, he listened to the president hold forth on the shortcomings of today's youngsters. The account had been opened with five hundred dollars, deposits made of paychecks as she received them. No other amounts coming in, outgoing amounts all looked like ordinary living expenses.

He chased his tail around campus for an hour looking for Salvatierra with no luck. Give it a rest. Get out to the Creighton place and waste more time searching for a notebook that isn't there. He drove through Keller Gate and headed the Bronco crosstown. Something in that house nagged at him anyway, like sand in his boot he couldn't shake loose. He didn't think straight these days, wasn't concentrating on the job, made him miss things. He'd always been good at the job. It was the one thing he had going for him, the one thing that had saved him from ending up dead or in jail like most of his childhood pals. Why he'd managed to escape that dead-end life, the poverty, a drunk violent father, street gangs and knife fights in stinking alleys, he didn't know. Maybe it had something to do with his mother. She had dreams and even the old man couldn't beat them out of her. It was still there all the same, his background, just under the surface.

He passed the fast-food places and used-car lots that trailed along the edge of Hampstead. The job was all there was. More than that led to trouble sure as God made little green apples. Conflicts battled in his mind. Self-preservation told him to move on; get out of town, cowboy, this place isn't big enough for both of us. Against that tugged desire. And deep down was another emotion, some mixture of pride and disgust at giving up without a shot. He drove by open fields. An old maroon Volvo came toward him heading for town and he glanced in the rearview mirror when it passed.

Egersund. That lady was guilty as hell, but he didn't know of what. Homicide? Why would a math professor off a typist in the English department? He needed to find out what Osey'd dug up on her.

He pulled into the gravel drive, cut the motor, got out of the Bronco and leaned against the fender to stare at the house. What had he missed? He rolled his shoulders in irritation, mind probably split a seam and started leaking sawdust, result of losing control and allowing headroom to adolescent yearnings.

Gawking at the outside of the house sure as hell wasn't going to tell him anything. He scuffed at sparse gravel, then started for the rear door.

A kid in jeans and blue down jacket wheeled a bicycle across the open field and came toward the house. Parkhurst raised an eyebrow. Math teacher meets kid in the woods?

The kid spotted Parkhurst. His face, which had been dreamy and relaxed, went tight. Parkhurst could feel waves of hostility rolling toward him.

"What's your name, kid?"

"Nick."

"Salvatierra?"

"So what?" He stood with one hand on the crossbar of the bicycle.

"So I've been wanting to talk with you." With a loose, easy

stride, Parkhurst ambled to the oak tree with the rope swing, folded his arms and leaned against the trunk. He knew this kid, not as an individual but as a type. He knew that look of bored insolence, the curl of adolescent underlip young males in their vulnerability take on to hide their fear of exposure, the don't-fuck-with-me stance. He might have been looking at himself twenty years ago. Nick faced him like a badass tough Hispanic street kid tempered by fighting his way through life. Parkhurst could see the cannon fire behind Nick's eyes and hear the distant rumble of the kid's own monumental war with the world.

"What are you doing here, Nick?"

"Communing with nature."

"By yourself?"

"Yeah, by myself. That a crime?"

"Depends on what you've done."

"Nothing." Nick studied him with bored, suspicious eyes.

"That right, Nick? Lynnelle Hames. You knew her, Nick?"

He shrugged. "So what if I did?"

"So I want you to tell me about her, Nick."

"I don't know anything."

"Come on, Nick, you can do better than that. Did you like her? Think she was pretty? Take her out? Take her to bed?"

"I don't have to talk to you."

"Wrong, tiger."

"Yeah? What can you do, cop? Bust me?"

Parkhurst grinned. "Beat the shit out of you."

Nick's knuckles tightened on the crossbar, his nostrils flared and his breath came hard.

"Don't try it, kid," Parkhurst said in a voice like silk. "I'm twenty pounds heavier and twenty times as mean."

"Yeah?" With casual deliberation, Nick lowered the bike, stepped back to face Parkhurst, flexed his hands.

Parkhurst shook his head wearily. "You're not very smart, are you, Nick?"

For a moment, Nick looked startled as though firm ground had given way to swamp, then he stuck out his jaw and clenched his fists. "You don't know anything about me."

"Wrong again, kid. I know everything about you. You came here all gung ho about education. Make something of yourself. Going to be great, right? Only it didn't work that way. You got here and it was a foreign country with a foreign language. The kids are different. They make you feel like a freak, look at you like something in a zoo. Makes you mad, doesn't it, Nick? You only feel like a man when you're playing basketball. Or is it football?"

"Football," Nick retorted, then glared, angry he'd given away even that much.

"These other kids may have it easier, some of them, but I'll tell you something, Nick. They're all just as scared, just as worried, and fighting just as hard to win their own game." If the kid would ever smile, he'd be movie-star handsome, but the sullen stare made him look like a killer.

"There's a time to fight, Nick, and there's a time to use your head." Parkhurst felt like he was quoting the Bible, or maybe it was Pete Seeger. Yeah, listen to me, kid. I've got all the answers. "When you figure out which is appropriate for a given situation, you might have a chance. Now we're going to start over and I'm going to ask you some questions and you try not to be a bigger asshole than you are. What do you know about Lynnelle Hames?" To a kid like this, Parkhurst was the enemy. He wouldn't want to open his mouth even if he knew anything.

Nick stared at him. "Knew who she was."

Parkhurst waited.

"She was a friend of somebody I know."

"Julie Kalazar?"

"Maybe."

"You come out here a lot?"

Nick shrugged.

"How often?"

"Once or twice."

Parkhurst would bet on that being a little short of true. "Anybody else ever out here when you were here?"

"Yeah. Julie."

"Did Lynnelle ever seem afraid?"

"She liked this dump. It doesn't even have any furniture."

"When was the last time you were here?"

Nick took a moment before answering. "I don't remember."

Now here we have a lie, Parkhurst thought. Why lie about that? "You don't seem to care about Lynnelle very much. Why'd you come?"

"Julie liked her."

"What do you know about Lynnelle's death?"

Nick's expression went just short of a sneer. "Didn't I already answer that? Nothing."

"What about Julie? She know anything?"

"You'll have to ask her."

Parkhurst wondered if Julie's mother knew about this friendship. From what he knew of Dr. Kalazar, he'd say the lady was a wee bit prejudiced. Could be why Julie was uptight, and had nothing to do with the murder. "You ever see Lynnelle with anybody?"

"I never saw her at all, except here and then she was with Julie."

"She ever mention any trouble with anybody?"

"We never talked."

"Anybody ever hanging around out here?"

Something shifted in Nick's bored eyes and for a second Parkhurst thought he might get an answer, then he could see Nick decide to keep dumb.

"Where's Lynnelle's family live?"

79

"Hey, man, I told you, we never talked." Nick scuffed at the mud with the toe of his Nike. "Take it or leave it. I can't tell you anything about her."

Parkhurst raised a skeptical eyebrow, waited a beat, then backtracked. "What were you doing here?"

Nick's sullen expression didn't change, but Parkhurst, veteran cop, sensed the flicker of apprehension and it made his antenna go up. "Who did you meet?"

"Nobody."

"Dr. Egersund?"

Nick snapped his fingers. "Oh yeah, I forgot. I came to get a math assignment."

"Were you born an asshole, or do you have to work at it? Dr. Egersund was here, you were here. I want to know what you talked about."

"She didn't even see me."

"Nick," Parkhurst said wearily, "I stomp freshman football players and rip them apart a little piece at a time. It makes me feel good the whole rest of the day. Why'd you come?"

Nick shrugged. "I like it out here. It's quiet. No trees where I come from."

Yeah. That got under Parkhurst's skin a little. It was the only thing the kid said that rang true. "What about Dr. Egersund? You see her?"

After some inner struggle, Nick said, "Saw her pick up something."

"What?"

"I don't know," Nick muttered. "Small. Picked it up and put it in her pocket." He lifted his chin defensively.

For the first time Parkhurst felt a touch of liking for the kid. Nick seemed to have some respect for this math teacher and regretted ratting to the enemy. Maybe there was hope for a hardass with respect for a teacher. Maybe said something for the teacher too.

He told Nick he could go, and watched with itchy dissatisfaction as Nick righted the bicycle and wheeled it around the house toward the driveway. I hope you didn't kill that girl, kid. I hope you make it. I hope you win your fight. He fished the key from his pocket and unlocked the back door.

As soon as he stepped inside, he had the feeling somebody had been here. Nick? Egersund? He sniffed and smelled nothing but mildew and dry rot. He went from room to room. Nearly as he could recall, nothing had been added or subtracted.

One nebulous quest at a time, he told himself, and starting in the kitchen he searched the place again. No notebook. And nothing set off light bulbs either, to spotlight the grain of sand.

From the bedroom doorway, he eyed the paperback books lined up under the window. A book? Was that it? Wasted this much time, why not waste more. Sitting cross-legged on the floor, he flipped through romances, science fiction, a few mysteries, a few fantasies of the sword-and-sorcerer kind.

Yeah. Two were different. *Momma, Where Are You*—not a mystery as he'd thought, but a story about an adopted child— and *Sins of the Fathers*, written by Keith Kalazar. Parkhurst read the jacket cover and raised an eyebrow.

Should have caught these two the first time. Would have, if his mind had been working right. He evened up the books against the wall, picked up the two that had caught his attention and left by the kitchen door.

Thirty minutes later, he trailed into the chief's office and dropped the books with a sharp smack on her desk.

She looked up and wondered what he was so pissed about. "What's this?"

"Wild geese, maybe." He tapped his knuckles against the desk. "I've just spent two hours at the Creighton place and that's all I came up with." He sat in the wooden armchair, slid down on his spine and placed his fingertips together.

"No notebook," she said. "Lynnelle kept it with her, wrote in it all the time. Innermost thoughts, presumably. It was important to her. What happened to it?"

"She either gave up childish things or somebody destroyed it. Maybe some of those innermost thoughts pointed right to our killer."

"It doesn't explain why we couldn't find any bills or correspondence or checkbook. Unless the killer destroyed all that too. Doesn't make sense. You think these books mean something?"

"Maybe. Lynnelle wasn't the serious, studious type. She read light fiction. Mystery, romance. Those two stuck out."

Susan picked up *Sins of the Fathers,* by Keith C. Kalazar, and read the blurb on the back cover. *Sally's new stepfather loved her very much. That's what he told her when he did those things. Their love was special, a secret. She was never to tell anyone.* "Incest?" Susan said to Parkhurst.

He shrugged. "A lot of that going around lately."

Could that be what Lynnelle was running from? It might explain why there was nothing of her background in that grim house; she covered her tracks.

"On the other hand," Parkhurst said, "she might have it simply because she knew the author."

Susan opened the book cover. No inscription.

Momma, Where Are You, was the story of an adopted child looking for her biological mother. Well now, was this the past Lynnelle came here looking for? "Biological mother," she said aloud.

"I did wonder if that might not be what we have in Dr. Egersund."

"That's quite a jump." Susan thought about it. "A child given up for adoption who returns years later."

"It happens."

"Yes, but does anybody care?"

He gave her an enquiring look.

"Care to the point of keeping it secret in a murder investigation. Or care to the point of killing."

"This is not San Francisco."

She was getting a little tired of hearing that.

"This is a small town, conservative, most folks go to church on Sunday. Even now they don't take lightly living together without benefit of matrimony. It's gossiped about and snickered about, fingers pointed."

"Egersund is an educated woman. Intelligent, accomplished. Why would she get all exercised and threatened by something long in the past?"

"She grew up here," he said. "Understand the circumstances. Twenty-some years ago, the whole thing would have been all wrapped around with secrecy and shame. Father a minister. We're talking serious, heavy-duty sin here."

"I can't believe it."

"Believe it. It's true."

Susan lit a cigarette and eyed him through the smoke. "Are her parents still alive?"

He nodded, got out his notebook and flipped pages. "Osey's still digging. Parents reside in Kirkwood, Missouri. The lady graduated with honors from the University of Oklahoma. Married, one son. Taught at Boulder."

"Any murdered clerk-typists while she was there?"

"No criminal record, very law-abiding citizen. Divorced. Started teaching at Emerson last fall."

Susan frowned, edged the books up evenly and shook her head dubiously. "That's building an awful lot on one paperback book."

"Yeah." He slid even lower and crossed his feet at the ankles. "Egersund is guilty of something. She was out at the Creighton place just before I got there. I saw her leaving and I even wondered for a minute or two if she'd been in the house. I also ran into Nick Salvatierra." He related his conversation with the kid. "Now just what was Egersund doing there?"

"You think she went there to meet him?"

"She didn't strike me as dumb and there are dozens of better places that wouldn't rouse suspicion. I'm inclined to believe him when he said he didn't speak with her. I definitely believe he saw her pick something up."

"Something incriminating she went back to find?"

"Well," Parkhurst said. "She didn't sprint right down here to show us what she found."

No, she didn't do that. "What was Nick doing there?"

"Yeah, Nick." Parkhurst shook his head. "I don't know about him, but I'll find out. Streetwise. All his defenses went up when he saw me. Set bells clanging in my head. He had the hidden caution that means he's not squeaky clean. And that one's hungry. He *wants.*"

"You saying he might be our killer? What's the motive?"

"I don't know." Parkhurst stood up, paced to the doorway and then turned. "One other thing."

"What?"

"If that book means anything and the girl was an adopted child, there might be another important figure in all this. The kid probably had a father."

"Anyone in mind?"

"No," Parkhurst said. "Except David McKinnon was handy on the scene."

He was gone before she could respond. She frowned, picked up the books, glanced briefly at each one and then stuck them in her shoulder bag. Quite possibly, they had nothing to do with Lynnelle's death, but it wouldn't hurt to ask Egersund another question or two. It was almost seven. She'd left the little cat alone for a long time again and wondered what kind of havoc it was wreaking. Put up a little higher on her list, find Sophie and get that cat back.

* * *

Receiver at her ear, Carena listened to the phone ringing in Topeka. Come on, Caitlin, answer. Where are you? Why haven't you called back? Carena twisted her fingers through the cord and stared unseeing at Alexa lying on the kitchen floor.

She clattered down the receiver. Phil probably neglected to pass on my message. Gingerly she rubbed her forehead, ignoring the low-pitched whirr of alarm in her mind. Aspirin, more aspirin. Taking a bottle from the cabinet, she shook two tablets into her palm, ran water in a glass and swallowed them. Alexa anxiously watched all her movements.

Right. Dinner. She hauled out a sack of kibble, dumped a goodly amount in a bowl, perked it up with some canned food and set it on the floor. Food, that's what she needed too, it might help the headache. Opening the refrigerator door, she stood gazing in, something she used to yell at Michael for doing.

Alexa finished off her meal, licked the bowl several times to make sure, then squeezed past chairs and stretched out under the table with a heavy sigh. Her eyes fixed on Carena with mute appeal. Carena's mind flashed on Caitlin, huddled under her desk, staring out from behind the chair legs with the same sort of imploring look in her eyes.

Carena had been seventeen, awakened in the middle of the night by singing coming from Caitlin's room. Frightened, Carena listened to the thin, high cadence of her sister's voice. She got up, tiptoed across the hall and knocked softly on Caitlin's door. There was no answer. She opened the door and went in.

A full moon shone through the window and spread a wide rectangle of eerie light on the floor. The bed was empty. Caitlin in her nightgown crouched in the kneehole of the desk, drawn in tight with her arms around bent legs.

"I'm tired," she said to something invisible across the room. "I want to go to bed."

She didn't appear to see Carena, even when Carena pulled away the chair and squatted in front of her. Caitlin's mouth was trembling and saliva dribbled down one corner.

"I already sang 'Abide with Me' and 'It Is Not Death to Die' and 'Just As I Am without One Plea.'"

"Caitlin." Carena took both her sister's hands and shook them. "What's the matter?"

"They're here again."

"Who?"

"They're singing and I have to sing with them."

"Who are they, Caitlin?"

"The dark angels."

"Where? Where are they?"

Caitlin pointed. "By the wall. Can't you hear them?"

"There's nothing there. Just the bookcase. You're having a dream."

Caitlin shook her head violently. "They want me to sing. I have to do what they want. If I don't, the crows will get mad."

"What crows?"

"On the windowsill. When I don't sing, they come and they scream at me. And sometimes they laugh, mean. They say terrible things."

"When did you start seeing things, Caitlin? You used to only hear voices. Are you sure you see them?"

"They'll hurt me."

"No, Caitlin, they can't hurt you. They're not real. Only in your mind."

Caitlin started shaking her head again. Carena, a hand on each side of Caitlin's face to stop the shaking, leaned close and looked directly into her eyes. "Caitlin, listen to me. Listen. I won't let them hurt you. We'll both sing, all right? But first you have to get back in bed. Come on."

She led Caitlin to the bed, fluffed the pillows behind her head and smoothed the blankets over her, then lay beside her and they both sang hymns to appease Caitlin's dark angels and the terrifying crows.

For some time, Carena had tried to tell her mother something was wrong with Caitlin. Her mother got angry. There's nothing wrong with Caitlin, she said. Caitlin just has too much imagination. She's always been that way. Even when she was little. She always had conversations with imaginary playmates and her dolls. Her mother clung to that belief until the first time Caitlin had hurt herself.

The dog barked and Carena jumped. Alexa scrambled up and trotted to the living room. A second or two later the doorbell rang. Now what?

Some of the tension eased when she opened the door and saw Chief Wren. There was nothing scary about this woman with her thick dark hair, blue eyes, fine cheekbones and small straight nose. She had a haughty look, like an ad for expensive perfume. Her soft gray skirt and blazer beneath the trench coat made Carena feel grubby in old tan pants and baggy green sweater. She fastened a hand on the dog's collar and kneed her back to let the police chief in.

"I won't keep you long," Susan said and thought, she's relieved it was me at the door. Susan sat on the couch and dropped her shoulder bag at her feet. Maybe I should have sent Parkhurst. "There are one or two things I need to clarify."

Egersund releaed the dog and eased into an old wooden rocker.

"Before I get into that, is there anything you haven't told me you'd like to tell me now? No? In that case, maybe you could tell me what you were looking for at Lynnelle's house."

"I've never been in her house."

"Never? Not this afternoon?"

For a moment, Egersund looked blank, then there was an *ob* expression on her face. "I did go out there. Not the house, the woods."

"Behind Lynnelle's house?"

"Yes," Egersund said as though wondering where this was leading.

"What time?"

"Around four-thirty or so."

"How long were you there?"

"About thirty minutes."

"What were you looking for?"

"I was looking for the dog," Egersund said sharply. "She got away and I went after her."

"You found her in the woods?"

"Yes."

"Then what?"

"I put her in the car and drove home."

"Dr. Egersund, it would be wise to tell the truth." She did not add, for a change, but allowed a hint of it in her voice.

"That is the truth."

"What did you find out there?"

"Find? What do you mean?"

"It's a crime to withhold evidence in a police investigation." She watched Egersund look down at her hands; they were holding onto each other as though for mutual support.

She looked up, met Susan's eyes and unclasped her hands. "I didn't find anything."

"Dr. Egersund, we have a witness. You picked up something in the woods. What was it?"

"What would I pick up? Dead leaves? I chased after the damn dog, tripping all over—" She broke off.

"Yes?"

"It's nothing. Just part of an old key chain." Egersund got her tweed coat from the closet, stuck her hand in the pocket and drew out the clump of damp blue feathers. "Is that what you mean?"

Susan held out her hand and the feathers were dropped into her palm. "If it's nothing, why did you lie about it?"

"I didn't lie," Egersund said tartly, seemed to feel that needed a little embellishing and added, "I simply forgot." She looked uneasy as though that sounded lame even to herself. She slid further back in the rocker and folded the coat across her lap.

"Where did you find this?"

"I didn't find it," Egersund snapped. "The dog did."

"Who does it belong to?"

"I have no idea. I've never seen it before."

"It's not yours?"

"No."

Susan gathered up her shoulder bag and got to her feet. Egersund rose also. At the door, Susan reached into the bag and took out the paperback books. "Are you familiar with these?"

Egersund took them, shook her head and tried to hand them back.

"Read the blurbs on the backs."

She turned them over. Susan, watching carefully, saw the little start of fear. She felt her heart pick up a beat. "It's about an adopted child. Have you read it?"

"No." The word came out flat and steady.

"They belonged to Lynnelle. We're wondering if perhaps Lynnelle, herself, was an adopted child. That would explain a few things that have puzzled us."

"Lynnelle was not my child."

Susan looked at her, letting the silence stretch. "Are you sure that's all you want to say?"

Carena withstood that hard knowing look and when Chief Wren left, poured a glass of red wine, found two more aspirins and gulped them down. I was wrong about this woman. In her own way, she's just as scary as Parkhurst. Carena rubbed fingertips against her throbbing temples. Chickens coming home to roost. Bad habit, in the face of adversity her mind scurried

89

around for apt quotations. "Ye have sinned against the Lord and be sure your sins shall find you out."

Her parents would find out. Her deeply religious father to whom so many things were a sin and her mother—also religious, as befitted a minister's wife, but more practical with it—would be shattered. "Trouble, thou wretch, that has within thee undivulged crimes."

9

"I DON'T BELIEVE it," Susan muttered as she pulled away. Kids are told from day one they're adopted; biological parents, adoptive parents all gather round in one big extended family.

She shook her head. Not true. Even now adoptions could be shrouded in secrecy. Her own family, for example. She had a cousin who was adopted. To this day, the kid didn't know, and he was in his twenties. Adoptees seemed driven to find their natural parents; struggled through all sorts of difficulties.

Susan nudged the heater up a notch. The weather had turned colder again, rain that had fallen earlier had turned to ice on the streets and glistened under her headlights. Every time the temperature dropped, she asked herself why she was still here and not in San Francisco, where she belonged. The radio crackled and she picked up the mike.

"Keith Kalazar's been on the phone," Marilee Beaumont said in her soft southern voice. Marilee was the dispatcher when Hazel went off duty. "He says he needs to talk to you."

"I'll call him. Anything else?"

"You wanted to know if anybody spotted Sophie? Ben Parkhurst just reported in. Saw her car on Essex. At the Lutheran church?"

The pickup tires skidded a bit as she made a right turn, cut past the campus and reached the church just as some meeting or other was letting out. The quilting ladies, she thought, since they all seemed to be female and mostly elderly. They made beautiful quilts and sold them to raise money. She intended to buy one before she saw Hampstead in her rearview mirror.

Lights on the outside of the church building reflected on the icy tarmac in the parking lot. She squinted at the quilting ladies filing out and flowing toward their cars and spotted Sophie in a long black overcoat as she broke rank and swooped toward her elderly Chevy.

"Sophie." Susan slid from the pickup, and her boot heels cracked sharply on the ice as she closed in.

The old woman peered across the dark lot, shading her eyes with one hand. "Evening." Her face was etched with fine lines, deeper lines creased her forehead and formed brackets from her sharp nose to her determined mouth. The long black coat was buttoned up to her chin and a black watch cap was pulled down over her ears, leaving spikes of iron gray hair sticking out around the edges.

"I want to talk with you," Susan said.

"Can't think why," Sophie said with a seraphic smile.

"The little cat cannot—"

"You need a cat."

"Sophie—"

"Everybody needs somebody to love."

"Yes, well, cats need company. I'm not home enough—"

"Poor little mite. Needs love. Been mistreated. You just don't worry about it. It'll all be fine. Plenty else to worry about with that girl getting killed. Find out who did it yet?"

"Did you know her?"

"Not to say know. Went 'round to see her about the time she moved in. Took her some pumpkin bread. Being neighborly, you might say."

Being nosy was closer to the truth, Susan thought, but she wasn't above taking information wherever she could get it. "What did you find out?"

"She wasn't easy when I came. Like she was nervous I might find out what she didn't want a body to know."

Susan suppressed a grin. That's exactly what Sophie would have had in mind.

"We chatted a bit like you do. Made me some coffee. More like weak water, not what I'd call coffee. But being nice and all. She was lonely really, and glad of any company. I asked where did she come from and why did she come here. She gave me one of those I-don't-want-to-say looks that always make me feel like asking more questions."

I'll just bet it did.

"She loved her dog. Told me she'd never been allowed pets because *he* was allergic. Stepfather, turned out. She hates him."

"Hates?"

Sophie sniffed, then exhaled in a puff of fog. "I may be old, but I can spot the difference between hate and dislike. She was all stiff and her face got pinched, and white around the nose. I got the idea he maybe mistreated her some way. I felt sorry for her. I hate to see innocent creatures mistreated. She said he didn't like dogs. He liked birds."

"Birds."

"Birds," Sophie said impatiently, as though she were talking to somebody slow-witted. "Watched them through binoculars. She worked, you know. Lynnelle. Gone most during the day. House wasn't always empty though."

"Somebody was there when Lynnelle wasn't home?"

"Little Kalazar girl, Julie. She'd go out there, meet her young man and they'd go inside."

"How do you know?"

"I just know."

Saw them, obviously. Probably lurking in the shrubbery. In

93

her assiduous devotion to needy cats, Sophie quartered the countryside and if she ran across anything interesting, she made it her business to poke her sharp nose into it.

"Now, just what do you suppose they were up to in there?" Sophie smiled and shook her head. "Wouldn't her mother have a fit, she was to find out. Audrey keeps close watch on that young'un's friends and weeds out the undesirables."

Sophie tugged the watch cap down to her eyebrows. "Can't stand around here talking all night," she said, clomped to her car and wrenched open the door. "The little cat needs shots. Get her to the vet real soon."

"Sophie—"

Sophie fired up the motor with a roar, then eased back and sedately rolled away.

Susan sifted through Sophie's information as she headed for home, trying to find the nuggets of fact. A hated stepfather? Only Sophie's interpretation. Damn it, why haven't we gotten onto the next of kin? Thirty-three hours since the body was discovered. What kind of drag-ass outfit are we, anyway?

What about the other little gem Sophie dropped? Nick and Julie using the house for a trysting place. Anything there? Could explain the second sleeping bag. Nick was a scholarship student and Hispanic. Would either or both make him unsuitable in Dr. Kalazar's eyes? The whiff of barely suppressed violence that Nick exuded was enough to make any parent nervous. Did Lynnelle threaten to tell Dr. Kalazar and one of them killed her? She gave them permission— why turn around and rat to Kalazar?

Susan pulled into the garage beside the little brown Fiat she hardly ever drove these days and, as she squeezed past, gave its dusty flank a pat and a promise for a spin. Soon.

The neighborhood kid she'd made friends with sat on the back step with her elbows on her knees and her chin in her hands, foil-covered bowl beside her.

"Hi, Jen."

"Hi," Jen said, an eleven-year-old uncertain of her welcome, but obviously glad to see Susan.

Cops don't have that many admirers that they can afford to pass one up. "Want to come in a minute?"

Jen tossed her brown ponytail over her shoulder. "I don't mind." She was a skinny kid in jeans and red ski jacket with unusual yellow-green eyes and a stubborn chin. A neat kid, smart and funny, with endless enthusiasms for anything new and a mind always looking for answers.

Dad had a new wife and Mom had a new boyfriend and when they weren't using Jen as cannon fodder in the battle between them, they were making her feel like excess baggage. Jen had the usual anxieties and confusions and fears that it was all her fault.

Susan hated it when kids had problems. It scared her and she was always afraid she'd say the wrong thing. "Does your mom know where you are?"

Jen shrugged. "She won't mind, she's on the phone with *Casey.*" Her mouth screwed up over the name.

"You could call and let her know."

"She'll talk forever."

"Well, you can keep trying."

Jen picked up the bowl and moved out of the way. Susan unlocked the door and snapped on the inside light. "Are you hungry?"

The kitchen looked the same as when she left; at least the kitten hadn't created any more rubble.

"I fixed spaghetti for supper. I brought you some since you never have anything to eat."

"Hey, Jen, that's nice." Susan tried not to be too effusive with praise. Jen got embarrassed. She hadn't received enough compliments in her young life and Susan tried to remedy that by throwing out lots of good words without overdoing it. Getting the balance right was a worry. "For spaghetti you deserve a reward. How about I let you beat me at Trivial Pursuit?"

Jen's face lit up with the sunshine grin she didn't use nearly enough. She was a wizard at the game and almost always won. "Shall I get it out?"

"You mind if I make a phone call first?"

The grin faded. "That's okay." In her world, adults made promises and too often didn't come through.

"It'll only take a minute. Before I do that I want to show you something."

"What?"

The dining room looked the same, except for tiny paw prints all over the clutter on the table. The living room—

"Wow," Jen breathed, looking around wide-eyed.

The two spider plants had been knocked from the mantle, the pots had shattered on the hearth and the plants were torn to bits, then scattered, along with the dirt, across the room. The kitten was crouched on the arm of a chair, brown paws tucked neatly under her beige chest, blue eyes slitted with the smug expression of a job well done.

Despite vigorous resistance, Hazel had managed to press the plants in Susan's hands. Killer hands. Even the sturdiest of plants shriveled up and died in her care. Hazel was almost as particular about finding homes for plants as Sophie was for cats. One unwanted gift destroys another.

"Are you mad?" Jen asked in a nervous little voice.

"I'm not pleased." Susan fingered a piece of pottery she and Daniel had bought in Mexico when they were on their honeymoon.

"I'll help you clean it up." Jen knelt by the chair and stroked the kitten who scampered up her arm and nibbled her ear. Jen giggled and cradled the kitten against her chest. "She didn't mean it."

If Susan thought Mom would stand for it, the kitten would be Jen's in a flash.

"What's her name?"

"She doesn't have a name. Can you come up with one?"

Jen nodded solemnly. "I'll think about it."

When they finished with dust cloths, brooms, dust pan and vacuum cleaner, the living room looked better than it had in a long time. Susan left Jen playing lurk-and-pounce with the kitten and went to phone Keith Kalazar. He answered immediately with a sharp hello.

"Chief Wren, Mr. Kalazar. I understand you were trying to reach me."

"I don't know where Audrey is."

Susan did not take the receiver from her ear and stare at it, but she felt like it. "I believe she's attending a conference in Dallas." Maybe he was even more vague than she'd originally thought.

"Yes." He paused to take a breath. "That's what I thought. The thing is—" He cleared his throat. "I just called the hotel."

"Yes?"

"Audrey never checked in."

10

"SOMETHING'S HAPPENED." Keith Kalazar rubbed an agitated hand over his well-trimmed beard and shook his head. "I know it."

At nine on Tuesday morning, he was seated in the wooden armchair in Susan's office and anxiety had him jumpy; leaning forward, leaning back, propping an ankle on one knee, tapping fingers against his thigh. Morning sun shone against the window blinds and spread a striped pattern across the floor.

"I knew it when he called." Keith jabbed a hand in a jacket pocket, the same fawn-colored jacket with the leather elbow patches.

"The conference coordinator," Susan said.

"Audrey didn't show up for her speech."

"When was the last time you saw her?"

"Saturday morning." He pulled out his pipe and smashed tobacco in the bowl.

"How did she seem?"

"Fine. Like always."

"She wasn't distracted, maybe thinking about the conference?"

"No. Oh, she did have her speech, glancing over it, last-minute checking."

"Was Julie there?"

Impatience crossed his face. "No."

"Where was she?"

"What difference does it make? She was around."

"What time did Audrey leave?"

"Ten-thirty. I put her suitcase in the trunk and she went off. She was leaving her car there so she'd have it when she got back."

"Tomorrow evening," Susan said.

He nodded. "Commuter flight to Kansas City and then the flight to Dallas. The same coming back."

"Was there anything at Emerson that was troubling her?"

"No."

"What about problems at home?"

"No." He patted his shirt pocket, then jacket pockets, then pants pockets, where he found a book of matches.

"Mr. Kalazar, I know this is difficult, but I need all the information I can get."

He tore out a match, struck it and held it over the pipe. "Nothing like that," he said shortly.

She waited.

He puffed on his pipe. "Maybe some minor worry about Julie."

"What worry?"

He moved a hand as though brushing that away. "Her grades have slipped a little. Audrey didn't like it."

"Anything else you can think of?"

He shook his head. "She just wouldn't do this."

"Did the two of you have a . . . disagreement?"

"Of course not."

Right, she thought, not really believing him, but not disbelieving him either. In any case, she decided not to push him on it at the moment.

After he left, she spent an hour on the phone before tracking down the conference coordinator, who was seethingly miffed because Audrey Kalazar had been a scheduled speaker. He'd been forced to find a replacement—at the last minute—and fill up holes in his schedule—at the last minute. He didn't sound too happy in his job.

Almost as much time was spent getting switched from extension to extension by the hotel in Dallas. "I'm sorry, I'm not authorized to give out that information. Would you hold?" Muzak each wait. She was fuming when she finally got a man who would talk. They must have run out of extensions. A room had been reserved for Dr. Kalazar but she had never checked in.

Receiver tucked against her shoulder, Susan rubbed her sore ear, then pressed a button and asked Hazel to send Parkhurst in. She ran over her scribbled notes. Audrey Kalazar had been last seen on Saturday, three days ago.

Feeling eyes on her, Susan glanced sidelong at the doorway. Parkhurst, in a navy-blue suit, stood there looking like he had an important appointment someplace else, dark eyes remote and guarded, slightly pinched at the corners as though he hadn't gotten enough sleep. Unexpected heat spread over her face. She stiffened her spine and took in a quick breath.

"You wanted to see me." His words came out flat.

So why did she get this sense of clamped-down anger? Back to the old resentments that she outranked him? Shit. I thought we'd gotten past that.

"Anything on Shoehorn?" Because the postman remembered the murdered girl receiving letters from someone in Kansas City with a last name like Shoehorn, they'd asked Kansas City PD to run a check on Lynnelle Hames. KCPD had come up empty.

"Osey's still working on it."

It was a longshot anyway, but right now the best they had. Why the hell couldn't they get anywhere on Lynnelle's family? Telephone records hadn't turned up anything useful; no calls conveniently made back home; no long distance calls at all. David McKinnon had arranged for the phone installation and the bills showed only the monthly charges with nothing extra. In his spare time, Osey was calling every listing in the Kansas City phone book that looked or sounded anywhere near Shoehorn. Susan was irritable, but it was better than nothing, and Osey kept beavering away. Susan told Parkhurst what she had on Audrey Kalazar.

"That explains it," he said with a quick smile. "Doctor Audrey Kalazar, vice-chancellor of Emerson, bashed in the head of a clerk-typist and took it on the lam." He paced through the stripes on the floor made by the sunshine and stood with his back to the window, interrupting the pattern and making it hard to see his face clearly.

She was awkwardly aware she'd been staring at him. "All we know at this point is she left with a suitcase on Saturday morning."

"Romantic weekend with a truck driver. Steamy, earthy sex."

She grinned. Controlled, fastidious Audrey? "Mr. Kalazar informed me, quite firmly, they were very happy." Husbands or wives with missing spouses always were. "They had no problems. No fights, no arguments, no disagreements."

"The perfect marriage."

"The only thing he admitted was that Audrey was concerned about Julie."

"What has the perfect daughter been doing to cause concern?"

"He was vague. Apparently Julie isn't doing as well in school."

"As well as what?"

"As Audrey thinks she should."

Parkhurst rubbed the back of his neck and let out a breath with an irritated huff. "We have one woman dead and another woman missing. What's the connection?"

"I don't see any."

"Emerson College. Kalazar is vice-chancellor, Lynnelle worked there and was a friend of Audrey's daughter."

"So what? We can make all sorts of associations like that. Nick Salvatierra is a student and a friend of Audrey's daughter."

He stared, brooding, at the shiny toes of his black shoes. "Nick's been on my mind. If he's not our killer, he's up to something and I'd like to know what."

"It's unlikely to have anything to do with Kalazar skipping a conference."

"Yeah. I think we should arrest Egersund and beat a confession out of her, then worry about Dr. Vice-chancellor."

"I think we should find Dr. Kalazar. Check with the airlines, see if she left here and got on the flight to Dallas."

He nodded impatiently. "Car?"

"Black Chrysler Le Baron, new." She flipped through her notes and gave him the license number.

He copied it down. "Susan—"

Something in his voice had her looking down at her pale blue silk blouse to see if she'd spilled coffee all over it. It had a fancy rolled collar that ended in a tie in front. She suddenly felt self-conscious. Frills didn't suit her. "What?" she said more sharply than she intended.

Ponderous silence.

"I'll lean on Nick a little," he said.

That wasn't what he'd meant to say. And when had he started calling her Susan? Chief was hard, it seemed to stick in his throat; usually it was a half-mocking Boss. "Parkhurst—"

"Don't worry. I won't leave a mark on him," he said as he left.

She felt uneasy, and not a clue why. Too much coffee. Irritation at time spent tracking Audrey Kalazar with a killer loose. Was there a connection? Retrieving cigarettes and lighter from the mess on her desk, she shoved them in her bag. Probably just too many cigarettes.

Osey Pickett, curved over his desk, said, "Yes, ma'am," into the telephone. Parkhurst sat at his own desk and waited. Osey's guileless blue eyes focused on him and Osey made a facial spasm of vexation.

"No, ma'am," he said and raked fingers through his straw-colored hair. "No, I don't think that's really necessary. Yes, ma'am."

He clamped down the receiver. "Damn it. That's the fourth one this morning." The phone rang again before he could remove his hand. "Detective Pickett, may I help you?" He listened a moment and then went into his "Don't worry about a thing, ma'am, we've got everything under control, rest easy" voice of dealing with the public.

Parkhurst looked at Osey and tapped his wristwatch. Osey nodded, said another "yes, ma'am" and hung up. "Everybody's worried. We getting anywhere on this murder? They're all rushing out to buy handguns. Afraid to go out at night. Don't want their kids working at the fast-food places and service stations. We don't do something pretty soon, they're going to be shooting each other in wholesale panic."

"Don't fret, son, it's all part of the job."

"Couldn't I just chase bad guys? I hate this shit. We aren't getting anywhere, are we?"

"Not so's you'd notice. Unless you're making progress with Shoehorn."

Osey grimaced. "Gone through about half the possibles. So far zilch. You wouldn't believe how rude some people are. Some of 'em think I'm an obscene caller. Some don't even bother to answer, they just hang up. I'd get along a whole lot faster if I didn't have to talk to all these nervous folks wanting to know if they should sleep with loaded weapons under their pillows. What's up?"

"We have work to do. Let's roll on it."

* * *

At the campus, Susan left the pickup in the circular driveway in front of the administration building and trotted up the front steps, then labored up to the second floor. The vice-chancellor's office was at the end of the hallway. Edie Vogel, expression remote, stared at a blank computer screen and when Susan walked in, Edie's head whipped up, panic in her eyes.

"Oh." She seemed to shrink back inside the boxy jacket of her beige suit. "For a second I thought you were Dr. Kalazar."

Sunlight angling through the window accentuated the dark shadows under her eyes and made her brown hair, cut into points around her face, seem like wilted petals. She looked more tired and haunted then she had when Susan last spoke with her. Obviously, there'd been no word about the missing child. Next to her name plate, Edith Blau Vogel, was a framed photo of little Belinda in a frilly pink dress.

"You expected Dr. Kalazar to be here this morning?" Susan scooted a chair from the wall to the front of the desk and sat down.

Edie, looking uneasy as though moving furniture wasn't allowed, shook her head. "No, not till tomorrow. Do you know where she is?"

"Not yet."

"Then something's wrong. She's always where she says she'll be."

"When was the last time you saw her?"

"Friday. She was here all day till four-thirty, then she said she'd be back Wednesday and left."

"Did you make the travel arrangements?"

"I always do whenever she goes anywhere. Hotel reservations and airline reservations and car rentals, all like that. I called Fran at the travel agency weeks ago about the tickets. One P.M. flight to Dallas Saturday afternoon."

"Did she seem bothered about something, irritated or worried?"

Edie's lips curved in a half-smile. "She was usually bothered or irritated about something."

"Any feuds going on? Resentments, jealousies?"

"With the faculty, you mean?" Edie shrugged. "Just the usual. Worry about tenure and getting department chairmanship and why their department doesn't get as big a piece of the budget. They're like a bunch of little kids."

"Anyone with a specific grudge?"

Edie's mouth curved again and this time the smile was almost real. "All of them one time or another. Dr. Kalazar's not exactly sensitive about people's feelings."

"Did anything unusual happen on Friday?"

"Well, she was furious at Dr. Egersund, like I told you. Read her out in this tight voice. Not shouting, you know, just mean and threatening. When Dr. Egersund left, oh boy, did she look mad. Her face was all white and grim. She better tippytoe pretty careful, because Dr. Kalazar gets really mad about mistakes and she doesn't give a second chance."

"Was she looking forward to the conference? Nervous about speaking? Excited?"

"Just the usual, I guess. Duty and all that stuff. Like gratified she was asked. She never had any trouble feeling important."

"Anything different about her? She didn't seem ill?"

"You mean like amnesia?" Edie grinned and Susan caught a glimpse of what Edie must have been like before her daughter was kidnapped. "She looked just healthy to me."

"Did she say anything before she left?"

"Are you kidding? A detailed list of all this stuff I was to do while she was gone."

"Thanks, Edie," Susan said as she stood up. "Did she ever mention Lynnelle?"

Edie leaned back in her chair. "Not to me, she didn't."

"I think I better take a look at her office."

Edie followed and took a quick glance around. She said it looked the same to her; nothing unusual, out of place, or missing. She went back to her desk and her blank computer screen.

The office was in a corner, second-floor front with windows on two sides. Susan stood a moment staring down at the driveway in front. A boy with an armload of books raced down the steps and, just as he reach the curb, dropped it all. Papers scattered in the wind. She watched him scramble and grab. Moving to the side window, she looked out at bare-limbed trees and pathways between buildings. It was just past noon and students in jeans and down jackets were swarming along the paths.

She turned to the desk in the center of the room. Audrey Kalazar was excessively neat, desktop bare except for desk blotter, pens and telephone. Even the drawers were neat with the usual assortment of pens, rubber bands, paper clips and note cards all in their respective places. In the top right-hand drawer was an appointment calender and she paged through it. Diagonal lines had been drawn through the three days of the conference. On Wednesday, February sixteen, was a penciled note: Herbert Ingram four-thirty. She checked the file cabinets for that name and came up empty. She flipped through files randomly, seeing no reason at this time to study them more closely.

There was nothing to suggest where Kalazar might be, or that she'd planned to go anywhere other than the conference, or even that she'd suddenly developed amnesia and was wandering around somewhere asking herself who she was. Susan didn't like this. Where was the woman? None of it made sense. Ha, unless Parkhurst was right and Audrey attacked Lynnelle and lit out. She went back to the outer office and asked Edie, "Who is Herbert Ingram?"

Edie thought a moment. "Nobody I know. Not a teacher, for sure. Maybe a student, but I don't recognize the name."

Susan told Edie to let her know if she remembered anything else and then stopped in at Registration. There was no student named Herbert Ingram.

Osey put the barbecued ribs on his desk with a stack of napkins handy, shrugged off his fleece-lined suede jacket and slung it across the back of the chair, then eyeballed his list of possible Shoehorns. The chief was getting a mite short-tempered about not finding the dead girl's family. She wasn't going to be too pleased they hadn't run down Kalazar either. At least he didn't have to tell her. Let Ben do it. Kalazar wasn't even due home till this evening. Maybe just took off somewhere on her own. Was strange, though.

Strange too that David McKinnon was paying the phone bills for the Hames girl. Why would he do that? Just a good guy? Chief letting judgment get skewed because he's a friend?

Most of the possibles on Osey's list didn't look all that much like Shoehorn to him. If he had anything else to dig at, he'd do it. Until then, he'd call every name starting with S, if he had to. Before he could pick up the receiver and get started, the phone rang.

"Evers, Oklahoma City. About that VW you're trying to get a line on?"

"Right," Osey said, making a shift in thinking to Lynnelle's car.

"Sorry for the delay. Salesman left one place and went to work at another. Took a while to find him. He took the VW as a trade-in, then turned right around and sold it to your girl. The Adam Henry didn't do the paperwork right."

Osey made a sympathetic noise. Adam Henry was polite talk for asshole.

"Help you any?"

"Not much but thanks anyway." Osey went back to his list. In the interest of time, he would punch in a number and ask whoever answered for Shelley. Mostly, he got, "Who? Wrong number."

Then things got a little more interesting. The name was Shoenhowser and the lady who answered had a daughter named Shelley.

Forty-five minutes and four phone calls later, he looked at his cold barbecued ribs and said, "I'll be damned."

11

It was afternoon before Parkhurst got around to Nick Salvatierra. In the hallway of the dorm, he could hear heavy rock music through Nick's door and feel the pulse of bass notes beneath his feet. He knocked once and, when he got no response, reached for the knob; finding it unlocked, he stepped in and closed the door behind him. Noise leaped at him like a snarling grizzly.

Nick, between mounds of clothes, books, papers and blankets, lay on the bed, one ankle balanced on a bent knee, foot jerking in time to the music. Startled, he snapped his head toward the door. "Hey, you can't—" He came barreling up.

Parkhurst shoved hard and Nick stumbled back, got caught by the bed and landed in a sprawl. Sullen hostility came down over his handsome face. Parkhurst strode across hockey stick, shoulder pads, helmet, cleats and snapped off the stereo. The sudden silence seemed to breathe like a living thing.

Nick rose. "You can't just walk in here."

"Sit!"

A long second went by before Nick sat back on the bed.

"A little chat, Nick." Parkhurst leaned against the wall by a bookshelf, books jumbled in crazy piles. "I think you have some interesting things to tell me."

One corner of the kid's mouth lifted in a sneer that said, no way, cop. Wouldn't tell you which way is up.

Parkhurst smiled, looked at the posters of rock musicians on the walls, clothes spilling out of the closet, and the football holding open a book on the desk. "Nice room."

He pushed himself from the wall, wandered to a speaker and ran one finger across the top, leaving a shiny streak in the dust. He picked up Calvin Klein jeans from the television set and dropped them on the floor. He was beginning to get an idea why Nick was so uptight.

At the desk, he leaned over to gaze at the Apple computer, then strolled past the foot of the bed to the other bookcase and touched a coffee mug shaped like the long-toothed Emerson wildcat, a pewter tankard with a Civil War flag stuck in it and a framed photo of Nick suited up in full football gear. Parkhurst's movements were lazy and offensive, calculated to hold a match to adolescent defenses, but he was alert to the slightest shift from Nick. The kid was on a short fuse.

"Lot of expensive stuff sitting around here." Parkhurst rested his rear against the edge of the desk. "Where's the money come from?"

"You got no right to ask."

"Oh, I think I do. I think illegal activities come right up there in my right to ask."

Nick shrugged.

"Don't want to tell me? Doesn't matter. I think I can guess. Got yourself a little business going, what you educated types call a cottage industry."

"It's the American way."

Parkhurst stared at him. The kid was smooth-skinned and clear-eyed. He didn't look like a user. "You a Buddhist, kid?"

"What?"

"You're messing up your life, Nick. Either you're an asshole or you believe you have another chance at it. Could be, I don't know, but I don't think you should count on it. Better you stop fucking up, in case this is your only shot." Parkhurst shook his head. "Besides, from the way you're handling this life you'll come back as a roach."

The sneer slipped slightly.

Bingo. The stupid little shit. "Not that kind," Parkhurst said. "Cockroach." He wanted to grab the muscled shoulders and shake the kid's head loose. "Mingling with all these privileged kids makes you want what they've got, doesn't it, Nick? You never will." Oh yeah, listen to me, my boy, I'll tell you a few ugly truths.

"You can sell drugs and buy shit like this." He waved a hand around the room. "But all the stereos and fancy pants in the world won't get you what they've got. That comes from background. You can't buy it and you can't change yours."

You haul it around all your life, Parkhurst added silently. From his father he'd inherited a violent temper and, as the old man got more abusive and progressively lost in the bottle, a hatred of drunks, a contempt for authority, but worst of all, a sense of failure. From his mother, he inherited something even more dangerous. Dreams, a love of books, and yearnings; undefined and consequently impossible to satisfy.

"You'll get your ass kicked right out of here."

"You got to prove it first, cop."

"Do I? You sure of that, Nick? A word or two in the appropriate ear and you'd be surprised what could happen." A little flick of fear went through Nick's dark eyes.

Parkhurst gave it time to take root. "Somebody like Dr. Kalazar might find it very interesting, don't you think? You know her, Nick?"

"No."

"The vice-chancellor? You don't know her?"

"What are you talking about?"

"Your girlfriend's mother."

"What about her?"

What indeed, Parkhurst thought. Resentment there. Julie probably kept him away from her mother and that made him feel like garbage. "You ever talk to her?"

"Why would I?"

It was a reasonable response. Parkhurst dropped that line of questioning. "What about Lynnelle?"

"What about her?"

"Why'd you kill her?" The edge of the desk was cutting into Parkhurst's butt and he shifted slightly. It wouldn't do for Dirty Harry to rub his numb ass.

"You'd like to hang it on me, wouldn't you? No way, cop. I didn't do it and you can't prove I did."

"In that case you won't mind telling me about her."

"I already told you. She was Julie's friend."

"You didn't like her much."

Nick shrugged. "She was all right."

Parkhurst waited.

"I didn't trust her," Nick said grudgingly. "She let us use her house sometimes."

"You and Julie?"

"Yeah. Julie was afraid of her mother so we had to be real secret." Nick spoke with the disgust of a hardass who's not afraid of anybody. "I just wondered what was in it for Lynnelle."

"Since you felt that way, why'd you accept the use of her house?"

Nick shrugged again. "Julie wouldn't go with me anywhere else in case somebody saw us. The place was a dump. Didn't even have any beds."

It occurred to Parkhurst that Nick might have a reason, besides satisfying his hormones, for meeting Julie at Lynnelle's. Only a step away was the thought that Nick could have killed Lynnelle because she discovered what he was up to.

Goddamn the kid. Even without a murder charge, he was in

a lot of trouble. Parkhurst crossed his arms and trapped his fists under his armpits. "My daddy use to tell me," he said, "if the freight train is coming in the tunnel, it's time to stop playing on the rails."

Nick eyed him warily.

"I'm the freight train, tiger. You better stop playing on the rails or I'm going to squash you flat."

Parkhurst left before he pounded the kid.

The Weymore Travel Agency was tucked neatly between Unerring Dry Cleaners and Fenn's Drugs on State Street a block below Main. Fran Weymore was the only good thing that came from an aerobics class Susan had mistakenly thought she wanted to take. She never could get too thrilled about exercise of any kind, but guilt or something had her out there pounding off miles. She was still waiting for that ecstatic euphoria that seemed to hit every other jogger. The weather here was such that only about three days a year were suitable for running; the rest were either too hot or too cold, so she'd looked around for an alternative. One aerobics class almost did her in. Thereafter, she'd substituted swimming.

Fran looked up from her desk with a professional smile when the door opened, then grimaced when Susan came in. "Oh, it's you."

"And it's good to see you too."

The office was equipped with a large desk, turquoise carpeting so thick you sank into it, curve-backed chairs in a pale salmon color and vivid-colored travel posters on the walls. Walking in was an experience to dazzle the eye. On a credenza behind the desk a pot of water simmered discreetly on a hot plate next to stacked boxes of the herbal tea Fran was addicted to.

"I don't suppose you've come to ask me to plan your trip to Europe." Fran wore a full turquoise skirt that matched the carpet, white blouse, a belt of silver medallions and white fringed boots; thirty-five and single, with a facility for collecting unsuitable men. Her hair color and style changed periodically. Today she had an abundance of wild red tresses cascading around her face and she did tricky things with eye makeup.

"New man in your life?" Each new relationship started out with a new hair color; maybe the thinking was if the color was right, the man would be right.

Fran grinned and tossed a lock of hair over her shoulder. "I haven't been a redhead in a long time. What do you think?"

"Looks terrific." Susan dropped into a chair, stretched out her legs and crossed her feet. "What happened to what's-his-name?"

"All those sports were starting to affect me. I was beginning to think about baseball. Why are you here? You want some raspberry tea?"

Without waiting for an answer, she swiveled and, digging her heels into the carpet, squeaked the chair to the credenza. She poured hot water in a cup and dunked in a tea bag, then squeaked back and offered the cup.

Susan shook her head. "Audrey Kalazar."

Fran swept a half-dozen bracelets up her arm with a silvery tinkle. "What's she done to attract the attention of the police?"

"Gone missing. She isn't at a conference she's supposed to be attending."

"Supposed to be?"

"She never turned up."

Fran stared at her blankly for a moment, then removed the tea bag and took a sip of hot red liquid.

"Did you see her on Saturday?" Susan asked.

Fran nodded.

"What time?"

"Eleven, a little before. She came in to pick up her tickets."

"What did she say?"

"Hand 'em over, or words to that effect."

"No 'hello, how are you, nice weather we're having, great to be getting away'?"

Fran blew gently over the surface of the tea and took another sip. "She picked up the tickets, stowed them in her purse and left."

"One o'clock flight to Dallas."

"Right. One P.M., Sunday."

"Sunday? Are you sure?"

"Of course, I'm sure," Fran said tartly.

"Sunday? She said she was leaving on Saturday."

"Don't look at me like that. Sunday afternoon flight to Dallas. Return Tuesday evening."

Susan slid lower in the chair and rested her head on the back. Dr. Kalazar told everyone she was leaving a day earlier than she actually was. Why the hell? Some plan, some activity she didn't want known? What, for God's sake? Giving the illusion the cat was away so the mice could play? Julie? Keith? She went somewhere before the conference? Where? Why?

Fran was watching her with eyebrows raised. "Something interesting going on in there?"

"Not yet."

"You want to see my records?" She sat the cup in the saucer with a clink and extracted a folder from the file cabinet. She showed Susan times and dates for Audrey Kalazar's flights.

"Thanks," Susan said.

Fran eyed her with a calculating look. "You work too hard, no social life. How would you like to meet a plastic surgeon? He could make you over to look like anybody you wanted. Or a composite. Nose from one, chin from somebody else."

"You're passing him on?"

Fran flushed. "I have something else going right now. Besides I kinda like being me."

"How would you like a kitten?"

Fran laughed. "Sophie finally got you, did she? You keep

refusing all these social offers and you're gonna end up just like her. Nuts."

When Susan returned to the pickup she found Parkhurst waiting, leaning against a fender with his arms crossed.

12

WHEN HE GAVE her a tight little grin, she felt a spurt of adrenaline. "What? Some progress for a change?"

"You might say that. A lead on Lynnelle's next of kin."

"It's about time. What have you got?"

"Stepfather. Right here in Hampstead."

She looked at him. "We've been chasing addresses and employers all over Oklahoma and Colorado and he's right here?"

"At the Sunflower Hotel. Care to go pay him a visit?" Parkhurst opened the door of the Bronco and she climbed in.

"What's his name?"

"Ingram." Parkhurst shut the door, trotted around to the other side and slid under the wheel. "Herbert Ingram."

"Herbert Ingram? Audrey Kalazar had him pencilled on her calendar for four-thirty today. How do we know he's at the Sunflower?"

"Osey spent his lunch hour making phone calls. The S's paid off. The name kind of like Shoehorn turned out to be Shoenhowser. Sound like Shoehorn to you? Not to me either. Osey got hold of Shelley's mother. She gave him Ingram. Dentist, lives in Kansas City. Osey got on to his secretary and she was the one who explained Ingram was in Hampstead."

"Lo and behold." She blew out a breath. "Get anywhere on Audrey Kalazar?"

"All negatives. She didn't get on the commuter flight to Kansas City. Her car isn't at the airport. Nobody saw her there. She didn't get on the flight in Kansas City to Dallas. So far all we have, she got in her car at home and drove off."

"She picked up her tickets." Susan told him what she'd learned from Fran.

The Sunflower Hotel was built in the early 1900s and refurbished fairly recently. The lobby had a lot of gold paint, Victorian furniture and heavy chandeliers.

Parkhurst rapped on the door of room 315.

A man in his fifties, wearing brown pants and a white shirt, opened the door; brown hair, bland round face and brown eyes that regarded them with friendly interest, a man who wanted to be liked.

"I'm Chief Wren." She held up her ID. "This is Lieutenant Parkhurst."

"What can I do for you?"

"We'd like to speak with you."

Ingram blinked slowly twice, paused then blinked again. "Why would the police want to talk to me?"

"We're conducting an investigation, Mr. Ingram. It's important that we talk with you."

"I must say, you're quite mysterious." He had a slight trace of a southern accent, so faint it was only noticeable on certain words.

A queen-sized bed with a pale-pink bedspread took up one side of the room. His suitcoat lay across the foot. Next to the bed was a table with telephone and small radio. Victorian prints hung on walls papered with a dusky pink stripe. Beneath the window were two chairs and a round table. In the corner stood a television set.

Susan settled in a chair and took note of the expensive

binoculars on the table, a book titled *Birds of Northeast Kansas* and a light gray muffler aflutter with blue jays. He backed into the other chair and sat leaning slightly forward, with the friendly look of a dog who hopes for a pat. Parkhurst stood with his back to the door.

Wishing there were some way to cushion or delay the blow, Susan spoke matter-of-factly. "As I mentioned, Mr. Ingram, we're conducting an investigation. Do you have a daughter named Lynnelle Hames?"

Ingram nodded and a wariness came into his eyes. He wasn't stupid; despite the flatness of her voice, he'd picked up on the sharper focus and was worried that something ugly was slithering around under the surface, something he probably didn't want to see.

"Would you happen to have a picture?"

Ingram looked at her, then reached into his back pocket and pulled out a wallet. He isolated a photo and handed it to her. It was two or three years old; Lynnelle, hair longer, stared defiantly at the camera with her mouth set tight, an anxious look in her eyes.

Ingram took it back and studied it closely, as though something about it puzzled him, then he tucked it carefully away. Finally, he said, "What is this all about?"

"Mr. Ingram," she said softly. "I'm afraid I have some very bad news." In flat slow words, she told him his daughter had been a victim of homicide.

"That's not possible." His pale hands, seemingly of their own volition, reached for the binoculars and cradled them in his lap. His head hunched down into his shoulders, his eyes slid from her to Parkhurst and then back to her, and finally down at his white pudgy fingers clutching the binoculars as though they were the only thing he had to hang onto.

"We'll need you to make a positive identification."

"You're telling me she's dead?" He stumbled on the last word, leaned his head against the chair back and closed his eyes. His breathing was so fast, she was concerned he might faint.

"Mr. Ingram, are you all right? Would you like a glass of water?"

He looked at her, eyes glistening. "Where is she?"

"At the pathologist's. Brookvale Hospital."

"You'll take me to her?"

"Do you feel up to it? Would you like us to call someone, a relative, friend?"

He stood up, moved to the bed, slowly put on his suitcoat, got a brown overcoat from the closet and just as slowly put that on. He simply stood there while she phoned Brookvale to alert the path department of their coming.

He was too pale. She shot a worried look at Parkhurst, who guided Ingram from the hotel and into the Bronco. He didn't ask any questions while they drove to the hospital and she let the silence hang in the air. Give him this brief respite; he'd need strength for the ordeal ahead.

A young lab tech held open the swinging doors for them. Ingram hesitated. She understood. When he went through the doors, she followed, Parkhurst behind her and the tech allowed the doors to swing shut.

A gurney with a sheet-draped form stood by the stainless steel table in the empty room. The tech scooted around them, reached for the sheet at the head of the gurney, looked at Ingram, then at Susan. She nodded. He folded the sheet away from Lynnelle's still gray face.

Ingram choked on a breath, clenched his white hands and seemed to sway. Quickly, Parkhurst was beside him, took his elbow and led him into a small waiting room off the hallway.

Ingram slumped on the black vinyl couch, head in his hands, shoulders shaking. Parkhurst went off to get him a cup of coffee, she sat in a chair at his right. For several minutes, she waited for

120

Ingram to gain control. At last, he took a handkerchief from his pocket, rubbed at his face and blew his nose.

Parkhurst returned with the coffee and placed it on the table near the couch, then stood just inside the doorway.

"Mr. Ingram," she said quietly. "Is there anything we can do? Are you sure there isn't someone we can call?"

"It's the shock. To see her like that—"

"Do you feel up to answering a few questions?" She waited while he straightened his suitcoat and took a sip of coffee. "Lynnelle was using the name Hames. Is it a married name?"

A second or two passed before he responded. "Stepdaughter. Lynnelle was my stepdaughter. I married her mother. Rose. Lynnelle was thirteen and then she became Ingram. But after high school when she left home— She wanted to be on her own. Young girls do," he said earnestly. "And then she—she wanted to go back to Hames."

"Why?"

He took a breath and exhaled slowly. "When I married her mother, Lynnelle wasn't— She resented me taking her father's place. Only natural. And then we made her use Ingram. I thought at the time it was a mistake, we shouldn't force her. But Rose wanted it, wanted us to be a family. What does it matter now? Why are you asking me all these questions? Why aren't you finding out who killed her?"

"It's helpful to know the background."

"How old was Lynnelle when Mrs. Hames adopted her?" Parkhurst asked.

Ingram looked at Parkhurst as though surprised he was still there. "She was just a baby. Rose never told her she was adopted. Lynnelle only found out after Rose died, when she was going through her mother's things. On top of her grief, she suddenly learned Rose wasn't her real mother. She was hysterical, crying that she didn't know who she was and everybody lied to her. I tried to comfort her but she—"

121

His voice caught and he bent his head. "I tried to help her. She's my daughter. I love her."

"What can you tell us about the adoption?"

"Such a pretty little girl," he said so softly she had to lean forward to hear him. "Quiet and sweet."

"The adoption, Mr. Ingram."

"Nothing. I don't believe even Rose knew. She was so delighted to have a baby, she didn't want to know. I think back in her mind, she was afraid Lynnelle wouldn't love her as much. I told her, Lynnelle, I told her I'd help. We could find her mother. But she—she wouldn't. She didn't want my help."

Gently, but relentlessly, Susan worked at getting information. Who were Lynnelle's friends, what did she like to do, did she have a boyfriend, did she mention any problems, any trouble with anyone, talk about her job, was she worried or anxious. Ingram, in a bewildered and confused manner, tried to answer, but it was clear he didn't really know much about his stepdaughter.

"When did you last see her, Mr. Ingram?"

He waited a moment as though it took some time for the question to reach him. "On Saturday. I saw her on Saturday."

The day Lynnelle was killed. "What time was that?"

"Around seven-thirty, I believe," he said slowly. "I went to her house, but she was going out somewhere, to see someone."

"Who?"

He just shook his head.

Dr. Egersund, Susan thought. "Since you were here on Saturday, Mr. Ingram, why are you back today?"

"I wanted her to come home where she belongs."

"She didn't want to go home?" Parkhurst asked.

Ingram rubbed his forehead, then pressed a thumb and fingers against his eyelids. Susan got the impression the question made him cautious. "She was upset, confused."

"You know a Dr. Kalazar?" Parkhurst's voice sounded harsh after Susan's quiet questions.

"I can't say that I do."

"No? You have an appointment with her."

Ingram nodded. "But I have yet to meet her. I've only spoken with her on the phone."

"Why did you want to see her?"

"I fail to see why the police are interested in my appointment with Dr. Kalazar."

Parkhurst put on his polite face of patient waiting.

Ingram blinked twice, paused, then blinked again, as though getting his thoughts together. "I wanted to explain about Lynnelle. She wasn't well. I felt Dr. Kalazar should know."

Parkhurst's expression changed from polite to suspicious. "Why?"

"In case Lynnelle said something that might be misunderstood."

"Like what?"

"I felt if I explained, Dr. Kalazar would agree Lynnelle shouldn't be working there."

"You wanted Lynnelle fired?"

"I only wanted what was best for her." Ingram pushed himself up from the couch. "I don't believe I can answer any more questions."

"Of course," Susan said.

When they got back to the hotel, Susan asked him, "Will you be staying for a while, Mr. Ingram?"

He looked at her and said vaguely, "I want to take her home. I'll bury her next to her mother."

After seeing Ingram safely inside, Parkhurst headed the Bronco back to the travel agency, where she'd left the pickup, and she glanced through her notes. Confirmation Lynnelle was adopted. Egersund had some more questions to answer.

"Well," she said to Parkhurst.

For a second he seemed startled, dark eyes suddenly wary. A little buzz of confusion broke up her thoughts. She looked away and fumbled for a cigarette. What did he think I was going to say? She sneaked a glance at him. If he didn't loosen his hands on the steering wheel, he was going to permanently lose all circulation.

What was the matter with him anyway? They'd finally arrived at a working relationship and now this. Goddamn it. She counted on him for clarifying her thoughts. Whatever he was stewing over, she wished he'd get it resolved. Put your personal life in order or leave it at home. "What did you think of Ingram?"

He grunted. "Lynnelle didn't want anything to do with him, told him to leave her alone. All this because she discovered she was adopted? Or was there something more in there?"

"He loved her."

"All kinds of things are done in the name of love."

"You suggesting he might have killed her?"

Parkhurst shrugged. "He tracked her down, said come live with me and be my child. She said get lost stepdaddy, I never liked you anyway. He could have gotten mad, hit her and drowned her in the creek."

"Why come back?"

"Find out if we were on his trail, realized people knew he'd been here and he'd better work up a good story. The appointment with Kalazar. Hell, come to take darling stepdaughter home in a box since she wouldn't go any other way."

He angled the Bronco in beside the pickup. It was three-thirty and she'd not yet gotten around to lunch. She started to suggest they stop somewhere for a sandwich, then changed her mind. She didn't want to put any more strain on the delicate balance between them. She stopped at a fast-food restaurant, ordered a cheeseburger and Coke and took them back to the pickup.

After two already, Sophie thought. Day's getting on. And those hard-boiled eggs she'd snacked on didn't take her very far. Parking the white Chevy at the edge of the park, she poked through the red and gold tapestry bag on the seat beside her. Cold enough, should keep people away. They scared the cat and she couldn't catch him even with dried liver treats.

Bag over her arm and black coat buttoned, she stumped toward the park, muttering to herself. Two women about to enter stepped out of her way, stared at her and decided to go someplace else. She darted across dead grass, skirted the pond and crept toward the shrubbery behind the band shell. The gray cat sometimes sheltered there. She'd been trying to capture him for weeks. Scared, he was, poor thing, ribs all sticking out. Must have been on his own a long time. At least, he was eating the food she left.

Squatting, she parted branches and peered into the thicket. There he was, huddled deep inside. She shook dried liver into a palm, held it out and crooned, "Hello, lovey. Yes, now. Food. Try a little. Just a little. So good."

As she murmured reassuringly, she crept closer. The cat inched backwards, watching her unwaveringly. He was so hungry, she thought sure he'd overcome his fear and try for the bait. Then she'd grab him.

Almost there. He was wary, but he stopped edging away. Just another two feet. Suddenly, he flattened and then was gone in a flash.

"Bah," she breathed and laboriously turned herself around to see what had frightened him. A boy stood in the shadow of the band shell, hands in the pockets of a blue letter jacket, gaze sweeping the park.

She squinted at him through the branches. Student. Bah. Ordinarily, she didn't pay much attention to students—they came and went, seemed faster all the time, and always stayed the same age—and they had a nasty habit of getting cats and then abandoning them when they left. She knew this one though. That Nick Julie Kalazar was so taken with. Why didn't he move on? The cat would never come back while he was there.

Cramps began to seize her legs and she shifted. Now, this is just ridiculous. She was starting to work her way out of the shrubbery when another boy in a gray sweatshirt jogged up to him. Why weren't they in classes? None of this wandering around when she was in school. Sat at a desk and paid attention.

They spoke to each other, but she was too far away to hear what they said. Nick took a small package from his pocket and the other boy took something from the pouch of his sweatshirt. They exchanged and set off in opposite directions.

At least they didn't hang around. Maybe the cat will come back. She waited. "Getting stiff as an old pump handle."

She thrashed her way out, then stood and rubbed one knee. Being old was exhausting. She clomped off around the band shell. One other spot the cat liked, beyond the pond. She couldn't find him there either. "Now, that's just too bad." She tucked away the dried liver and went back to her car.

Clouds like a thin layer of grimy cotton covered the sky as she drove out of town and into the country, all set for home. A gray cat popped out of the ditch on her left and streaked across the road in front of her. Stomping on the brakes, she watched with a sigh of relief as the cat skimmed down the opposite ditch, leaped up the other side and picked its way daintily through the empty field toward a grove of trees.

It couldn't be the homeless waif from the park. He wouldn't be way out here. Well, she'd just better see. You never knew. And cold as it was, he might need a warm stove to sleep by. Upending the tapestry bag, she dumped the contents on the seat beside her, scrabbled through the pile for the cat treats, dropped them back in the bag and hung it over her arm.

She crossed the ditch, scooted under the barbed wire and paused to catch her breath. With long strides, she set off for the trees. Way before she reached them, she slowed, walked softly and chirped to the cat.

Her eyesight was excellent—especially long sight—even if she was on in years, and her head darted this way and that, looking for movement and a small spot of gray.

Suddenly, she pulled herself up short and squinted. Down there, just under the trees. Now, what on earth is that doing there? Muttering to herself, she went to find out.

13

SUSAN BIT OFF a chunk of cheeseburger, then started the pickup and eased out into the traffic. The radio crackled. Transferring the burger to her left hand, she picked up the mike.

"Wren," she mumbled with her mouth full.

"I've been trying to reach you," Hazel said.

Susan swallowed. "I stopped to grab something to eat."

"Hamburger, I suppose, and french fries," Hazel said in tart reproach. "You know—"

"Don't say it."

"—that's not good for you."

"It's food and it's quick. What's up?"

"Sophie called."

"Now what?"

"She found Audrey's car."

The entire force was on the lookout for that car and Sophie found it? Goddamn it, no telling what evidence she messed up. "Where's Parkhurst?"

"On the way." Hazel gave her the location and instructions on how to get there.

Susan tore off a chunk of burger, washed it down with a swig of cola and headed out of town. The sky was a uniform gray, the

128

color of lint in the pockets of jeans. So much for sunshine, and the day had started out so promising.

Two and a half miles from town, she spotted Parkhurst's Bronco parked at the edge of a graveled road and pulled in behind. The three strands of barbed wire had been cut and moved to one side. A car had churned through the mud getting into the field, but heavy rains had obliterated any distinctive treads and whatever footprints there might have been.

She crossed the field and went down the slope to a grove of trees. Audrey Kalazar's black Chrysler, mud-spattered and rain-streaked, was nosed up to a tree trunk. Parkhurst and three uniformed officers, along with a sheriff's deputy, were combing the area. He gave her a shrug to indicate they'd found nothing so far. It was already after four o'clock; there wouldn't be much daylight left for searching.

Sophie, long black overcoat flapping around her ankles, stood some distance away, like a mourner waiting for the funeral to begin. No doubt, Parkhurst had told her to get lost and that was as far as she'd go.

Osey Pickett, enormous hands and feet seeming to get in the way as usual, was going over the car. As Susan approached, he tossed straw-colored hair from his face and gave her an aw-shucks grin. He looked like a hayseed and played it up for all it was worth. When she first knew him, she'd had severe doubts about his mental ability, but she'd learned many things in the year she'd been here and right near the top was that Osey's amiable manner was an effective cover for an exceptionally alert mind.

"Anything?" she asked.

"Dings and scratches," Osey said. "Some fresh, from driving through the trees. Fingerprints on the passenger side, a few in the back. Only smudges on the wheel. Whoever drove last wore gloves. Keys were in the ignition."

The fistful of keys he handed her were attached to a silver

letter A. How very like Audrey Kalazar to brand what was hers. They bounced in her hand with a solid clink. The blue feathers Egersund had found apparently hadn't come from Kalazar's key ring. Feathers weren't her style anyway, silver was much more fitting. The car was empty and, like everything else Audrey Kalazar owned, immaculate.

"Hey," Sophie called, creeping closer. "Shouldn't you open the trunk and see if Audrey's inside?"

Audrey was not in the trunk. There was nothing in the trunk but a jack and a spare tire, and even they were immaculate. No suitcase, no handbag or briefcase.

The last of the daylight was rapidly fading, the sun managing a dying streak of orange.

"Anything?" Susan asked Parkhurst.

He shook his head. "We'll go at it again in the morning."

She tossed Kalazar's keys and he caught them with an upraised palm. "See what they belong to," she said and left him and Osey to get the car towed in.

"Something's happened to Audrey," Sophie said, striding along beside as Susan started back up the slope. "She's a woman always where she says she'll be. Good as her word and never allows anybody to question it. Even herself."

Susan's mind was working along the same lines.

"Now that husband Keith," Sophie said. "What kind of a man sits on his backside all day making up stories? Up to things." She clucked like a broody hen.

"What things?"

"Not for me to spread tales."

Ha.

"Wouldn't do to bring trouble down on foolish people who should know better. Weak, you know, and then making excuses."

"What are you talking about?"

"Susan, you ought to keep your eyes and ears open. Otherwise, how you going to know what's going on?"

"Sophie, if you know anything, I expect you to tell me."

"Already told you all I know. If I knew any more, don't you think I'd pass it on? Now, you just better get busy finding out what's become of Audrey." With a sweep of her coattails, Sophie slid into the Chevy.

George Halpern, seated at his desk, tossed down his pen when Susan came in, leaned back and clasped his hands across his rounded midsection. "What did you get from the car?"

"Nothing that leaps out at first glance." She dropped into a chair, slouched and stretched out her legs. She'd learned a lot about being chief in the past year, much of it from George, and she still relied heavily on him. Without him, her facade of cool poise would have been exposed for what it was. "Tell me about Keith Kalazar."

"Anything in particular?"

"I'm not sure. Sophie threw out some kind of hint he was up to something."

"We're listening to Sophie now?"

"Why not? She tracked down Audrey's car. That's more than we were able to do."

George took off his wire-rimmed glasses, making his pale blue eyes look tired, and rubbed the bridge of his nose. She felt a twinge of guilt; letting him work too hard, relying on him too much.

He put back the glasses and his eyes shapened into focus. "Keith is a local boy made good. Father worked at the lumber mill. Friendly man, liked to talk, went fishing whenever he got the chance. Used to be some of the best catfish ever around here. Mother died in childbirth. They had the two girls and then Keith and then the last little girl. The whole bunch was taken in and raised by the mother's sister. Don't know that she was exactly pleased, but she did it. Keith was a handsome boy, always had girlfriends in tow."

"Would he have known Carena Egersund?"

"Sure. She was a Gebhardt back then. They were kids the same age, went to school together right on up through high school."

"Did they have a love affair that might have resulted in a child?"

"You looking for a connection between Audrey's disappearance and Lynnelle's murder?"

"I don't like coincidences. And the timing is right."

"It's possible," he said doubtfully. "As I remember her, Carena was quiet and studious. Not much of one for the boys. Had plans for herself. Always looking out for a younger sister. Something not quite right about that one, as I recall."

Picking up the pen, he tapped it against the desk while he thought. "Seems to me Carena left at the beginning of one summer, right after she graduated from high school. Off to work someplace and then on to college in the fall. The family moved to Missouri right around then. And if I remember true, Keith left at the end of that same summer. I doubt you can make much of that. He got himself a scholarship and went to school somewhere too. Colorado maybe. He was the only one in the family to get an education. They were all right proud of him, even if they were bewildered by what he chose to study."

"What, ballet?"

"Worse than that." George smiled. "Psychology. He taught at Emerson a short time, then married Audrey and pretty soon he quit teaching and commenced to write."

"Can you tell me anything about Audrey?"

"Not much, she's not local. Not greatly liked, puts people's backs up. Respected, though. Knows her job and does it like God talking to Moses."

"Happy marriage?"

George rubbed his jaw. "Oh, I think probably so. She runs things, acourse. Any threat of rebellion is squashed before it gets started."

"Keith puts up with that?"

"Well, she sees to it that he has the good life. Beyond that, I expect he just quietly eases around to whatever he wants."

"What has he been up to that I ought to know about?"

"Now there, I can't help you."

Susan sat straight and sighed. "You haven't been very helpful, George."

"Sorry, ma'am. We try our best," he said with a twinkle. "You're always too impatient."

"Yeah. I want solid results within forty-eight hours or I slump into a decline."

"Go on home. Have a little something to eat, relax, watch a little television. Tomorrow might bring something new."

"That's what I like about you, George." She got to her feet. "Always optimistic."

"It all turns out the way it turns out," he said with a dry whispery laugh.

"Shove it," she said. "And go home yourself."

It wasn't very late, only a little after six-thirty, she thought as she collected her coat. That left a whole evening with nowhere to go at the moment on Lynnelle's murder or Kalazar's disappearance. A good time to get started on packing Daniel's clothes. Busy hands allow the mind to roam; right-brain, left-brain stuff. Except handling Daniel's things wouldn't be a mindless task.

It wasn't like her to put things off. As a kid, she always wanted to be first to read her class report, first in line at the dentist, homework done at the beginning of Christmas vacation. Get it over with. She'd been putting this off for over a year.

She started the pickup, turned on the headlights and pulled out of the lot, then dawdled along toward home. She could drop by Fran's. She needed to talk with her again anyway. Fran was the last person to see Audrey Kalazar. Susan cut left instead of right at Main Street. If Fran hadn't eaten yet, maybe she'd like to have supper someplace.

Fran lived in one half of a duplex, a neat white frame with red brick facing that sat on the center of U-shaped Beacon Street. The owner lived in the other half, a man in his seventies who kept a fatherly eye on Fran and worried mightily about the constant turnover of males in her life. You need to marry a nice young man and settle down, he repeatedly counseled her.

As Susan got out of the pickup, three teenage girls drifted by on the sidewalk. Their hairstyles were identical, skimmed flat on one side of the head and frizzed out in a wild bush on the other, as though they were passing through hurricane gales. The streetlight glittered on about six earrings apiece in the exposed ears. Susan smiled to herself. It was the sort of look that had the old folks shaking their heads. She caught a snatch of their twittering conversation.

"So I go, 'Anybody that diddle-head is unreal!' and he gets this scrunched-in face and he goes like, 'Hey, well how was I supposed to know . . .'" They trailed a cloud of heady perfume.

Susan pressed a thumb against Fran's doorbell.

"You look tired," Fran said.

"That's not tired, that's hungry. You feel like going out for something to eat?"

"I have wonderful stuff in the crockpot. Stew that's been stewing itself all day. My mother's recipe. Give me your coat." Fran wore what looked like a kung fu outfit in dark-green silk that swished as she padded barefoot into the living room.

Susan plopped into a low squishy chair of psychedelic greens and blues. Fran sat cross-legged on a couch piled with pillows of every possible color from white to pale yellow to oranges, reds, blues, greens, all the way to black. She liked vivid colors and unusual fabrics and surrounded herself with odd mixtures of each that somehow worked, in a stimulating sort of way.

"You sure it's only hunger?" Fran asked.

"Yep. Well, maybe a little of putting off going home."

"Ah." Fran looked at her with a squint of dawning perception. "You still haven't gotten rid of Dan's stuff."

"I can't even bring myself to look at it."

"I could take care of it for you, if you want," Fran said gently.

"I can't do that either. But thanks."

"Glass of wine?" Fran asked.

"Why not." Susan didn't drink much; she didn't much care for the taste of alcohol. Nicotine was her drug of choice.

"You're at it again."

"What?"

Lowering her chin, Fran spoke in a deep ponderous voice. "All right, I have to do this. Now. Get in there and get it done." She raked fingers through the glorious cascade of red hair. "Why do you beat up on yourself all the time?"

"So I get things done."

"Why do you have to get things done? It's highly overrated, if you ask me." Fran unfolded herself from the couch and flowed into the kitchen. A moment later she returned with two glasses of red wine, handed one to Susan and reinserted herself among the pillows. "Drink your wine and stop fretting. When you're ready, you'll do it."

"Thank you, *Reader's Digest.*"

Fran grinned. "Any time." She emerged from the pillows and padded off to the kitchen again. This time she came back with two steaming bowls of stew, put one on the table at Susan's elbow and the other on the coffee table, then went back for hot rolls, butter and the wine bottle.

Susan dipped a spoon in the stew and took a cautious taste. "Good," she said and scooped up another spoonful. "Very good. I made stew once. It didn't turn out like this."

"When your father dies when you're twelve and your mother goes into the catering business, you learn to cook. How come you ended up being a cop?"

"One of those quirks of fate that have the gods slapping their knees and howling with laughter."

"So tell me."

"I was trying to prove to my father that he couldn't run my life. So I looked around and deliberately chose something guaranteed to make him furious. It turned out I was good at being a cop, and I liked it."

"Why stay here? Not that I'm not glad you're here, but if I thought I could support myself in San Francisco, I'd be gone tomorrow."

"After Daniel died there didn't seem any point to anything. And nobody believed I could handle the job. I had to prove something, and then—" Susan shrugged. "I'm still here."

Fran broke open a roll and smeared it with butter. "I heard you found Dr. Kalazar's car."

"Actually, it was Sophie."

"Any idea why Audrey didn't get on the plane to Dallas?" There was an odd note in Fran's voice.

"How do you know she didn't?"

Fran's eyes slid away and focused on her bowl of stew. "Doesn't everybody?" She stirred, rounded up a carrot and conveyed it to her mouth.

Probably so. "Tell me again about seeing her on Saturday." Fran told her.

"I was hoping for something like she just happened to mention Rio de Janeiro is beautiful this time of year."

"Ha. The Audrey Kalazars of this world don't chitchat with the likes of me." Fran tilted up her glass and drained it. "What does Keith say?" Again that odd note.

Keith? Susan looked at her. Oh damn. Fran was somehow involved? A part of Susan's mind wanted to let it go. Another part, the professional part, suddenly stood at attention. "How well do you know Keith?"

"Oh, you know, as well as you know people."

"Like him?"

"Sure. Why not?"

Susan wished she'd just gone on home. She took a sip of wine; it tasted sour. "How long have you known him?"

"All my life, more or less."

"When did you last see him?"

Fran stiffened. "You're questioning me."

"Sorry. It's my cop's mind."

"I thought we were friends. You come into my house and eat my stew and all the time you have sneaky plans to question me like some kind of suspect."

"That's what cops do, ask questions."

"Goddamn it. Friends talk to each other. They don't set clever little traps to fall into."

"Fran—"

"Forget it. Just ask your damn questions. Go ahead. What do you want to know?"

Sometimes Susan hated this job. "Since I've known you, you've had three different men in your life."

"So?"

"New hairstyle, new color. And you've always told me about them."

"So?" Fran said again.

"You haven't mentioned the new man."

"So?"

"Is he married?"

Fran glared at her, opened her mouth to say something, changed her mind, then said, "What if he is?"

"Is it Keith?"

Fran gave her a long look as she struggled with herself. Susan kept quiet; she could see that Fran wanted to tell her.

137

"No," Fran said.

"No?"

"No, it's not Keith." Fran grabbed a pillow and crushed it to her chest.

"Frances—"

"I hate that name."

"I know." Susan loved the name, because she'd loved her aunt Frances van Dorn.

"It doesn't have anything to do with—" Fran waved a hand.

"Then there's no reason not to tell me."

"Damn it, I've never had a cop friend before. Is this how it goes?"

Oh, Fran, I'm afraid so.

Fran plopped the pillow in her lap and picked at the cording. "It's Osey," she mumbled.

"What?"

Fran raised her head, eyes snapping. "You heard."

"Osey?"

"You see?" Fran pointed a finger accusingly.

"Why all the secrecy? Osey's—" She stopped; Osey was Osey.

"That's exactly why. You're about to make a joke. He's not your dashing hero type."

"He's a good—" Susan was about to say a good kid and then thought she might have an inkling why Fran was embarrassed.

"Right. Kind, loyal, trustworthy and true or whatever all that boy scout stuff is."

"What does that mean?"

Fran gave her a wry little smile. "He's too young."

"Why did you say he was married?"

"I didn't. I was just mad. How could you think I was that dumb?"

"Look, Fran, I'm sorry." Susan struggled out of the clutches of the chair, reached for the wine and topped off her glass. It kept her from smiling fondly; and she sure didn't want to do that. Fran would never forgive her.

"Well, don't be so quick with your suspicions. I'd never take up with a married man, and if I did it wouldn't be Keith. He has to ask Audrey's permission to go out and mail a letter."

"You think he's unfaithful?" Something like seventy-five percent of married men were, but that left the other twenty-five percent.

"Oh, he probably has some sweet young thing he meets in remote places."

"Who?"

"No idea. He hit on me once. I make travel arrangements when he does book tours, sees his editor, whatever. He asked if I'd like to meet for a weekend in New York City. When I said no thanks, he pretended it was all a joke."

As Susan finished her stew and mopped up the last spicy drops with a piece of bread, she wondered who, if anybody, Keith had been romancing and if it had anything to do with Audrey's disappearance. All they had to do was find out. Simple.

Sure. Just like they'd been so sharp this far.

14

As Susan switched on the kitchen light, she braced herself for the latest kitten destruction, and looked around in surprise. The kitchen was no more of a mess than it had been when she'd left. Only so long could you tell yourself your mind was on higher things, then you had to start wondering if you weren't simply a slob.

The whole house was just as she'd left it, except the damn cat was gone. She searched from one end to the other. Could it have sneaked out when she left that morning? The poor little thing would freeze. In the bedroom, she pulled open a drawer for a flashlight to check outside and a furry little brown face stuck itself around the lamp to peer into the drawer.

"Where the hell have you been?" The amount of relief sluicing over her exposed a worrisome sense of ownership. She changed into jeans and sweatshirt, then devoted thirty minutes to the kitchen; clearing the table, stacking dishes in the dishwasher and wiping countertops. With a great sense of virtue she enjoyed a long hot bath, then took herself off to bed and snuggled under the down comforter.

Sleep eluded her. While her mind chewed over the possibility of Keith and weekends of illicit romance, errant thoughts flitted around the idea of Fran and Oliver Charles Pickett, affectionately known as Osey. Pretty brave of Keith, if he was dillydallying someone. Audrey was not a woman to quietly look the other way. She was more apt to be enraged and start handing out punishment. The thought of Mrs. Vice-chancellor enraged was awe-inspiring. Was any of this connected with Lynnelle's murder?

Outside, the wind blew and tree branches rubbed against the house with a dry creak. Ask Parkhurst, maybe he'd come across some grapevine hearsay. When she drifted off, she dreamed a black panther with glowing yellow eyes was chasing her with loud eerie screams through thick trees.

She woke sticky with sweat. Hair-raising panther cries came from downstairs. Leaping out of bed, she headed for the door, smacked a toe on her way through and stumbled downstairs. In the living room, the kitten yelling its head off, clung like a burr to the top of the drapes. Jesus. How could anything so small make so much noise? It didn't want to let go either and once free dug all its needle-sharp claws into her shoulder.

Nothing like a jolt of adrenaline to ruin a night's sleep. She stacked pillows behind her head and groped for the lamp switch, squinted at the sudden light. Three-thirty. She read Keith's book *Sins of the Fathers* until her body stopped jangling. The wind died down and she finally felt sleep creep over her. Just before her mind shut down, she thought somebody had said something she should remember.

She didn't wake until eight, feeling logy and irritable. She pulled on sweatpants and sweatshirt, did a few desultory stretching exercises and kicked herself out for a run, telling herself how good all this was for her, how much it was going to clear out the mental cobwebs. The sky was a pearl gray, making it seem earlier than it was and not improving her mood. She pounded heavy-footed for three blocks, puffing like a steam kettle, frigid air biting into her lungs. Screw it. It was too cold. She headed for home at a fast walk.

Jen, in jeans and red ski jacket with the hood up, came clattering down her front steps, textbooks clutched in her arms. "Hi," she said in a disgruntled fashion.

"Anything wrong?"

"Mom won't let me do anything."

Oh oh, this could be sticky. Susan didn't want to make any critical comments about Mom.

"I have to come straight home from school all the time. I can't do anything. I can't go to the library, or feed the ducks. I can't even go over to Judy's. All because of some stupid old killer."

"She worries about you."

"I guess." Jen kicked at dead grass with the toe of her Reeboks. "You going to catch this guy?"

"Sure."

Jen didn't seem satisfied.

"Are you scared, Jen?"

"Nah, what would a stupid old killer want with me?" She shifted her books to the other arm. "Is it dangerous being a cop?"

"Sometimes maybe, but not very often."

"What if something happens to you?"

Oh, that's what this was about. "I'm very careful so that nothing will happen to me."

Jen scowled. "Like look both ways and don't talk to strangers?"

"You got it."

"Was Dan careful?"

Tread very softly here. "Yes, Jen, yes he was. But sometimes things do happen. Not very often though."

Jen's yellow-green eyes showed the scorn she thought that was worth. "Why can't you let somebody else do it?"

"It's my job, Jen."

"Have you ever been hurt?"

Oh shit. Don't lie to a kid. Don't scare the hell out of her either. "Once."

"Bad hurt?"

"Pretty bad. But, hey, I'm still here."

"Well, you just better watch out, that's all." Jen stomped off.

It's hard when you're eleven. And maybe it never gets easy; if you care for someone, you're at risk.

She showered, brushed her hair and applied some makeup to cover the ravages of too little sleep, then dressed in a charcoal suit and pale blue blouse. As she munched through a bowl of Cheerios, she glanced over the newspaper. Headline:

DEATH SPREADS FEAR.

Fearful that a killer may strike again, business people are
hiring security guards and residents are staying home
and talk of carrying guns for protection.

"Just what we need," she muttered, shoved the paper aside and picked up Keith's book to read while she finished her coffee. The thought she'd had just before falling asleep poked around in the back of her consciousness and finally surfaced. Casey. Jen had said Mom was talking on the phone with Casey.

Susan closed the book over one finger and looked at the cover. Keith C. Kalazar. K. C. Casey? Drink some more coffee, your mind's still asleep.

The thought stuck with her while she brushed her teeth, wouldn't let go. It's ridiculous. Not possible. A wild hare. Comes from not enough sleep, making some nonsensical jump between O.C. and K.C.

All right. It's nonsense. Go talk with the woman and rule it out.

Drawing in an irritated breath, she slipped on her trenchcoat, grabbed her shoulder bag, told the cat not to have any wild parties and paced up the street to the next block.

The house was a white woodframe with a steeply pitched roof, a porch that ran the length of the front and a large many-paned window that looked out over the porch.

"Oh, Susan," Terry Bryant, Jen's mom, said with a start of surprise. Her usual twinkly smile was a little brittle around the edges. She'd been a high school cheerleader and never quite got out of the habit. She blinked her mascaraed lashes.

"May I come in for a minute?"

"Oh well, yes, I guess so." Terry flipped back the fluffy brown hair that curled down around her shoulders. "I'd offer you some coffee, but I really need to get to work."

Susan didn't know her very well; their acquaintance mainly consisted of a hello and a nod when they happened to run into each other. Terry was the sort that always tried to please; thirty-three, a couple years younger than Susan, dressed smartly in green skirt and sweater that matched her green eyeshadow. She worked part time at Rieff's bookstore.

"It'll only take a minute." Without waiting for an invitation, Susan sat on the couch. Keith's book lay on the coffee table; his picture on the back cover smiled out at her. She glanced at Terry who inched uneasily onto a chair. Maybe this wasn't so farfetched.

"If it's Jen, I'll tell her to stop bothering you."

"Jen never bothers me. If I had a daughter, I'd like her to be just like Jen." Terry didn't seem too pleased about that; the little hero-worship on Jen's part stirred up jealousy. "What do you know about Audrey's disappearance?"

Terry gave a nervous little laugh. "Me? Why would you think I'd know anything?"

Susan eyed her steadily; Terry started to fidget. Hit her with it and see what happens. "Because you're having an affair with her husband."

Terry's face flamed red. Right on, Susan thought.

"I don't know what you're talking about."

"Oh Terry, that isn't something you can keep secret." Susan tried for a calm voice of omniscience.

"It isn't what you think." Terry looked down at her black high-heeled shoes.

Susan kept quiet.

"We were in love." Terry's chin rose defiantly, or defensively.

Susan nodded, wondered if Terry realized she'd used the past tense. She suspected Terry repetitiously picked at the situation in those four A.M. moments when the mind perversely chooses imagined dialogue instead of sleep.

"We didn't mean for it to happen. He's a wonderful man, a wonderful writer. He's warm and sensitive and—"

"How long have you been seeing each other?"

"About eight weeks. It just happened. We would chat when he'd come into the store. I told him I was trying to write and he asked me about it, and he offered to look at my work. He helped me, gave me encouragement. And then—" Terry plucked at the pleats in her skirt.

One thing led to another. "Did Audrey know?"

Terry shook her head. "He was going to tell her. He really was. It's just that—"

Waiting for the right time, no doubt. "Do you think he got—angry with her?"

Terry looked horrified. "Did something to her, you mean? No!"

"How can you be sure?"

"I just am. He's not that kind of man. He'd never do anything like that."

"Who knew about you and Keith?"

"Nobody."

"Jen?"

"Of course not. It's not— I always call him K.C. She doesn't— Nobody knows."

"Terry." Susan came down heavy to keep up the I-know-it-all act.

"We were very careful." Obviously Terry's conscience was bothering her to the point where she wanted the relief of confession; maybe even a little part of her wanted to punish Keith for not telling Audrey.

"Where did you meet?"

Terry scrunched further back in the chair. "Different places. Topeka mostly. Sometimes in Kansas City. When Jen was at school or staying with her father. We'd go to dinner, sometimes a movie and—"

Check into a motel. Susan felt sorry for her. "You did see each other here on occasion."

"We never did."

Susan looked her disbelief.

"Only once. By the creek." Terry studied the bright red nail polish on the hands in her lap. "We didn't know anybody was living there," she murmured.

"Where?"

Terry looked up, then away. "The old Creighton place."

Oh shit. "Lynnelle saw you."

Reluctantly, Terry nodded.

Damn, Susan thought, I wanted a connection between Lynnelle's murder and Audrey's disappearance. Now I've got it. Jen's mom. Beware what you wish for.

"There you are," Hazel said when she walked into the department. "The mayor's on the phone."

"What does he want?"

"The latest on Audrey Kalazar, and where is the budget."

"Tell him I'm not in yet." Susan turned around and marched back out. She hadn't done anything with the budget except haul

146

it around with good intentions. She also hadn't talked with David since the body was found; with Parkhurst throwing out dark suspicions, that was something she'd better do.

David McKinnon's office was on a side street three blocks from the center of town, in a square red-brick two-story building. She'd met him the year before when she needed an attorney to help her release her rights to the farmland her husband had owned jointly with his sister. At that time David had only been in Hampstead a little over a year and was still picking through the emotional baggage of divorce. She was trying to survive the loss of her husband. After Daniel's death, she resigned from the whole male-female thing; the risk was too great and the cost too dear; cold showers were always available and hardly cost anything.

The elevator in David's building was carpeted—floor, walls, ceiling—in a tweedy brown. Certainly was quiet. Maybe better to concentrate on the horrors that awaited at your doctor, dentist or attorney.

The reception area was one of hushed prosperity, with comfortable chairs and Impressionist prints on the walls. A capable, middle-aged woman with the unlikely name of Gwyneth guarded the door to the inner sanctum; she took her responsibilities seriously. Formidable lady. Brought to mind the woman who'd taught Susan's eighth-grade geometry class.

"Good morning, Mrs. Wren. May I help you?"

Never once had the woman called her "Chief" Wren. The feminists still had a long way to go in Hampstead. "Would you ask David if he would see me for a minute?"

"Have you an appointment?"

Gwyneth knew full well she didn't. "No."

"He's awfully busy," Gwyneth said with a smile that managed both doubt and regret. "Could it wait?"

"No."

With a sniff, Gwyneth pushed a button on the phone and murmured into the receiver. "Go on in," she said when she hung up, her tone just short of "and don't waste too much of his time."

David rose from behind his desk. At nine-thirty, he'd already shed his blue suitcoat, loosened his tie and rolled up his shirt-sleeves. Pale sunshine from the window at his back leant a saintly aura to his blond curly hair and sculptured features. He looked tense with the slightly weary distraction of unhappiness. "Would you like some coffee?"

"The dragon lady doesn't want me to stay too long."

"We'll drink fast. Have a seat. I'll be right back."

She waded through gray carpeting and sank into a black leather armchair that creaked like a ship under sail. His office—two walls of floor-to-ceiling bookshelves with impressive leather-bound tomes, desk stacked with legal papers and files—brought back feelings of her childhood. It had the same air of expensive success as her father's, the same odd mixture of reassurance and intimidation.

David returned with two mugs, handed her one and sat behind the desk. "Weighty thoughts on your mind?"

"Tell me about Lynnelle."

"You getting anywhere?"

"What did she tell you about her background?"

"Typical cop. Never answer a question. I've already told you everything I know."

"She had a notebook, loose-leaf binder, you ever see it?"

"No."

"When she called you Saturday evening, did she sound frightened?"

"Leading question," he said with a dry smile. "She sounded—" He thought a moment. "—a little breathless."

"And what did you think that meant?"

"Now you're sounding like a shrink. I'm not sure I thought about it at all."

"Think now." Despite the underlying sexual pull, they'd always been easy with each other. Now he seemed stiff; it worried her, made her determined to find out what was going on.

He picked up his coffee, leaned back and took a sip. "Come on, Susan, what's all this about?"

"It's about finding a killer."

He waited, polite attentive look on his face.

"Indulge me a little," she said. "Throw caution to the winds and speculate."

"It won't help you any."

"You never know. What was your impression of her?"

"A young lady with a lot of demons. I felt sorry for her, somewhat responsible. And before you ask, my feelings were strictly paternal."

"How paternal?" No matter what Parkhurst thought, the likelihood that David was Lynnelle's father was practically nil. Twenty-one, twenty-two years ago, he'd lived in Boston; very unlikely he could have known Carena Egersund.

"Excuse me?"

"Never mind. You said she called you Saturday night about seven."

He nodded. "She sounded tense, determined." He paused. "Maybe a little nervous, maybe a little frightened. It was a brief conversation. She said the furnace had conked out. I told her I'd come by and take a look. She asked if I'd come in the morning. She'd be fine until then, she had the Franklin stove and she had something planned for the evening."

"What was it?"

"She didn't say. I didn't ask."

Going to see Egersund, Susan thought, and was personally

betting the young lady had said, Hi, Mom. I'm your daughter. "Did she tell you she was an adopted child?"

"No, Susan. I really know nothing about her."

"You said she had demons."

"You asked for impressions."

"What gave you that impression?"

He sipped coffee. "I saw her maybe half a dozen times. She seemed young for her age." He glanced at a framed photo of his own daughter sitting on the corner of his desk, a lovely young woman with long blond hair and David's blue eyes. "Laura at sixteen is more mature, more sophisticated."

Laura lived in Boston, Susan thought, with a moneyed background; that may have something to do with it.

"Lynnelle was closed in. When she came to me about living in that ramshackle house, I asked a few questions and barriers went up all over the place. She had a lost look, hurt—angry."

"Did she ever mention her stepfather?"

"She never mentioned anything about herself or her family."

"Didn't you find that a little odd?"

"You're pumping a dry well, Susan. I've told you everything I know."

No, she thought, you haven't. Why not? Parkhurst was sharp. Had he picked up something she'd missed because of friendship? She sipped coffee and let seconds tick by. Traffic sounds came from the street outside, and one impatient toot of a horn.

"All right, David. What is it? What do you know you're not telling me?"

His blue eyes sharpened; he leaned forward and picked up a pen, tapped it against his thumb. "What are you, a witch?"

"Just a cop with experience."

He looked at her for a moment. "I can see you're reading in things that are not there and jumping to conclusions. Saturday was not the best night of my life." He rubbed his forehead with

150

his fingertips and leaned back. "My wife was getting married Sunday afternoon."

"Ah, that's a hard one."

He gave her a sour smile. "We've been divorced for over two years. But on Saturday night, she didn't seem ex- at all. I was digging up bones."

"Oh, David, I don't know what to say. I'm sorry."

"I was programmed for success, sailed along through school, everything happened at the right time. Good law school. Partnership track with a good law firm. Met the right people. Made the right moves. Married the right woman, had the right child. Made partner. Worked sixteen-, eighteen-hour days. Typical success story."

"No time for your family."

"Hey, I was providing. It wasn't my job to have time for my family. One day I woke up and I was forty-one years old and my wife was gone."

"You loved her?"

"Now there's an interesting thing. The day she told me she was leaving was the first time I noticed her in over a year. Being true to my kind, only after she stopped loving me did I realize how much I loved her."

"Did you tell her you loved her?"

"I was a husband. Of course, I didn't tell my wife I loved her."

"You always make jokes at serious questions?"

"Absolutely. For a long time I couldn't breathe when I thought about her. Bad jokes were the only thing that held me together."

"You ever try tears?"

"I only cry at cheap moments. Marching bands and graduations. My daughter's boyfriends."

She smiled.

"As Saturday evening wore on, I developed an attack of the grues. I hadn't made any right choices in my life, it had all gone sour, nothing was ever going to go right again." He made a dismissive sound of disgust as he shook his head.

"I started worrying about that damn Franklin stove. No telling how long since it's been used, what kind of shape it was in. I imaged the fucking thing blowing up, setting fire to the house and Lynnelle burned to a crisp."

He fiddled with the pen, drawing small circles on the desk blotter. "I had to go out there."

"What? What time?"

"About eleven-thirty."

"Goddamn it, I should arrest you for withholding."

"Actually, I didn't. You asked where I was from eight to eleven. I answered. Truthfully."

"What about helpfully? Now we're finally discussing all this, maybe you wouldn't mind telling me what happened when you drove out there, to a house that you own, on the night when the young lady who was living there got struck on the head and left to drown in the creek."

"Nothing happened. I drove out. The house was still standing, not engulfed in flames. I knocked on the door, got no response and left."

"Was her car there?"

"I didn't see it. It may have been in back. I only went to the front door."

"You didn't see anything?"

"Not a thing. Oh, a car going in the opposite direction."

"Did it come from Lynnelle's?"

"Not that I know."

"What kind was it?"

" 'Sixty-five Mustang." He smiled tiredly. "I owned one once. Sweet little car. I totaled it. Felt like I'd lost my best friend."

"Only the driver? No passengers?"

"Only the driver, and I can't give you a description. Male, female, young, old, I don't know. It was too dark and raining too hard. My guess would be a young male, but only because that's the kind of car a kid might have."

"Why didn't you tell me this?"

He took a breath and let it out slowly. "I'm sorry, Susan. I don't know. I went a little nuts. It was embarrassing. If you want to know the truth, it scared me a little. I simply didn't want you to know."

At her desk, Susan read reports while Parkhurst paced. A fluorescent bulb in the ceiling fixture flickered periodically, driving her nuts. Three calls during the night from an elderly widow reporting suspicious noises. Responding officers found nothing.

A man heard someone in his kitchen and fired a revolver at his teenage son who'd come down in the middle of the night for a snack. Fortunately, the guy was a bad shot. Shit. They better get this cleared up before the next idiot killed his kid.

"Nick is peddling weed." Parkhurst tapped a knuckle on the desk, paced to the window and rested his rear on the ledge. "I think he has his warehouse out there."

"Why didn't we find it?"

"Smart kid. Way too smart for dumb cops. The little shit. He has an opportunity, and he's going to blow it. He could have killed Lynnelle because she found out what he was up to."

"Does Julie know about the drugs?"

"Might not bother her. The old line about it's no worse than alcohol and their elders and betters guzzle that."

"How does Dr. Kalazar's disappearance fit in?"

"Maybe through daughter Julie," he said.

A shade reluctantly, Susan told him of Terry Bryant's affair with Keith and Lynnelle seeing them by the creek.

"Either one or both together may have whacked Lynnelle."

She didn't like that scenario; Jen had enough problems. "Then got rid of Audrey? And did what with the body? And if they'd removed the problem why do anything to Audrey?"

"Leaving the path clear for true love."

She tensed her shoulders. "I don't know. I keep feeling there's something here we're not seeing." She scattered through the reports looking for her notebook and flipped pages. "Egersund had an argument with Audrey. Find out what that was about."

"Anything else?"

"Yeah. Ask Egersund what kind of car her son drives."

Parkhurst raised an eyebrow.

She told him what she'd learned from David.

Parkhurst grinned. "So your friend the attorney has been lying to us."

15

CARENA LOCKED HER office and left the building with a feeling of relief. One more day of school over, even if it was only Wednesday. Two more days and then a weekend. All this lying and dithering was pulling her deeper in trouble, and making her short-tempered and irritable. At least, she hadn't been arrested yet. Damn it, she looked at problems, figured all the possibilities, then chose what seemed the best solution and tried to carry through as well as she could.

Twenty-one years ago, God help her, she'd tried to do the right thing. Agonized and worried, struggled with the fear and guilt, tried to ease the sense of shame and sin. Once the baby was born and given up for adoption, she'd worked on the theory that it was over, past, and was naive enough to believe the whole thing *was* over, a closed system.

Ha. She should have applied a little math. Godel's theorem. Any closed system, no matter how perfectly closed, always produces facts that are true, yet can't be proven from the elementary propositions of the system.

The wind had a sharp sting and nudged along a cluster of fleecy clouds in a faded blue sky. Briefcase in one hand and the other hand in the pocket of her tweed coat, she headed down a slope toward the parking lot and ran into Julie Kalazar and Edie Vogel on the driveway by the administration building.

Edie, eyes watery and nose red, sneezed into a soggy tissue. "Sorry," she said and poked the tissue into the pocket of her dark-green coat. "Lousy cold."

Carena nodded sympathetically and turned to Julie. "Any word about your mother?"

Julie, in jeans and blue down jacket, armload of books clutched to her chest, shook her head miserably. The wind tossed a strand of straight brown hair across her face and she tried to brush it aside with a raised shoulder. "Everything is so awful and now—" The books slipped, she grabbed at them, then dropped them all and burst into tears.

Carena and Edie gathered up the books and stacked them in Julie's arms. Carena patted her shoulder, wishing she had some words of comfort. Julie wandered off.

"I think she had a fight with her boyfriend." Edie sneezed and scrabbled in her pocket for another tissue. "It's too much on top of Lynnelle and her mother and everything."

"Did you know Lynnelle pretty well?"

"We were good friends. She had troubles and I've got troubles and that made—" Edie crushed the tissue in her hand. "Like a bond."

"What troubles did Lynnelle have?" Carena shifted the briefcase to her other hand and stuck the cold one in her pocket. She preferred to think Lynnelle had been a longed-for child, cherished and coddled, with a storybook life.

"Sad things, hard things." Edie patted her nose with the balled up tissue. "Oh, I wish— I just wish—" She blinked pale lashes wet with tears. "Lynnelle wanted something good to happen. But that's life, huh? You hope and you plan and you try and what happens? Like she said, a broken pumpkin." Edie suddenly looked frightened.

Thinking of her daughter, Carena thought, and sick with worry.

"I'm rambling," Edie said angrily. "Don't pay any attention." She sneezed again. "It's just this dumb cold."

"You shouldn't be standing around out here. You need a comforter and hot tea."

Edie almost smiled. "You sound just like my mother."

"We can't help it. Mothers are programmed that way."

Carena crossed the street and went to the parking lot. A student trudged past with her head down and her shoulders hunched, tears trickling down her cheeks.

Everybody I run into is crying. As Carena got in the old maroon Volvo and turned the ignition, she felt like crying herself. The starter made a slow *ugh, ugh, ugh*. Come on. Don't do this. Please don't die on me.

The motor wheezed, coughed, and she fed it more gas. It caught, faltered and, after she held her breath, decided to run. All right. Good reliable Swedes. Well, except for her ex-husband. She let the motor warm up before she backed out and set off for home.

A black Bronco was parked in front of the house when she got there. Oh no. As she pulled into the driveway, Ben Parkhurst got out of the Bronco. She drove into the garage, cut the motor and, in the rearview mirror, watched his approach. He moved inexorably toward the garage. Like Nemesis. No, that couldn't be right. Nemesis was female. Like Alastor. What would he do if she slammed into reverse and screeched off with a smoke of rubber? Probably set up roadblocks. She opened the car door and slid out. Inside the house, Alexa set off a clamor of welcome barks.

"Dr. Egersund," Parkhurst said with a nod. "I'd like to ask you a few questions."

No more questions. Not now. I'm too tired to see the steel traps. "Do I have a choice?" she snapped.

157

He smiled. "Yes, ma'am."

By God, the man can smile. She couldn't have been more startled if a stern rock face on Mount Rushmore had cracked a grin.

"There are always choices," he said. "But some are wrong."

His light tone confused her. Wrong choices? Story of my life. I schemed and planned to have a baby adopted, married the wrong man, came back to Hampstead, where I spent the first part of my life trying to get away from, withheld information and now I stand here, like "the man in the synagogue with an unclean devil, in front of authority and power who commandeth the unclean spirits to come out."

A giggle rose in her throat. Oh my God, I probably look an obvious mass of quivering guilt. "What questions?" She raked fingers through her short blond hair and then wished she hadn't. It probably stood on end, making her look like a guilty madwoman.

"Could we go inside?" he asked mildly.

"No."

Somewhere behind his dark eyes there lurked a detached amusement. She felt foolish, but like a recalcitrant child, having taken a stance was forced to stick with it and shiver in the cold. The dog continued to bark.

Parkhurst leaned against the rear fender of the Volvo, relaxed and apparently unaffected by the cold. "Last Saturday night," he said. "Your son was here?"

She waited. You're not going to bring Michael into this.

"What time did he arrive?"

"About eleven, I think."

"You're not sure."

"About eleven," she repeated.

"You were at home when he got here?"

"I've already told you."

"You got home at what time?"

"Close to twelve."

"Where were you?"

"I already told you that too. Several times. Driving. Just driving."

He stared at her impassively, reeking disbelief.

"I often do that when I want to think." Oh hell, stupid thing to say. His intent was to goad her into saying something and she had obliged.

"What were you thinking about?"

When she didn't respond, he said, "Rainy night, cold. The thinking must have been important to keep you out in that kind of weather."

Her mind scurried around for an apt quotation. Stop it. Pay attention.

"Thinking about Lynnelle? Wondering what to do about her?"

Bang on, she thought and tried to stare just as impassively as he did. "I teach, Lieutenant. Sometimes it's a difficult job."

"I see. Maybe you were thinking about your argument with Dr. Kalazar."

That wasn't a question she expected, or even worried about a whole lot. She relaxed a little.

"What was that about?"

"Actually, I'm not quite sure."

"I see," he said again and seemed to imply a wealth of seeing.

"It was about Julie."

"What about her?"

"She's in my calculus class, bright young lady. She started out doing very well. In the last four or five weeks, she's slipped way down."

"Dr. Kalazar blamed you?"

"I expect she blamed Julie."

"What was Dr. Kalazar angry about?"

Carena took a breath and let it out slowly. "I've been a

teacher for a long time and I know when a student has a problem he or she can't handle. They have a lot of pressure; from peers, from parents, from school, from all sorts of directions. Julie wasn't able to concentrate. I suggested talking with a counselor might help."

"Dr. Kalazar was upset about that?" he said with skepticism.

"Yes, Lieutenant, she was *upset*. I had no right to interfere. She knew what was best for her daughter. If Julie had a problem Julie could come to her."

"Dr. Kalazar threatened to have you dismissed."

"She couldn't. Not for that."

"What could she have you dismissed for?"

"Nothing," Carena said.

"You're not worried about your job?"

"No." Well, maybe a little. She might see to it that I'm not on the staff next year.

"Where did all this driving on Saturday night take you?"

"I don't remember."

"Out to Lynnelle's house?"

"No."

"You don't remember where you went, but you remember where you didn't go?"

Her fingers strayed to her temple where a little throb meant the start of a headache. "I didn't go out there. I went— I don't know where I went. I just drove, through town and around the campus and—west. I drove west. In the country. Just around."

"Did you see anybody?"

"I maybe did. It was late. Nobody I knew. Only another car or two. I wasn't paying attention." I didn't know I was going to need an alibi.

His flat eyes held hers in a steady gaze. Like jacking a deer, she thought. And I'm just as paralyzed and just as scared.

Parkhurst nodded. "Thank you, Dr. Egersund. You've been very helpful." He pushed himself away from the fender and drifted toward the driveway, as silent and deadly as a predator.

Have I, indeed, and what does that mean? At least he's leaving.

Just outside the garage, he turned. "Oh yes, one other thing. What kind of a car does your son drive?"

Maternal instincts raised their hackles. "Why?"

"Simple question. If you won't tell me I'll find out another way."

"An old Mustang. 'Sixty-five. Metallic green."

"Thank you. Good evening."

She watched him go down the driveway, get in the Bronco and pull away. Why had he asked about Michael's car?

Alexa kept up her little woo woo woo cries of joy when Carena came into the screened back porch. "Okay, okay, I'm coming." Juggling purse and briefcase, she found her key and stuck it in the lock. Alexa sniffled and scratched along the inside of the door. As soon as it started to open, the dog plunged out and stood on her hind legs with an elephantine wiggle. Carena knelt and hugged her. "Oh dear, Lexi, it's all getting worse and worse." The radio clock on the cabinet read four-thirty. She found aspirin and swallowed two and wondered if Michael would be in yet.

She tried his number and was a little surprised when he answered. "Hi, sweetie, this is your momma."

"Ah. *Guten nachmittag, Mutter.*"

"And a good afternoon to you too, *sohn*. How's everything?"

"*Gross.*"

She laughed. "Is that German or English?"

"Half and half. German is gross. And that's English. You okay, Mom?"

"Oh, fine. What are you up to besides German?"

"Oh, this and that." There was a pause and then he said, "I'm going to have dinner with Dad."

"That's nice, honey." She was sorry she'd asked. Michael

161

always felt uncomfortable mentioning his father and she didn't quite know how to make him feel easy with it, let him know it was fine with her that he loved his father.

"Michael, last weekend when you were here?"

"Yeah?"

"You tried to see that young woman Lynnelle Hames."

"Uh-huh."

"You said you went to her house."

"I drove around, finally found the place. She wasn't home. Why?"

"Did anything happen? Did you see anybody?"

"Huh-uh. What's up, Mom?"

"Tell me about going out there. What happened?"

"Why do you want to know?"

"Could you just do it? Indulge your old mother."

"Well, I guess, but—"

"Just do it."

"Okay," he said, drawing the word out. "It was raining. Windshield wipers, swipe-swipe, swipe-swipe. Long driveway with potholes full of water. I was thinking, wrong again, and then I came to the house. Looked abandoned. Dilapidated. Porch light on, though, and a light on inside. I knocked on the front door. Nobody came. I was leaving when this monster came rushing around from the back. I thought, this is it. The end. Slavering beast rips apart brilliant student."

"Big white dog?"

"Yeah. Wet and bedraggled. The thing barked at me and raced back and forth like it wanted me to follow. Lassie, you know? So I did."

"You followed the dog?"

"Not very far. Around to the back of the house. Big old tree. Creepy. I mean we're talking Halloween III here." He hummed an ominous da da *da* da. "I mean the rain and the dark. Owl

162

going *who who*. Then there was this clap of thunder, like a cannon. I went straight up about six feet."

He was silent a moment, then said, "I did see something."

"What?" she asked with a sharp intake of breath.

"Nothing dangerous, Mom. Don't worry. Big flash of lightning. Okay? Can you picture it? Rain, trees, owl, thunder, then this lightning. Whole world got bright for just an instant. About fifty yards away, a bunch of trees." He paused. "I thought I saw somebody standing there."

"Who was it?" She felt a pulse beat in her temple.

"It was only for a second, you know, and I sort of thought— Well, I thought it was you. Dumb, huh? Then I figured I imagined it."

"What did you do?"

"Nothing." He gave an embarrassed laugh. "Unheroically, I scarpered, as my Brit mate would say. Why you want to know all this?"

"Well, Michael, she was— Oh, honey, something awful happened."

She told him about Lynnelle's death but said nothing about being a suspect or the police asking about his car.

"God, Mom. I don't get it. I mean, why? She—" His voice was strained and suddenly sounded much younger. "She kind of reminded me of Timmy. Remember Timmy?"

"Yes, darling, I do." Timmy and Michael were fast friends when the boys were twelve.

"Like she needed looking after, you know? Just like Timmy, stumbling over stuff and losing his lunch money and nobody paying attention and always being in the wrong place at the wrong time. I mean, if you're friends, you're friends and you stick up for 'em."

"Yes," she said. She let him talk as long as he wanted and when he ran down she told him she loved him.

"Love you too, Mom."

She listened for the click, then hung up. Chickens coming home to roost. She stared into the refrigerator for a time, then abruptly took out the bottle of white wine, poured a glass and sat at the table. Alexa squeezed underneath and flopped across her feet.

Guilt, that old shrunken deformed devil guilt, hissed in her ear. Ssinsss. "Ye have sinned against the Lord and be sure your sins shall find you out." You thought adoption was the end of it? What happened to that child? You never thought to find out.

When I thought of her at all, I pictured birthday parties, loving mother tucking her in at night, doting father taking her for pony rides. Troubles, Edie said, Lynnelle had troubles—bad things, hard things. Carena shook her head and trickled more wine in the glass. Every child thinks she—or he—has troubles. Lynnelle was adopted by good people who wanted a child. She was cared for, loved.

The old devil shook with wheezy laughter. You took care of a problem and then washed your hands of it. Swirling the glass, she held it toward the light and watched the pale liquid circle. "Pontius Pilate took water and washed his hands."

She banged the glass down on the table. When I start quoting scripture it's time to take steps. She squinted at her watch; five-fifteen. Steps better wait until tomorrow. I can either find something to eat or sit here and get drunk. "It is good neither to eat flesh, nor to drink wine." Or maybe I could get the mail.

Pushing herself away from the table, she stood up, took another sip of wine, then went through to the living room and opened the front door. The dog snaked past and bounded off.

"No! Alexa!" Carena raced down the steps. "Alexa! Come back here!"

The dog was already out of sight. Goddamn it. How would you like to stay out there? She stomped back inside for her car keys.

She parked at the rear of the malevolent-looking house, black against the slate sky with a pale moon rising behind it half-hidden by a trail of clouds. Shivering, she got out of the car. What if it didn't start when she got back in? That didn't bear thinking about. Michael was right, this place was creepy.

Don't get spooked by your own imagination. Get the dog and get out of here.

"I knew you would come."

Carena's hair stood on end. Pale moonlight filtered through the branches of the oak tree. A figure in a raincoat sat in the rope swing, hands gripping the rope on each side. Carena thumbed on the flashlight.

"Caitlin!"

Caitlin turned her head away from the light.

Carena knelt in front of her, looking up at her face. "What are you doing here?"

"I belong here."

"You certainly do not." Carena rose. "Come on, let's go."

"It's quiet here. Can you hear the quiet?"

"You're freezing. We have to go." She tried to pry Caitlin's cold fingers from around the ropes.

"It's warmer inside. There's a sleeping bag."

Carena could not get Caitlin's hands to release their grip. Stay calm. She stopped pulling at Caitlin's fingers, took a breath and spoke normally. "How long have you been here?"

"It's my fault."

"Nothing is your fault. Caitlin, listen to me. We have to go."

"Nothing can hurt her anymore."

"Caitlin, give me your hands."

She stared over Carena's shoulder. "They're coming."

Heart pounding, Carena swung the flash around. Glassy eyes glittered in the light. Alexa bounded toward them from the woods, pranced up to Caitlin and scrubbed her face with a wet tongue.

"Oh, Carrie, isn't she beautiful?" Caitlin's voice lost the eerie,

165

distant tone and with tears running down her face, she slid from the swing and threw her arms around the dog.

"Caitlin, how did you get here?"

"I can't remember. It scares me when I can't remember. It's going to be bad again."

"No, Caitlin." With a hand under one elbow, she urged Caitlin to her feet, brushed the tangled hair from her face and rubbed a thumb across the tears.

"She's hurt herself." Caitlin nodded at Alexa who had flopped down and was noisily licking one front paw.

"We have to go now," Carena said and nudged Caitlin toward the car.

Alexa limped alongside.

16

Alexa jumped in, spread herself across the backseat and licked her paw. Carena settled Caitlin, shivering and teeth chattering, in the front, buckled the seat belt around her, and made sure the door was locked, wishing there was some way to prevent it from being opened. She could almost feel Caitlin slipping away inside herself.

The drive to Topeka was a nightmare. They sang hymns. Whenever Carena tried to stop, Caitlin got agitated and Carena was afraid she would fling herself from the moving car. The road stretched endlessly, hypnotically in front of the headlights; the windows were fogged, the heater droned, and they sang.

By the time they pulled up in front of Caitlin's house, Carena was hoarse. She got out of the car, went around to the passenger side and helped Caitlin out. A porch light went on, the front door opened and Phil came out on the porch. For a moment, he stood there, then ran down the steps.

"Where the hell have you been?" He grabbed Caitlin's arm and she shrank back against Carena.

"Let's get her inside," Carena said through clenched teeth. Damn him, why did he always attack. The throb in her temples grew worse.

In the living room, a pleasant room with soft shades of green, pale-green carpet, paler green walls and flowered chairs, they got Caitlin to the couch and wrapped her in a blanket. She was quiet now. Curled like a fetus, face turned away, she was starting to withdraw into the deep stillness that made Carena want to cry.

Phil Avery looked down at his wife with fatigue and anger. He was in his mid-forties, a stocky man with a few strands of gray in his carefully combed brown hair and a heavy jaw that always looked in need of a shave. He wore dark suit pants and white shirt with the cuffs turned up. He had a square face that looked tired, the skin was soft and pinched around his eyes and mouth, and his eyes were slightly bloodshot.

"I'll call her doctor," he said in a dead voice.

Carena sat beside her sister and crooned softly, brushed hair from Caitlin's face. "I'm sorry, darling. I know you can hear me. Just listen. I love you. I'm so sorry this is happening again. Just remember you'll get better. You've done it before. You rest, heal yourself. Don't give up."

When Phil came back, she stood. "How long has she been gone?"

He rolled down his cuffs and buttoned them. "Since Saturday night?"

"Why didn't you let me know?" The headache surrounded her eyes in a tightening web of pain.

He glanced around for his tie, found it over the back of a chair and slid it under his collar. "Dr. Brock said I should take her in to the hospital. He'll meet us there."

Carena hated to see Caitlin small and still in the sterile room with its white walls and smell of antiseptic. Twice before she had gotten real bad, babbled about her dark angels and terrifying crows, and cut her wrists. Carena kissed her motionless sister and said she would be back very soon. The tears she was trying to hold back dribbled down her face on the drive home.

Caitlin will get better, Carena told herself in much the same tone as she had used with her sister. She has before. As long as she was in the hospital and sedated, at least she couldn't hurt herself.

It was after midnight when Carena got home. She undressed quickly, dropped her clothes on the end of the bed and climbed in. Pulling the covers up to her chin, she closed her eyes.

Was it some predetermined genetic code that decreed Caitlin must carry all the family pathology? She was the best of them, the brightest and the kindest and the softest and the most gentle. Was that why? If Martha Ann hadn't died, would Caitlin still be battling her dark angels? Or would they be safely locked away in some far corner of her mind?

Martha Ann, curly-headed baby, unexpected and the darling of the family. Martha Ann, who had only two years of life. Caitlin was looking after her, had taken her outside to play and Martha Ann wanted her pink teddy bear. Caitlin went in to get it and, in that brief moment she was gone, Martha Ann grabbed the garden rake near the metal end and darted for the steps going down to the driveway. She fell. The tines pierced her throat.

Tears filled Carena's eyes and ran down her cheeks. Much later, she had taken the hose and washed the blood from the driveway.

Students hated eight o'clock classes and tried with creative endeavor to avoid them. This class seemed endless, and the kids who couldn't fit in calculus at any other period looked semicomatose—those that weren't studying for their next class or watching the clock or asleep with their eyes open.

Carena slogged on, not very inspired, not raising a spark of interest. Julie Kalazar, her best student at the beginning of the semester, now close to failing, looked scared. Nick Salvatierra, whom she'd struggled hard with, had reverted to his sullen scowl. When the period finally ended, she went to her office and phoned Phil at work. He was short with her. He didn't like grim reality intruding into his professional world, the one he could control, the one where he invested most of himself. He had nothing new to tell her about Caitlin. She punched in another number and made an appointment with David McKinnon. Even that much felt like action and the rest of the classes weren't quite so burdensome.

At four, she walked into David McKinnon's office. With a smile, he rose from behind his desk, came around it and extended a hand to shake hers. Dark suit, discreet tie. A very good-looking man; she'd forgotten how good-looking. Her ex-husband was very good-looking. Handsome men expected, as some sort of rightful due, pampering and kowtowing. She perched on one of the two black leather chairs beside a low round table. Maybe coming here was a mistake. He wasn't the only attorney in town. He regarded her with eyes a remarkable shade of blue. Even though the office was sufficiently warm, recessed lighting making it seem pleasantly light after the gloom outside, she shivered and kept her coat on.

"Would you like some coffee?" he asked.

"What I'd really like is an aspirin."

"I can probably provide that." Picking up the phone, he spoke to his secretary and a moment or two later, she brought in a tray with two mugs, cream and sugar and a small bottle of aspirin. Taking the tray from her, he murmured his thanks and she withdrew. He put the tray on the low table in front of Carena and sat in the other chair. She unscrewed the bottle cap, rattled two tablets onto her palm and swallowed them with a gulp of scalding coffee.

"What can I do for you?" he asked.

"I think I'm going to need an attorney."

"Why do you need an attorney?"

"I think I'm going to be arrested for Lynnelle's murder."

"Why do you think that?"

She looked past him at the cold gray sky out the window and then down at the mug clutched between both hands. I should have thought more before I came, figured out how much to tell him.

"There are three people you should never lie to," he said quietly and sipped coffee.

She looked at him.

"Your physician and your attorney."

She waited and when he didn't go on, she asked, "Who's the third?"

"Either God or the IRS, I forget."

The laugh bubbled out. "God was a big issue in my life. I don't recall much mention of the IRS."

"Why do you think you'll be arrested?"

"They think I've been lying to them."

"Have you?"

She hesitated.

"Whatever you tell me is privileged. I can't be forced to reveal anything to the police."

"I know that," she said and added quickly, "I didn't kill her."

"You have information you haven't told them?"

"It's not— Nothing that will help. Nothing about the murder. If I did, I would— I'd tell them."

"It'd be more helpful, if you'd tell me the stuff that goes between the pauses."

She tried a smile that felt sickly even to her. "Aren't you supposed to be on my side?"

"Absolutely." He gazed at her with sharp intelligence.

Too sharp. All she wanted was an attorney to represent her if it came to that, not a ferret.

"You're trying to protect someone," he said.

"Myself," she snapped.

"You're afraid whoever it is might have killed her."

"No." The aspirin hadn't helped any and pain throbbed in her temple. "I'm afraid the police will think so." Especially if they talk with Michael and he tells them he saw me out there.

"Lynnelle thought you were her mother."

"I'm not. I wasn't. How do you know that?"

"An inference from questions asked by Chief Wren." He studied her closely. "You know who her mother was. Someone close. Friend? Relative? Sister?"

Oh hell. *Trouble thou wretch, that has within thee undivulged crimes.* "She was fifteen and scared to death." I was just as scared and trying not to let her know. "We never told anybody."

"Your parents?"

She shook her head. Good people, her parents, her kind gentle father would never have pointed a stern finger at the raging blizzard and proclaimed, Out! But they would have been devastated. "I was enrolled at the University of Oklahoma for the fall and I told them I had to be there for the summer. I made a big deal about going to a strange place and I wanted her to come with me."

That awful summer. Unbearably hot. The crummy apartment with weeds growing through cracks in the walls. The crummy job cleaning toilets. The nosy landlady with her sly, knowing looks. "The adoption was arranged through a physician."

"Why did Lynnelle think you were her mother?"

"I don't know. We told so many lies. Caitlin never used her real name."

Something flickered in his blue eyes and for an instant, he seemed to look through her.

"She was Karen Hart. Half the time I think she actually believed it. If Lynnelle in her search came across my name—I had to have a job, identification." She sighed. "If I were searching for someone, I might think Karen Hart was a phony name for Carena Gebhardt." With both hands, she raised the mug and sipped coffee, fighting down a sense of failure and betrayal.

"Why are you trying to keep all this a secret?"

Because I don't know where Caitlin was that night. I'm afraid she was there, I'm afraid it was her Michael saw. "She's never been very strong. Her worst nightmare, the child would one day show up. She never told anyone. Not her husband and—well, he isn't a very understanding man."

"You're afraid she killed Lynnelle," David said gently.

"No. She could never kill anybody. She's sweet and kind and loving, but she has fears and demons and sometimes she gets lost inside herself."

Again, she caught a thoughtful inward look in his eyes. It made her uneasy. She knew nothing about this man, not even how skilled he was as an attorney. "How long have you lived here?"

If he was surprised by the question, he didn't show it. "Over two years."

"What made you choose Hampstead?"

He smiled. Charming smile, she thought with all her cynical distrust of attractive men.

"It was more a matter of leaving where I was. This is somewhere between there and the place I should have gone."

"Stuck a pin in a map?"

"Not quite. I used to have relatives here."

"Who?"

"An uncle. Howard Creighton."

She remembered Howard Creighton. There was some scandal about his son—what was the son's name—and he committed suicide.

"I worked for Uncle Howard one summer years ago when I was a kid."

Years ago? How many years? She'd never met him, she'd remember if she had. Could Caitlin have known him? Caitlin

173

was friends with—Lowell, that was his name—and she could have been around when David was there. Caitlin had refused to say who the father was. She'd dug in her heels with unshakable stubbornness. *He can't help,* was all she'd say.

Drizzle streaked down the windshield and the wipers only smeared it. *So much for confession,* Carena thought. *I always suspected unburdening your soul wasn't all it was cracked up to be. Oh, come on. David McKinnon could not be Lynnelle's father. God wouldn't display such a bizarre sense of humor.* Consciously, she relaxed her shoulders, but it didn't relieve her uneasiness.

At home, she turned on the kitchen light, blinked a bit at the brightness and snapped on the radio to interrupt her thoughts. Tea was what she needed. She ran water in the tea kettle and set it on the stove, then shrugged off her coat and draped it over a chairback. A weather forecaster said rain turning to snow later in the day. Alexa, favoring her right foreleg, limped to the door and pressed her nose against it.

"I suppose you need to go out." Carena attached the leash and opened the door.

The cold drizzle was not to Alexa's liking and she had to be coaxed from the screened porch, then took care of her needs quickly and lurched back inside on three legs. Carena knelt to examine the sore paw. Lexi turned her head away as though she couldn't bear to look. It was bad, pads split and swollen and pus-filled. Nasty. *Why didn't I look at this before?*

The tea kettle shrieked, startling her and she rose to turn off the burner. In the phone book, she found veterinarians, slid on her coat and loaded Lexi in the Volvo.

Two people waited ahead of her in Dr. Newcomer's office, an elderly woman with a black cat in a carrier and a man with a quivering cocker spaniel. Carena sat on a beige vinyl couch that squeaked whenever she moved and Alexa plastered herself against Carena's legs.

A gust of cold air blew in when the door opened and Chief Wren, in a grey trenchcoat and carrying a cardboard box, stepped inside. Carena's pulse jumped and she took in a breath of antiseptic air. I'm going to be arrested in a vet's office, hauled away in handcuffs. Close your mouth and try not to look like a scared rabbit.

Susan, hoping this wouldn't take too long, glanced around. People waiting. Damn. Come back another time. She started to leave, then noticed Carena Egersund looking like an animal run to ground. Ah, maybe this wasn't such a waste of time. Combine responsibilities of pet ownership with hotshot police chief on heels of suspect.

Resting the box on the counter, she spoke to the receptionist, then stepped around a trembling cocker spaniel and walked over to Egersund, who watched with worry and apprehension all over her face. If only I knew the right buttons to push, Susan thought. "I understand you consulted with David McKinnon."

"Spies, Chief Wren?"

Susan smiled. Apparently, the woman wasn't as unstrung as she looked. They were speaking softly, but the other people in the room watched curiously. Egersund seemed to take heart from their presence, as though thinking Susan wouldn't attack savagely in front of witnesses. The woman was wrong about that, but Susan wasn't sure enough for a savage attack.

The vinyl squeaked as Susan sat down. She placed the box on the floor, pulled off her gloves and shoved them in her pocket. "We've located Lynnelle's stepfather. I'll let him know you have the dog."

"Stepfather," Egersund repeated.

"You knew she had a stepfather?"

Egersund loosened the fingers clutched in her lap and absently patted the dog.

"Her father died," Susan said in a low voice, "and her mother remarried when Lynnelle was thirteen."

"Her mother. Have you talked to her?"

"Her mother died two years ago."

The elderly lady with the cat carrier was summoned into the inner office. Egersund watched her go. "I'm sorry," she said so softly Susan had to lean closer to hear her.

She looked like a woman with too much to bear. For a moment, Susan felt compassion, then she pictured Lynnelle dead, blond curls plastered around a gray pinched face, twenty-one years old. Professional detachment slid back into place. "Sorry for what?"

Egersund seemed to pull herself together even more and some of the tightness left her voice. "For a lot of things. For Lynnelle, her mother, her stepfather."

Susan wasn't sure the stepfather deserved any sympathy.

"I didn't kill her," Egersund whispered.

Maybe not, but something weighs heavy on your conscience, Susan thought. The lady with the cat left and the man with the cocker dragged it into the office.

Alexa nosed the box on the floor and Susan moved it further under the couch. "What's wrong with her?" Susan nodded at the dog.

"Just a sore foot."

Right on cue, Alexa raised her paw. Just then the examining room door opened and the cocker flew out, scrabbling for escape, and the receptionist nodded at Egersund who led away a reluctant dog.

Twenty minutes later, Susan placed her cardboard box on the examining table.

"Chief Wren," Dr. Newcomer said with surprise. He was a large man with a thick chest, heavily muscled arms and huge hands with springy pale gold hair on the backs and square blunt fingers. Dense, dark-gold curls framed a wide face and sleepy-

176

lidded amber eyes slanted away from a Roman nose. He looked like a benevolent lion. "What have you got?"

"A kitten."

"Involved in some kind of crime?"

"No. Well," she grinned, "not that I know of, it came from Sophie." She unfolded the flaps. The kitten, crouched in a corner with her ears flattened, hissed when she reached in. "I brought her in for whatever immunizations she needs."

He turned to a cabinet for small vials and syringes. "What's her name?"

"She doesn't have a name. I didn't plan on keeping her."

"Oh, yes?" A deep rumble came from his chest—a laugh, she assumed—and he upended a vial and withdrew liquid into a syringe.

The cat spat and swore and it took both of them to hold her down. Small she might be, but she intended to fight valiantly to the end.

"The Samoyed you just saw," Susan said. "What's wrong with it?"

"Beautiful animal, sweet-tempered. She managed to drive a mess of wood slivers into her paw. Old rotted wood."

"How did it happen?"

"I'd say digging at old lumber, something like that."

"Will she be all right?"

"Should be fine. If I got all the splinters out. Some infection, but antibiotics should take care of that." He pinned the spitting, squirming kitten with one hand and stuck an otoscope into her ear. "Terrible thing, the young lady getting killed."

"Did you know her?"

"She was in a few times. Once the dog picked up a tick. She was afraid it was some kind of life-threatening growth. Every ounce of love and longing and need went into that dog. People need someone to love who loves them back. If they don't get it with humans, they turn to pets."

"Good for the pets."

"For the owners too. That young lady had a lot of needs. She told me she had a cat once but was forced to give it up because her stepfather was allergic to animals. She was a very—sensitive young lady."

"In what way?"

"Maybe the word is lonely or lost. I asked her if she was nervous living way out there. She wasn't." He released the kitten, who leaped into the box, crouched and glared with blazing eyes.

"She said she fit right in."

Fit right in. At that wretched place. Lynnelle's life must have been pretty empty if moving in there felt like fitting in.

Dr. Newcomer leaned back against the cabinet with his hands flat on the counter top. "I hope you nail whoever killed her."

"I will."

He nodded. "Nice healthy little kitten you have there."

I guess so. She folded the flaps and scooped up the box. The nice healthy little kitten started yelling as soon as they were in the pickup. Susan dumped her at home and set off for the station.

Head down, she slogged through the rain toward the door. A thought sailed by and slid down somewhere under the slush in her mind.

"There you are," Hazel said when she came in.

"Yes. Why?"

"Oh, nothing urgent. The chancellor called demanding to speak with you. He wants to know why you haven't found Dr. Kalazar. He wants you to call him immediately. The mayor called. He wants you to call him immediately. David McKinnon called. He didn't say what he wanted so I don't know if it's immediate. The newspaper called and wanted to know the latest about Lynnelle's murder. And Mrs. Melshan called and demanded to know why there isn't a crosswalk on the street between the library and the parking lot. She's tired of walking to the corner to cross the street. Susan, are you listening to me?"

"Yes." She flipped through messy mental files trying to retrieve the thought that got away. "Is Parkhurst in?"

"Yes, he—"

"Would you ask him to come into my office?"

"Yes. Susan—"

She wandered into her dark office and dropped into the desk chair. Come on now. Dr. Newcomer talking about Lynnelle. Lynnelle liked that malevolent house. She loved the dog. Dr. Egersund now has the dog. Injured foot. Splinters.

"You wanted to see me?"

A figure stood backlighted in the doorway and through some distortion of dimness and wavery lines of rain streaking down the window pane, she saw a childhood memory. She was twelve and in a hurry that rainy evening because she was late and it was dark. She wheeled down a hill on her bicycle, zipped into the street and was hit by a car.

When she opened her eyes she was dazzled by a man in a silver cape silhouetted in sparkling light. Tristan coming for Iseult. Later, her father told her the man had been a policeman in a raincoat.

The figure in the doorway hit the light switch and bulbs flickered on. She blinked. The image moved into focus and became Parkhurst in a shiny wet raincoat. He couldn't have been there long; she'd have felt his presence.

"You wanted to see me," he said again.

Uh, yes. She wanted to see him. She forgot why. She lit a cigarette. Rain trickled down the window. The silence got heavy. He shrugged off his wet coat. The defective bulb flickered and acted on her like a fingernail on a blackboard. Board. Black. He was dressed in black; black pants, black turtleneck sweater. He moved like a panther. That stupid dream. Forget it.

"You all right?" he asked.

179

Think about splinters. Old weathered wood. Why would the dog scratch at old boards? The thought Susan had been tracking suddenly surfaced; she stared at Parkhurst.

He raised an eyebrow. "You subject to some kind of fits?"

"I know where Audrey is," she said quietly.

17

Snowflakes drifted around them in the darkness as they stood under the trees, staring down at the weathered boards over the abandoned well. They spoke in hushed tones like a little band of medieval grave robbers and their breath made puffs of frost in the cold air.

"You can see the scratches," Susan said, moving the flashlight over the boards. "Something in there interested the dog."

Parkhurst, collar of his gray coat turned up, shoved his hands deep in his pockets. "Could be a rat."

Osey, in hiking boots and light-brown sheepskin jacket with beige cross-stitching, glanced from her to Parkhurst, then crouched and peered with beady-eyed intent at the rusty nails as he focused his flashlight on each one.

"They been lifted." He straightened up in a series of awkward jerks.

"How deep is it?" she asked.

Osey shrugged and looked around as though judging distances. "Twenty feet maybe hereabouts."

"Water?" Parkhurst said.

"Probably."

"How deep?"

181

Osey screwed up his mouth and wrinkled his forehead. "No way to tell till I get down there."

With a frown, Parkhurst looked around, half-turned and looked back in the direction of the house. "Where was the dog when Lynnelle was killed?"

"She must have been out," Susan said. "Because she was out the next morning when David and Egersund found the body."

Parkhurst scowled. "Why didn't she attack the killer?"

"Well—" Osey lifted his shoulders and crossed his arms. "That lil' dog just ain't the kind that attacks." The dog in question was in no way little, but Osey tended to use the word in affection rather than description.

"Right," Parkhurst grumbled. "Let's get on with it."

Osey inched the lab van in under the trees as far as he could—she hoped he'd be able to get it out again—and they set up lights. He and Parkhurst manhandled a winch from the van to the side of the well and got to work removing rusty nails and then lifted rotten boards.

"We've got somethin'," Osey said, rocking back on his heels.

Yes. A faint musty sweetish odor of death and decay tainted the clean cold air. Could be a rat, she reminded herself, to slow her racing pulse.

Crouching forward, Osey shined a flashlight down the inside of the well, brick-lined with a row of rusty metal rungs running down one side. Far below, the light fanned out, bounced off slimey bricks, and dissipated like translucent fog against black night.

"Water down there all right," Osey said. "Hard to tell how far." He looked at her. "We could drop in a rock and count till we hear the splash."

"No!"

He grinned. "Joke, Chief."

Ha ha. Hidden beneath that country bumpkin exterior lurked a good investigator, but now and then he couldn't resist getting a rise out of her by playing the dumb hick; too often, she fell for it.

"You okay to go down there?" Parkhurst asked.

"Sure." With his usual amiable willingness, Osey ambled off to the van to change into a wet suit. She'd never known anyone as affable and compliant as he was. His appearance reminded her of a scarecrow, tall and lean, and he moved with a disjointed awkwardness. When he clomped back, he sounded like a rubber raft on a choppy sea.

"You be careful," Parkhurst said as he buckled a webbed safety harness around Osey's chest and attached a line from the winch.

"Don't worry, Mom." Osey adjusted a light—the kind used by underwater divers—on his forehead. Gingerly, he put his foot on the top rung and bounced lightly. "Seems okay. Mortar's a little crumbly round these bricks."

He went down a rung and rested his elbows on the rim. "You reckon this is why I became a cop?" He pulled the mask over his face, stuck the air hose in his mouth, and with a jaunty wave started down.

Slithery sounds of rubber against brick drifted up, but the winch line stayed easy as he worked his way down. Watchful silence seemed to creep in with the falling snow. Atmosphere. Auras. Had Lynnelle found them welcoming? Susan didn't feel any welcome, or malignancy either, only this watchful waiting. Bullshit. Irritably, she cinched tighter the belt of her trenchcoat.

Parkhurst, snowflakes dusting his shoulders and glistening on his dark hair, waited motionless, breathing a thin stream of frost, a gloved hand lightly on the line. He'd be terrific on a stakeout, all that ability for unagitated waiting. She hated waiting; impatience acted on her like hives, making her itch and twitch. She tried to curl her cold toes inside her boots and shifted her feet.

Splashing came from the well and Osey yelled, "Ooo-kay!"

The long syllables split through the stillness like the ripping of cloth.

His head popped up and he jerked off the mask. "We found it."

"Audrey Kalazar?" Susan asked.

"Don't know. A body, all right. Wrapped up like a package."

"How deep's the water?" Parkhurst asked.

"Not more'n fifteen feet."

Jesus. Osey was groping around at the bottom of a black well in fifteen feet of water. Shivering, she hunched her shoulders.

Osey went back down to attach lines to the body. Several minutes later, he climbed out and Parkhurst worked the winch, slowly bringing the body to the surface. Wrapped in black plastic trash bags and tied with thin rope, it streamed water all around as they maneuvered it to the ground.

"Suitcase down there," Osey said, "and a couple other things." He slapped the mask back in place and started down again.

Some moments later, there was a tug on the line and Parkhurst winched up the suitcase. Osey reappeared with a handbag slung over his shoulder and a briefcase in one hand.

"I think that's all," he said as he handed them over to Susan. "But I want to check something."

"It can wait till morning," Susan said. "Get out of that wet suit and into some warm clothes."

"A couple a minutes," Osey said. "There's something funny about places in the mortar."

"Osey—" Parkhurst growled.

"One quick look." He climbed back in and his voice came up with a hollow sound. "Body bumped some coming up. Looks like—yeah, crumbling away."

Susan shined a flashlight down on his head. Three rungs down, he scratched and picked away at the mortar, flakes and bits and chunks plopped into the water.

"Knock it off," she ordered. "You're contaminating the site. Get out of there."

"Oh. Right. I just—" From between the bricks, he eased out a flat packet.

Telling the family was always the worst of it, Susan thought as she poked the doorbell. Keith Kalazar opened the door and the look of friendly inquiry on his face slipped into brittle caution when he saw her.

"It's about Audrey," she said.

He seemed to sag and, holding tightly to the edge of the door, he stared blankly past her shoulder and down the flight of steps behind her, as though he hoped she might turn and walk away. "Come in," he said thickly.

She followed him into a large kitchen with recessed lighting in the high ceiling and hardwood floors polished to a glossy shine. Audrey's absence was evident in scuff marks on the floor, smudges on the gleaming cabinets and dirty dishes on the ceramic-tiled countertops. A rumpled newspaper lay on the light-colored round wooden table, along with an ashtray filled with pipe debris.

"Coffee?" He motioned her toward the table and pushed up the sleeves of his brown sweater, got out filters, fit one into the coffee machine and spooned in grounds. He was putting off the moment of bad news and concentrating on the familiar. She felt sympathy. He had a lot of difficulties ahead, and the police poking into his affairs would compound them.

While the coffee dripped through, he stood with his back to her, leaning slightly forward, arms outstretched, hands clutching the edge of the countertop and his head bowed. His shoulders shook and he mumbled, "I never would have—"

She didn't hear the rest. He poured two cups, carried them to the table and carefully eased himself into a chair. Not looking at her, he sipped hot coffee as though it might bring some relief.

185

"I'm sorry, Mr. Kalazar. We found your wife's body earlier this evening."

"What——?" he whispered, cleared his throat and tried again. "What happened?"

"We don't know yet."

"I'll have to tell Julie," he said bleakly and set the cup down. "And Audrey's parents. They live in Florida. They're retired." He looked at his watch. "I don't know what time it is in Florida."

He picked up the cup and studied it. "Where?"

"Where did we find her?"

He nodded.

"In the abandoned well at the Creighton place."

"She drowned?"

"We won't know until after the autopsy."

He covered his face with his hands and sat very rigid in an attempt to control his emotions. If he had known his wife was dead, or if he had killed her, he was a terrific actor. "Is there anything I can get for you?" she asked when he got himself under control and sat straighter, squared his shoulders.

He shook his head, apparently not trusting himself to speak.

"I could call someone. Your Doctor. Reverend Mullet?"

"No."

"I'll leave now." She stood. "Call me if you think of anything that might help."

Tired and angry, sorry for the Kalazars and keyed up by finding the body, Susan headed for the hospital. She'd left Osey and Parkhurst to handle the removal of the body and by now Audrey Kalazar should be in the morgue.

In the parking lot, she turned off the motor and took a cigarette from her bag. The flare of the lighter hurt her eyes. Leaning back, she sat in the dark and smoked the cigarette. It was snowing hard, flakes swirled around the parking lot lights creating silvery haloes, and the red neon of the emergency sign winked and shimmered. Another search of the well and the woods was in order, but that had to wait for daylight. The snow wasn't going to help any. Some lucky officer got to freeze his butt off standing guard. She crushed out the cigarette and went inside.

On the stainless steel table in the autopsy room, water still oozed from Audrey Kalazar's sodden clothing. Susan wrinkled her nose at the pungent odors and tried not to breathe deeply. Owen Fisher, dressed in gray pants and white shirt, hands clasped behind his back, prowled around the table and gazed at the body from different angles with bright interest.

The strong overhead light glared harsh and uncaring on the dark bloated features. Short gray hair pasted to the skull, pin-striped suit and white blouse, neat black pumps still on her feet. Her hands showed the dimpling effect of long immersion, but very little decomposition was evident because of the coldness of the water. Audrey had been a small woman and in death seemed even smaller; it was the force of her personality that had lent size to the living woman.

"Well?" Susan said. Every conversation she'd ever had with Dr. Fisher seemed to start that way.

He reached for a pair of latex gloves and stretched them over his long-fingered hands. Squatting, he peered closely at the skull and lightly, almost like a caress, ran his fingertips over it.

"Head injury," he murmured as though talking to himself. He looked on every body as a fascinating mystery he was privileged to unravel.

"Cause of death?"

He rose, giving her a look of mild reproach. "I'll do the autopsy first thing in the morning. Then I might have some-thing."

"How long has she been dead?"

His dark eyebrows drew together. "You're asking me to reach a conclusion before I've examined the facts."

"Yes."

"Well, I can safely say she probably died around nine twenty-five."

"That much I know." Audrey's watch, the face circled with diamond chips, had stopped at that time, probably shortly after it hit the water. "What day is more what I had in mind."

He nodded judiciously. "I believe that's going to be an interesting challenge."

"Owen, would you give me an informed guess? From superficial examination, based on your years of experience and your expert knowledge, has she been dead for anywhere around four days?"

His eyebrows did their thing again, but amusement glinted briefly in his hooded eyes before they turned blandly thoughtful. "That seems possible," he said.

All right. The two deaths were connected; they had to be. It was too much to believe two killers were roaming around this quiet little town with wide clean streets and conservative citizens. Why Audrey? She knew something about Lynnelle's death? What, for God's sake? And how did she know it?

"After the autopsy," Dr. Fisher said, "I might be able to tell you something." Pathologists never liked to commit themselves until after cutting, peering, snipping and prodding. Even then, it was only within a set of limits, never unequivocally on the nose.

Snow was still falling when she left the hospital and meandered through the dark streets on the north side of campus. They were mostly deserted, the good citizens probably preparing for the ten o'clock news before retiring to bed. Except at the Kalazars. She hoped Keith and Julie were able to give some comfort to each other.

On Victoria Street, she pulled up in front of David McKinnon's two-story white shingle, pleased to see lights still on inside. When she slid from the truck, the cold hit her and she hugged her trenchcoat around her, plowed through drifts to the porch, slipping slightly on the steps. She poked the doorbell.

The porch light blinked on and David opened the door. "Susan," he said with surprise. "Looking for a port in a storm?"

"Something like that. May I come in?"

"Of course." He took her coat and hung it in a closet, then led her into the living room.

"You've been eating salami," she said. The garlic smelled wonderful after what she'd just left.

"Leftover pizza. Marvelous things, microwaves. Would you like some?"

She hesitated only a moment. The last solid food she'd eaten was the cheeseburger six hours ago. When she nodded, he set off for the kitchen and she settled on the couch, long and low, of a deep blue color, new since the last time she'd been here. For months there'd been only a card table and two folding chairs, as though he were camping out. Now the place looked like somebody had moved in. It was warm and pleasant with polished wood floors and oriental rugs in ivory and blues, Impressionist prints on the walls, silver candlesticks on a dining room table.

He set a plate on the oak coffee table in front of her, two generous slices of pizza, piled with salami and dripping cheese.

"Beer?"

"No. Thanks."

"Ah," he said. "Business then, and not pleasure."

"Don't be so smart."

"Designer water? Coffee?"

"Instant will do. You don't need to grind exotic beans and brew up excellence."

"Your education has been sadly lacking in some areas."

"Hey, I'm only a dumb cop."

The coffee appeared, boiling hot. He fetched a bottle of beer, took a long swallow and sprawled in the easy chair, which gave a soft sigh. She felt like sighing too. The adrenaline jazzing

189

through her system ever since they'd opened the well ran out, leaving her with all the energy of a large rock. Ridiculous thoughts skated across the surface of her mind. He looked good, even in faded jeans and old gray sweatshirt. Why not hurl herself in his lap and run her fingers through his blond curls?

The thought startled her. Not since Daniel died had a thought like that come to her. She wrapped both hands around the cup and took a sip. Too hot. Risk ruining a good friendship? Get a grip on yourself. And remember you're here on business.

Carefully, she approached a slice of pizza, trying to keep control over long strings of cheese. She chewed and swallowed. "Dr. Egersund came to see you," she said.

"She did."

"She tell you she was Lynnelle's mother?"

He smiled. "Is that what this is about? You know I can't tell you what she said."

"Good old privileged information. Just thought I'd give it a try."

"Now that's out of the way, would you like a beer? No? So why have you come?" His tone more than the words hinted at cozy possibilities.

Didn't seem like such a bad idea. Must be unused hormones. She picked out a disk of salami and poked it in her mouth. Getting involved was too open to pain. Never again.

She could hear her father's approval—just the kind of man you should be with. That was enough right there to make her turn away. Stupid leftover from childhood, this perverse instinct to mutiny.

Her father was an attorney, had wanted her to be one. She graduated from law school and passed the bar exam, all according to his plan; then became a cop because she was afraid she'd never be good enough, never measure up to his standards.

"We found Audrey Kalazar's body," she said.

"Body? She was killed?"

"She was indeed."

"Where?"

"Where killed? I don't know yet. Where found? Abandoned well. On your property. Did Lynnelle ever mention it?"

"A well? Of course not. Why would she?"

"We also found something else in the well." She watched him for a reaction; if he gave any, she couldn't see it.

He waited, enquiring look on his face, took a swallow of beer. "You going to tell me?"

Why not? She was too tired to set little verbal traps and pounce when he fell in. It had been a long day, the room was too warm and her mind was too soggy. He was too sharp for traps anyway. "Bonds."

"Bonds?" He plunked the bottle down and stared at her.

"When did you get this annoying habit of repeating what you're told? Bearer bonds. Sealed in mortar between bricks in that well. Several packets, apparently. We don't know yet how many. More thorough investigation in the morning."

"Bonds," he said as though they were something he'd never heard of before.

"There you go again."

"I'll be damned. You found old Uncle Howie's fortune."

"You knew nothing about them?"

"Come on, Susan. Do I look like the kind of man who'd leave bonds in a well?"

No, he didn't.

"Howie went sort of nutty after Lowell died."

"Lowell?" Now she was doing it.

"Howie's son. Committed suicide."

Oh, yeah. George had told her about that.

"Well, well. Small wonder nobody ever found anything."

"Lynnelle ever give any indication she had found them?"

He shook his head. "She couldn't have. What would she be doing in the well?"

Stealing bonds. Though how she'd know they were there to steal was a good question. How many people examine abandoned wells just on the off chance? Someone killed her to get greedy hands on them? They were legally David's, although he might have a hard time proving it if someone else had possession.

"Whoever killed Lynnelle killed Audrey Kalazar?" he asked.

"Anything you can tell me to help?"

"I wish I could," he said.

What did that mean? He wished he had information? Or he wished he could tell her information he did have?

She sipped coffee that was finally cool enough and tore off a bite of pizza. She chewed slowly and swallowed. "You called me this afternoon. What did you want?"

For a moment, he looked blank. "Oh that. Dr. Egersund started me thinking."

He paused long enough that she prodded him. "About what?"

"That old house." His eyes seemed focused inward.

"Why did talking with Egersund make you think of that?"

Slowly, he shook his head. "Just remembering stuff from years ago."

"What stuff?" she prodded again. The warmth and the food and the comfortable couch were making her drowsy; her mind wanted to drift, not ask questions.

"I worked for Howie a summer when I was a kid."

Her mind snapped alert. "When would that have been?"

"Twenty years, maybe more."

"Did you know Carena Egersund then?"

"No." He shook his head, started to say something, then changed his mind. "No, nothing like that and now I think about it, it's probably not important. You probably already know about the kitchen cabinet."

"What about it?"

"Tall narrow cabinet by the stove. The floor boards lift out

192

and there's a space underneath. Secret compartment," he added with a smile.

"How do you know this?"

His smile grew broader. "Do I assume from your tart tone that you didn't find it? I happened to see Lowell replacing the boards one time. He was such a funny kid, and it was obviously something he didn't want anybody to know about that I never mentioned it. I forgot all about it until this afternoon."

"Funny in what way?"

He thought for a moment. "Troubled. I don't really know. I was only a kid myself and I just thought he was weird. I didn't know how to talk to him so I left him alone."

Buried treasure, secret compartments. What next?

18

"Any other little items of interest you can tell me?" she asked.

"Nope. No more pizza either." He wiped his hands on a paper napkin, balled it up and tossed it on the fire. "More coffee?"

She looked at her watch. After eleven. "May I use your phone?"

"It's in the kitchen."

The bright overhead light gleamed on white ceramic tiles and white porcelain appliances. Either he was very tidy or he had some efficient person keeping things clean. Maybe she should ask him; her own kitchen could use this kind of attention. The phone sat on the corner of a cabinet and she picked up the receiver and punched in a number.

"Yeah," Parkhurst said, sounding irritated. Eleven o'clock on Thursday night. Had she interrupted something?

"It's Susan. I'm headed for the Creighton place. I'll come by and pick you up in ten minutes."

"Why?"

David came in with a stack of dirty dishes and put them in the sink.

"I'll explain later," she said to Parkhurst and hung up.

"I don't suppose I can convince you to stay awhile," David said.

"Sorry," she said, mind back on track, the investigation taking over.

"Always the cop." He got her coat and held it while she slid her arms in the sleeves.

Parkhurst lived on Walnut Street in a neat brick Tudor tucked in behind two large bare-limbed trees. He stood on the curb, breathing steam, and he yanked open the door as she pulled up. "What's going on?" he said as he slid in.

"I've been talking with David McKinnon." She told him about the false floor in the kitchen cabinet.

Snow sparkled under the headlights when they left Hampstead behind and rolled along the unmarked country road, snow tires biting in with a solid grip.

Parkhurst snugged up the seat belt. "Why didn't he tell us this earlier?"

"He only just remembered."

"What's his motive for telling us now?"

"He only just remembered."

"Ha."

"You think he had some ulterior motive?"

"Yeah."

"What?"

White teeth flashed in a quick smile. "Not apparent. Anything else he just remembered?"

Like he fathered a child twenty-one years ago? "No." She gave a brief recap of their conversation.

Arms folded, he glared through the windshield. She darted a glance at him. He seemed angry, fogging up the windows with it. She pushed on the defroster. The pickup plowed through virgin snow at what she felt was reasonable speed given the darkness and road conditions, but it did slide once or twice on the curves. Each time he tensed and caught his breath. At the long driveway up to the house, she made the turn too tight and the pickup skidded. She overcorrected, then straightened and got it under control and plowed on.

"Stop!"

Automatically, her foot hit the brake, the pickup slewed in a half-circle. "What the hell—"

He hit the door handle and took off.

"Parkhurst—"

For a moment, she sat stupidly staring through the open door at the falling snow. Goddamn it. He just teetered over the edge? He's trying to say something about my driving?

Reaching across the seat, she punched open the glove box and retrieved the flashlight, then got out. Cold wind pinched her face and she tucked her chin in her collar, cinched her trenchcoat and plowed through snow, flicking the light back and forth over his footprints, rapidly filling with snow, leading across the open field toward the woods. She floundered, sliding on hidden weeds and uneven areas. At the edge of the trees, she hesitated. Somehow she'd lost the trail. She cast the light around. Under the trees, the snow was less dense, but if there were prints she couldn't spot them. Hearing the crunch of a foot against snow, she switched off the light and stood motionless.

"You don't need to stand there in the dark."

She flicked on the light and shined it in Parkhurst's face. "You mind telling me what that was all about?"

"I saw someone."

"Who?"

"Thought I saw someone."

"You can see in the dark through a blizzard?"

"No." His teeth flashed white in a wolfish grin. "But whoever I was chasing could. Disappeared in a wink. Didn't make any noise either."

"Police! Stay where you are! Put your hands up!"

"Chief Wren," she said and briefly held the light pointed up to illuminate her face.

"Oh geez, Chief, ma'am. I'm sorry." Officer White, dressed like an Eskimo, holstered his gun with a rather shaky hand. "I heard somebody running and then I heard voices."

"Anything been happening out here?" Parkhurst asked.

"No, sir."

"You hear anything earlier?"

"Uh—no, sir. A time or two I thought I did. But just the wind, you know."

"You didn't see anybody?"

"No, sir. Just you."

"Where were you a couple minutes ago?"

"Right there stuck to the well."

Parkhurst nodded. "Get back to it. We're going to take a look around."

"Yes, sir."

Susan and Parkhurst tromped through the woods, shining flashlights around and found nothing.

"Apparently didn't leave any footprints either," she said dryly as they mushed back to the house.

"It's snowing," he said.

"You imagined it," she said.

"Yeah, maybe. I saw a shadow and then it was gone." He unlocked the door, reached in for the light, then waited for her to go in ahead of him. Leaping around after shadows seemed to improve his mood.

It was colder inside the house than outside. The cabinet, built into the wall beside the ancient gas stove, was five feet high, two feet wide and two feet deep. It had three shelves with a few cans, mostly dog food and a twenty-five-pound bag of dry dog food on the floor.

They scooped up the cans, removed the shelves and knelt to

peer at the floorboards. She held the light while Parkhurst tapped the boards and, leaning on a palm, put pressure on various spots. The boards seemed solid.

"You suppose McKinnon looked in here before he told us about it?"

"Just figure out how to get in."

"If we don't find anything, McKinnon got here first."

"What's this prejudice you have against David?"

Parkhurst took the light from her, squeezed his shoulders inside and stuck his nose inches from the baseboards. He grunted, backed out and straightened up on his knees to get a pocket knife. Carefully, he inserted the blade behind the baseboard and wiggled it gently, then applied more force. The baseboard popped out.

"Not nailed in," he said and pulled out the other three.

The floorboards, fitted tightly together, lifted easily. They looked at each other with smug looks of congratulation and then practically slugged each other aside to see what they had.

Notebook. Ordinary blue-gray three-ring binder. Lordy, Lordy, what have we here? She got her hands on it. The space, only about two feet square, also had bills, checkbook, letters from Shelley, canceled checks and a scattering of receipts for paid bills and purchases.

"Why didn't we find this before?" she said.

"You want to kick me a few times? Then I'll go kick Osey a few times." He made neat little stacks, as he separated bills, letters, receipts. "Why'd she hide all this stuff away?"

"I think she was secretive by nature. It probably appealed to her to have a secret hiding place. And maybe she didn't want stepfather Herbert going through this." Susan picked up the binder. "Let's get out of here before we freeze to death."

They gathered everything up, placed it in a paper bag and left.

* * *

With Parkhurst right behind her, she trudged through snow toward her house.

"You ought to leave a light on," he said.

"I didn't plan on coming in this late." She unlocked the door and flicked on the kitchen light. Mess, big mess. Dirty dishes, full ashtrays, table littered with books and papers. No telling what kind of chaos the kitten had added.

Parkhurst's eyes held a glint of amusement as though he was aware of her discomfort. With a glance at the table, he said mildly, "Maybe the other room?"

She led him through the dining room, turning on the light as she went, and was relieved to see the kitten hadn't destroyed the living room in her absence. Lynnelle's binder clutched to her bosom, she stood looking around, feeling like a hostess caught unaware and wanting to make apologetic noises. Shit, this isn't a social call. So what, if he thinks I'm a slob.

She dropped the notebook on the coffee table and switched on lamps at either end of the couch. "Drink?" she asked, slightly less than gracious.

"Sure." Shrugging off his jacket, he tossed it over the back of the easy chair and pushed up the sleeves of his white cable-knit sweater.

In the kitchen, she shed her trenchcoat, clinked ice into two glasses and tipped scotch over it. She sipped from one and grimaced, dumped it in the sink and put water on for coffee. When the tea kettle shrieked, she spooned coffee crystals in a dirty mug and added hot water.

Resting on his heels, Parkhurst crumpled newspaper under logs in the fireplace and struck a match. Great. Those were the papers she was saving to read when she got the chance. She handed him the scotch. He smiled tightly, lifted the glass in her direction and took a sip, then picked up the binder and settled cross-legged with his back to the fire.

She joined him, legs also crossed Indian-style, fire warming her back and read over his shoulder.

The first page, ordinary lined notebook paper, was dated June 13.

TODAY I AM NOBODY

Parkhurst looked at her, raised his eyebrows and turned the page. "My past is a shoebox," he read aloud.

> *An old shoebox covered with dust way at the back of my mother's closet. Rose's closet. From now on I'll call her Rose. She lied to me. Everything was a lie. All those times she told me she loved me and I was so special. Lies! How could she do that to me! I'll never trust anybody again!*

Looking over his shoulder, Susan could see that the handwriting had deteriorated as numbed bewilderment boiled over into rage. Adoption papers were clipped to the next page, followed by an old letter addressed to Rose. Lynnelle had underlined several sentences. Susan leaned closer to decipher the scrawl.

> *Rose, I know how much you want a baby, but there's an awful lot of risk in adopting. I wish you'd think about it more. You never know what you'll get. What kind of people does this baby come from?*

"Aren't people wonderful," Parkhurst said sourly.

They were sitting so close their knees were almost touching and she was acutely aware of the smell of him, a clean smell of soap. She stretched her legs out straight and thought he knew exactly what she was doing. She reached over and flipped the page.

The altered birth certificate had the name of the hospital where Lynnelle was born and the name of the attending physician. Mother—Rose Vivien Hames. Father—Richard Alan Hames. The date, time of birth, sex of baby and weight. Below was a copy of the original birth certificate. Mother—Karen Hart. Father—unknown.

"Ah." She squinted, leaning even closer. "Karen Hart. That sound like anyone we know?" She turned her head to glance up at him.

He was looking down at her. Firelight threw shadows across his face, highlighting his cheekbones, leaving his eyes in darkness. A pulse fluttered in his throat. The fire snapped with a shower of sparks. She jumped, smiled—it felt like stretching a mask—took the notebook and plopped it on her thighs. Parkhurst sipped scotch.

She read aloud.

> *Had a big fight with Herbert. He tried to tell me Rose loved me. She only did what she thought was best. He's so sorry I had to find out this way. He's so sorry I'm so upset.*

> *June 14*
> *It's almost midnight and I'm writing this in bed. I've been thinking all day. I have to find my mother. Karen Hart. I'm leaving tomorrow. I'll tell Shelley so she won't worry, but no one else and make her promise never to tell Herbert where I am. Not even her mother.*

> *June 17*
> *I did it! I did it! Here I am in Oklahoma City. City of my birth! I waited until Herbert went to work and then I left. I'm staying in a motel. Not a very nice one, but it's okay. I can't wait for morning. First thing I'm going to buy a car with the money Rose left me. Then talk to Dr. Gorman who delivered me.*

Maybe he even knew my mother personally. Like a friend of the family or something. Maybe he knows where she is!

June 18

Got a car! My very first car! It's yellow. Only good thing today.

Dr. Gorman isn't even here any more. He died two years ago. Nobody at the hospital knows anything or they won't tell me anything.

June 19

I went to see Mr. Lavery, the attorney. I made an appointment so he'd have to see me. But he couldn't tell me anything. I guess I believe him. He seems okay and acted like he'd like to help me and everything, but he said he didn't know anything at all about my mother. Only her name. I already know that. I won't give up.

June 22

I didn't know I could be so lonely. I've been thinking a lot about Rose. I thought I hated her, but I don't anymore. I wish she were here so I could talk to her.

July 4

Fire crackers. Seems like I don't have much to celebrate.

July 12

I have a job! Receptionist at Belker's Electronics. And I found a place to live. Only one room but it's all mine. I even bought furniture—a sleeping bag and a lamp. That's all I need anyway, plus some dishes and stuff. And best of all I have a telephone. I called Shelley. Was she ever surprised. She promised to write to me.

July 24

Drove to Clayton today. Hardly anybody still there that I used to know. The Johnsons and the Meyersons. They were real surprised to see me and said how sorry they were about Rose.

I've written to everybody I could think of. All Rose's friends and her cousins and everybody. Nobody seems like they want to talk about my adoption. They didn't know anything about the girl. That's what everybody calls my mother. The girl. Maybe that means she was very young. Everybody asks why I want to know all this. Forget about it. It doesn't matter. Rose was your mother. Get on with your life.

Aug. 5

Herbert found me! Shelley told. Everybody always believes him when he looks so sincere and says how much he loves me. He loved me all right! I hate him! I hate him! I told him to leave me alone. I never want to see him again.

It's two in the morning. I keep thinking about all those times when he loved me. And told me never to tell. Our special secret. He did those things because he loved me so much. Why didn't she protect me? She should have protected me. I hate him!

"Not real fond of stepdaddy." Parkhurst tipped an ice cube in his mouth and crunched down hard. "Bastard." He set down the glass and took the notebook. Bending over it, he read:

Sept 1

My birthday. I'm 21 years old. I wonder if my mother is thinking about me. Shelley called. All I did was cry. She said I should get myself a birthday present. Something very special. Special! Special! Special! I got a dog. Alexa is the most beautiful, sweetest dog in the whole world. Went to the animal shelter. Terrible sad place. I wanted to take them all. Alexa *knew I came for her. As soon as she saw me she made this big commotion. Both of us just thrown away. Now we have each other!*

Silently, he glanced through several pages, muttering, "Nothing but passages of discouragement and despair. Ah, things are looking up."

Oct 14
I got an idea. I saw a movie this evening and I got so excited I wasn't even paying attention. It was about putting ads in the personal columns of newspapers.

Oct 15
I did it! I did it! Would anybody with information about Karen Hart, who had a baby on September 1, twenty-one years ago please contact me. Can't wait to get a paper with my ad.

"Got five responses." he said, running a finger down the page. "None of them what she was looking for. Here."

Nov. 22
Gladys Shumacher rented an apartment to my mother! She's pretty old and kind of nosey. She has a canary she calls Billy and she was putting newspapers in the cage. She said something just drew her eye to my ad. So she saved it and then thought about it for a long time and finally something just told her to answer. Lucky for me!
Two girls, she said rented the apartment. Real polite and quiet. One of them was pregnant and Mrs. Shumacher thought she was about fifteen. She called herself Karen Hart. Mrs. Shumacher gave me this sideways look, like she knew what that meant. But she couldn't really tell me much except no mail ever came addressed to Karen Hart. Hardly any mail ever did come, but if any did it was addressed to

"Well, well, well," Parkhurst said.

"What?"

"Addressed to Carena Gebhardt."

"Let me see that." Susan grabbed back the notebook, thinking this Three Stooges routine was ridiculous. She continued from where he left off.

> *The letters came from some place in Kansas. Mrs. Shumacher couldn't remember where. And she thought there was something from the University of Oklahoma.*
>
> *Carena Gebhardt is my mother!*

The sentence, written over and over, covered an entire page.

Susan quickly skimmed through the following pages. Lynnelle obtained a copy of Carena's birth certificate giving her the names of Carena's parents and an address. Attempts to reach the parents by phone and letter were unsuccessful. They had moved away and she didn't know where. For a time she seemed stymied again and then she made repeated visits to the University of Oklahoma. Carena Gebhardt had attended. From old yearbooks in the school library, she discovered that when Carena graduated her last name had changed to Egersund. Lynnelle fired off letters seeking a copy of a marriage license and finally got one. Carena Gebhardt had married Gerald Egersund.

Now she had another name to search and again a long period of no progress. Finally, simply for the sake of activity, she began looking up Egersund in phone books at the public library. Since it was an uncommon name, fortunately for her and her phone bill, she didn't find many. One listed in Tulsa turned out to be Gerald Egersund's mother. She told Lynnelle Jerry was teaching at the University of Colorado.

Parkhurst moved closer. Susan positioned the notebook so he could see better. She kept skimming. His breath brushed her ear. On September 9, Lynnelle packed up her clothes and her sleeping bag and her dog and moved to Boulder where she poked into the life of Gerald Egersund.

Parkhurst tapped the page. "Here we come to Egersund's kid."

> *September 13*
> *I have a brother! Neat! Neat! Neat! His name is Michael.*

Susan nodded, and ran her gaze down the page. Lynnelle found another secretarial job and started hanging around campus, frequenting the student union and the library, chatting with students, deliberately placing herself in Michael's path.

> *September 24*
> *Today I met my brother. I like him! I like him! I didn't tell him. It's fun knowing things nobody else knows.*

"Indeed she liked him," Susan said. "Wrote down every word he said, where they were at the time, and what he was wearing."

At the end of November, Lynnelle loaded up her VW again and came to Hampstead. Having finally found her mother, she was suddenly hesitant and afraid, and couldn't bring herself to confront Carena Egersund. She looked for a place to live and ran across the Creighton place.

> *Found a house to live in. All by itself out here. Been abandoned. Looks lonely. Just like me. I figure I fit right in. Ha ha. Plenty of room for Alexa. There's a creek and the woods are great.*

She settled in, explored the woods with the dog and spent long periods of time by the creek. On the tenth of December she got the job at Emerson.

> *Clerk-typist. Not very grand. But I can be near My
> Mother.*

She began to watch Carena Egersund, follow her, drive by
her house periodically.

Parkhurst raised an eyebrow. "Maybe the good teacher was
up to something she didn't want known."

"Like what?" Susan asked skeptically and read aloud of Lynnelle's friendship with Edie Vogel.

> *She's nice. I like her. We talk. She told me about her little
> girl. Kidnapped by her ex-husband! How could anybody do that!
> She's really worried all the time. I wish there was some way I
> could help her. She says I help just by being her friend. She's
> hired this private detective. It costs a lot of money, but she says
> it doesn't matter how much it costs. All she wants is her little
> girl back. I kind of told her about Herbert.*

"Kind of," Parkhurst muttered.

> *And she told me about the house, the man who killed
> himself. I can sort of understand. I've felt that way. You just
> think you can't go on.*

Scanning again, Susan quickly ran past general thoughts
about people Lynnelle knew, pep talks with underlined sentences berating herself for not having the courage to approach
My Mother. She mused about her friendship with Julie and
letting Julie use the house to be with Nick.

> *What would Julie's mother do if she knew!*

"Motive of sorts for young Julie," Parkhurst said.

"Maybe." Susan shook her head dubiously. "Nice polite

child. Well brought up. Life very much regulated by her mother. Doesn't feel right."

Parkhurst snorted. "Feelings yet."

Jan. 14
> *Today Lexi chased a fox. Good thing she didn't catch it. It probably would have beaten her up. I saw Julie's father down by the creek. With a woman. He seemed like such a nice man. I was wishing I had a father like him. I don't think I'll tell Julie.*

Susan tapped the page with a fingernail. "This a pattern with Keith?"

"Surprises the hell out of me. I'd think he'd need to ask permission."

> *Herbert found me. He won't leave me alone. Shelley promised.*

"Good old Herbert," Parkhurst said. "Doesn't give up easily, does he?"

> *I'm afraid Nick is keeping drugs here somewhere. I won't allow it!*

"What about Nick?" Susan asked.

Parkhurst took in a long breath. "Hard to say. I can see him mad at the girl and offing her, but how did Audrey get mixed up in it?"

"Good question. She must have known something about Lynnelle's murder. What it could be or how she could know it is another good question."

"Easily answered if Keith did the killings. Get rid of Lynnelle and his wife and live happily ever after with girlfriend Terry Bryant. Works the same way for Terry. Fits even better."

Susan nodded reluctantly. She hoped it wasn't that way. Not Terry, not Jen's mom, but wanting didn't make it so. Turning the page, she read,

I found a secret hiding place! It had this note in it.

The note was a sheet of typing paper, yellowed with age that had one sentence printed neatly in the center.

I wish it could have been different.

Susan's throat tightened as she read the calm desolation in the single sentence.

"By damn, a suicide note," Parkhurst said.

"Did you know him? Lowell Creighton."

"Before my time. Poor bastard."

I feel so sorry for him. I know about when things are so awful and you can't stand it and there's no way out.

The last entry was dated February 13.

Herbert was here again, all sloppy and crying and promising and pretending to love me. I hate him! I hate him! If he doesn't leave me alone I'm going to ask Mr. McKinnon to get him arrested.

"Let's make it Herbert," Parkhurst said. "I'd like that slime-bag locked up."

"There's the little matter of Audrey."

"We'll think of something."

Closing the notebook, she brought her knees up and rested her shoulders against the hearth. Parkhurst did the same. The silence grew heavy. She was aware of his quiet breathing and noticed she had adjusted her own breathing to match his. The clock on the mantel ponderously struck twice.

He looked at it, jumped up and shrugged on his jacket. "I think I better split." He left abruptly. A second or two later there was a soft tap on the door. She opened it.

"Sorry to bother you, ma'am," he said with a dry smile, "but I don't seem to have a car."

19

THE FIRST TIME the mayor called on Friday morning, Susan was in the shower and she dripped on the carpet while she listened.

"What the hell is going on? Audrey Kalazar is an important person in this community. How could this happen? Is this the kind of image we want to send out to the world? The vice-chancellor of Emerson College! Murdered and stuffed in a well. It'll be on the news. In the papers. What are you doing about it? I want it taken care of immediately. You understand? Immediately." He faded away muttering threats and regrets and the possibility of her quick dismissal.

Not if I can help it, she thought grimly. I might not want to spend forever here, but you won't give me the axe. I'll leave when I'm damn good and ready.

The second time he called, she was munching toast and she listened to it all over again while she watched the kitten dip a paw in her coffee. The awful part was, she halfway agreed with him, felt a sense of responsibility.

"Don't forget the fair opens this afternoon," he said with an abrupt change in subject. "At least make sure that comes off without a hitch."

"I'm sure there won't be any problems." George was taking care of all that; he had everything under control.

When the mayor hung up, she dumped the coffee in the sink and headed for the hospital.

The snow had stopped, but the streets were full of ice and slush and that meant on top of everything else, the day would be full of fender benders the officers would have to sort out.

Owen Fisher, in surgical greens, was just completing the external exam of Audrey Kalazar's body, and dictating his findings into a cassette recorder, when Susan entered the autopsy room. He switched it off and looked at her.

"The settling of the blood along the right side of the body indicates she'd been dead for some hours before she was dropped in the well," he said. "Primary cause of death appears to be blunt trauma, the mechanism most likely subcranial hemorrhage."

Susan tried to take shallow breaths through her mouth to avoid the full impact of the odors, but it didn't help a whole lot.

"Notice the dilation of the right pupil," he said. "She was alive when she was hit."

"Was death immediate?"

He nodded. "Nearly instantaneous. Not much clotting. No vomiting or bite marks in her mouth. Nothing that suggests seizures."

He made an incision from ear to ear across the scalp and peeled it away, front and back, to expose the skull. The high-pitched shriek of the saw tearing through bone made Susan's teeth ache. When he turned the saw off, the sound still buzzed through her head. Neatly, he removed the top of the skull and thoughtfully studied the surface of the brain before he switched on the recorder. "Skull fracture with associated subdural hematoma."

With both hands he lifted out the brain and weighed it, then made thin slices, examined them under a strong light and put samples in bottles. He made a Y-shaped incision and opened the chest and abdominal areas, then removed each organ, described it and weighed it, sliced each one and put samples in bottles. Except for the very beginnings of arterial sclerosis, Audrey had been in good health. He scooped out the stomach contents and bagged them for the lab.

Susan was very interested in what the lab might find in its analysis of stomach contents. She knew from talking with Keith—assuming he wasn't lying—when Audrey had last eaten. The lab results would tell approximately how many hours had passed before she was killed; that might be the closest Susan would get to time of death.

When Dr. Fisher had switched off the recorder, Susan asked about the weapon.

"Right-angle corner, heavy enough to cause the skull damage with one hit. Smooth. Hard enough that there was no fragmentation. She was struck one blow, from the front, probably by someone right-handed."

When Susan left the hospital, she drew in great breaths of fresh cold air. Not a whole lot of help; that particular smell stuck with you. She lit a cigarette to try to cover it, but it was still there, way back in her throat.

At her office, she yanked the blinds all the way up to let in the watery sunshine, stacked the reports of the two murders on her desk, got herself a mug of coffee and started at the beginning. How did these murders fit together?

Nick Salvatierra and his drug peddling. Lynnelle suspected. Did Audrey also know?

Stepfather Herbert. Maybe had a reason to kill Lynnelle, but Susan didn't know what it might be and she could see no reason to off Audrey. Even if somehow Audrey knew about the sexual abuse—and that was unlikely unless Lynnelle told her; even more unlikely—no reason to kill Audrey. In Susan's experience, sex offenders simply denied, they didn't kill the accuser.

Keith Kalazar and Terry Bryant, Jen's mom. That made more

sense than anything else, but for Jen's sake Susan hoped it wouldn't turn out that way.

Carena Egersund and all this business of the illegitimate child.

Susan shoved both hands through her hair. From what they had so far, she might as well put all these names in a hat and draw one. Bloody hell, what am I not seeing?

Shuffling through paper, she found her cigarettes and lit one, leaned back to blow smoke at the ceiling. A spider was working a web on the light fixture; most inept spider she'd ever seen. It clumsily examined the site, then fell three feet straight down, clung to the thread by one leg and flailed the others frantically in the air. Laboriously, it climbed back up the thread and fell again.

"I know just how you feel," she said.

A tap sounded on the door. "Am I interrupting something?" Hazel, with a white carnation in her auburn hair, came in carrying a square plastic container.

"Not so's you'd notice," Susan said.

"Here." Hazel plopped the container on the desk. "You skipped lunch again."

Susan looked at her watch; three-thirty. Eating wasn't something she felt much like doing after watching an autopsy.

"Eat it. It's good for you," Hazel said with motherly firmness.

Susan moved a handful of reports and the budget stared blank-faced up at her. With two murders on her hands, it was way down on her list. Try to work on it at home this evening, she thought and removed the lid of the container; carrots, cauliflower pieces, two apples and a pear, a small dish of almonds. She picked up a carrot stick and crunched a bite. Right about now the mayor should be all set to give his speech for the opening of the fair. The one that started out, "We are a community, a fine community with caring in our hearts," and ended with "helping those less fortunate among us."

She decided to skip it and read reports while she munched through Hazel's offering. As the afternoon went on, the sun gave up its feeble attempts and let the clouds take over. She switched on the desk lamp.

The phone rang, startling her and she snatched the receiver. "Yes, Hazel."

"The mayor's on the line. He sounds upset."

He was not only upset, he was sputtering. "Get yourself over here! Now!"

"Mr. Bakover—"

"The community center." He hung up with a bang.

She pushed a button to get Hazel. "Where's George?"

"We've had a slew of minor traffic incidents. He went to help."

The parking lot at the side of the brick building was almost full; the Helping Hand Fair was one of those not-to-be-missed occasions. Some considerate volunteers had shoveled the lot clear of snow, leaving the mounds heaped along the curb.

Everything looked quiet and normal. Whatever the problem was, it hadn't spilled outside. For a moment, she hesitated between using the rear door, or trudging around to the front. The rear, she decided when she slid from the pickup and the wind hit her; the rear door was closer, and the temperature had dropped again. A solid blanket of clouds completely obscured the sun and the wind was fierce. People were going in and out the back door and none of them seemed concerned with anything more than getting out of the cold. She slipped and slid across the walk and reached the door just as two teenage girls, bundled up in parkas, were coming out. Each held a small shiny-decorated box and they were poking through them with fits of giggles.

Susan grabbed the edge of the door before it could close. One of the girls looked at her and elbowed her friend.

"I'm looking for Mayor Bakover," Susan said. "Do you know where I can find him?"

"I don't know, but if you go that way," the girl gestured over her shoulder at the flight of steps leading down, "be careful of the goats. One of them bites."

They scooted off barely able to keep upright for their laughter. Susan went into the entryway and the wind whipped the door shut behind her. The flight of steps that went up had a door at the top, propped open, and she could see people milling around, hear the loud buzz of conversation. All ordinary. A corridor to the left led off to the coatroom; no activity there.

She trotted down the stairs and went into the large room crowded with people. Here too, nothing seemed out of the way; the room had been partitioned into booths along the walls and in the center with aisles through them for the people to pass by and peruse the goods. After the gloom of outside, it seemed brightly lit from the overhead lights, and some participants had added lights of their own to better display their wares. The place smelled of perfume and wet wool and baked goods and popcorn.

Mrs. Mayor stood surrounded by a group of indignant and gesturing ladies and she zeroed in on Susan at the same time Susan spotted her. Without a word, Mrs. Mayor cruised through the ladies like an icebreaker. She wore gray today, skirt and sweater and the ever-present strand of pearls, every hair as perfect as the last time Susan saw her.

"I just told you, didn't I? I told you, there would be trouble. Having those kids involved! This is what comes of it. Martin is looking for you upstairs."

"What's the problem?"

"Those kids! The very idea! Never have we had anything like this. It'll probably get in the paper."

"Kids." With a sinking feeling, Susan looked at several four-

or five-year-olds playing tag around the legs of the adults, and knew they weren't the kids under discussion.

"Are you trying to be smart with me, young lady?" Mrs. Mayor gave her a withering look that had probably been in her family for generations.

"I don't understand what you're upset about."

"Upset?" If anybody as refined as Mrs. Mayor could be said to screech, this was it. "Booth twenty-seven. Those college kids. Just you go and see what they're doing. I want them out of here. I want them arrested. You just come with me. I'll just show you—"

Before she could steam off with Susan in tow, a timid soul with gray hair trapped in a bun scurried up. "Oh dear, Rita. The popcorn machine seems to be jammed again and all those youngsters are waiting. Really they're getting very impatient. And I must say, I can't blame them."

"Oh, my heavens, do I have to do everything? Don't fuss, Dora. I'm coming." Mrs. Mayor shook her finger at Susan. "You just go and take care of it. I'll let Martin know you're here."

What the hell could "those college kids" be doing? Selling kisses? Auctioning their underwear? So far, panic hadn't set in. Outside of the clutch of irate ladies around Mrs. Mayor, nobody seemed unduly bothered. She noticed Henry Royce, the *Hampstead Herald*'s editor, wandering around with what passed for a smile on his jowly face. He stopped to talk with his lanky, shaggy-haired photographer.

Susan meandered past booths of pottery, knitted baby sweaters, cookies, cakes and jars of pickles, and found booth twenty-seven way in the back. Whatever was going on, they were getting a lot of attention. Two goats, one with horns, were tethered to each side of the booth by a short rope. They had lettered signs hanging around their necks, but she couldn't read them; one sign had twisted to the side, and Nick Salvatierra was standing in the way of the other. She noticed everybody but one little girl was giving the goats a lot of space.

This what the fuss was about? Get rid of the goats; livestock shouldn't be around all this food. Across the aisle, the lady in the booth displaying bouquets of paper flowers was looking at all the activity around booth twenty-seven with, Susan thought, a certain amount of envy.

The little girl, about four years old, clutching a bag of popcorn, stood staring solemnly at the goat with horns, now and again munching a kernel of corn. The photographer snapped her picture. The goat snaked out its head, snatched the popcorn and ate it, bag and all. The little girl just watched with grave interest.

Only college kids were gathered around the booth; laughing and joking, shoving each other and pointing. Julie Kalazar wasn't there, but the three R's stood behind an array of jewelry spread out on the table; more jewelry hung on the makeshift walls at the sides and back. On one end of the table were decorated boxes like the ones the teenagers had. The jewelry glittered and glistened in the light; earrings and brooches, all made with round flat discs an inch and a half in diameter, covered with sequins and beads and small stones; bright glittery greens, reds, blues, gold and silver; some with small jaunty feathers. They were attached to three-by-five cards.

"The cops," Nick said with a sardonic smile, and stuck his fingers in the back pockets of his jeans. "Link arms. We shall overcome. Go limp when they drag us away."

"Oh, chill out, Nick." Renée shot him an irritated look and pushed thick curls of red hair away from her face. She wore earrings of bright emerald green that flashed when she moved, and had a feathered brooch of blue and green stones pinned to her black jumpsuit.

"Ask why she's here," he said. "I'll lay you odds it's not to buy jewelry."

"I've had a complaint."

"Imagine that. And here we're being all law-abiding."

"Nick—" Renée said.

He shifted and crossed his arms.

"I don't see why," Renée said to Susan.

Robin, fiddling with the end of her long blond pigtail, had on red earrings with gold stars and quarter moons, a red brooch on her gold sweater.

Roz, with a look of wary defiance on her face, stuck out her chin, making her earrings, silver sequins with long strands of gold beads, dance and tinkle. They looked very fetching with her long slender neck and short-cropped dark hair. She too had a brooch pinned to her overlarge white sweater. "We refuse to leave," she stated.

"You can't make us," Renée said. "We followed all the rules. We made all this." She gestured in a circle around the display. "By hand."

Roz gave a snort of laughter. Renée looked at her, then back at Susan. "We paid the entry fee. And we're donating all the money. We're not selling any of this." She patted the stack of AIDS information pamphlets. "Just giving it away, if anybody asks. We're not pushing it. It's just sitting here."

"What are you doing?" An indignant mother grabbed the little girl's arm and yanked her away; the little girl stared back over her shoulder with a bemused expression.

"The goats?" Susan thought they must have stayed up all night, every night, getting all this stuff made.

"Here." Renée handed her a card with a brooch of iridescent blues and greens. COMING AFFAIRS was printed on the card.

"Watch it," Nick said. "You'll get run in for bribing a cop."

"Light off, Nick." Renée glared at him and he grinned and backed away. The goat nipped at him and he jumped smartly to one side.

Susan read the hand-lettered sign hanging around the goat's

neck. *Do you really love me, Billy?* She looked at Nick, looked at the three R's, then sidestepped two paces to read the sign on the horned goat. *I kid you not.* Laughter fizzed in her throat. Now, she was getting an inkling of why Mrs. Mayor was so incensed.

"There you are!" Mayor Bakover bore down on them, face red enough to suggest an impending stroke. "I was waiting for you upstairs. We cannot have this!" He banged his cane against the wooden floor with a resounding thump. "What kind of example is this? There are children here!"

"Yeah," Nick muttered. "Better they should get AIDS."

The mayor turned on him with a furious scowl, then swept the three R's with the same look. "I've informed them they are to leave. They have refused. Get them out of here. And remove all this—" Words failed him.

"We won't go!"

"We're entitled . . ."

"You can't . . ."

"What laws have we broken?"

"Living in a police state."

Before the situation could get any hotter, Nanny goat took the matter out of Susan's hands. Nanny calmly ate her tether and trotted off to greener pastures. On the way, she paused to sample some silk-screened fabrics. The woman at the booth shrieked and made shooing motions. Nanny moseyed along to the pies and settled in. A crowd packed around, hooting and yelling.

The mayor spun on his heel to see what all the commotion was about and the end of his cane struck Billy on the rear. Billy, bucking and lunging, pulled down one side of the flimsy partition. It crashed over on the three R's. Earrings and brooches scattered. Billy took off. Nick grabbed at him and got bitten for his troubles. Billy, kicking and bucking, overturned the pie table and careened into a row of jams and jellies. Jars tumbled and shattered. Like a rodeo cowboy, Susan tackled Nanny, who was headed determinedly for a blueberry pie. Nanny twisted her head and bleated indignantly in Susan's face. A flashbulb exploded.

Oh shit, Susan thought, I'm going to see my picture in the paper.

It wasn't until hours later that she had a chance to look closely at the jewelry the three R's had made. The flat round discs beneath all the sequins and stones and feathers of Coming Affairs were condoms. The bejeweled boxes held undecorated condoms, lubricant, and instructions for the use thereof.

20

CARENA LAY IN bed trying to gather the necessary energy to get up. It was after ten. With the curtains closed, the room was dim. Another dreary day. She'd been staring at the ceiling for over two hours. Saturday, errands to do. And she needed to go in to her office. In her unorganized haste to see David McKinnon, she'd left her briefcase with the papers that needed grading. Always papers to grade. Talking with McKinnon maybe hadn't been such a good idea. *Doesn't matter; he can't repeat anything I told him. Oh Lord, I'm tired. Maybe I should just stay in bed all day.*

That way I'll never get any coffee. Caffeine, a little impetus stirring through my bloodstream.

A wet nose poked her arm, sympathetic brown eyes peered at her.

"You'd like something to eat, I suppose?" Lexi brushed her tail back and forth on the carpet.

With a weary sigh, Carena dragged herself out of bed, slipped on a fuzzy blue robe, jammed her feet into warm slippers and plodded to the kitchen. She dumped the last of the dry food in the dog bowl, put water on to heat and checked the refrigerator. Just enough milk for her coffee. Add a trip to the market to her list.

After a cup of coffee and a piece of toast, the last of the bread too, she showered and dressed in dark-green pants and bulky white sweater, took her tweed coat from the closet and dug car keys from her purse.

The sky was gray and the campus hills white with snow, the bare-limbed trees had snow-covered branches. Gloved hands in her pockets, Carena trudged along a path crisscrossed with footprints. Off to the right on an intersecting path, a kid in sweat pants and Emerson sweatshirt jogged toward her, then stopped short. Nick Salvatierra. Before she could get a hand from her pocket to wave, he angled off uphill at a fast lope.

At the fork, she veered left toward the math building and set a brisk uphill pace that had her breathing heavily. A student in blue down jacket with the hood up, hurrying along a side path, almost bumped into her. For a moment, Carena didn't recognize Julie Kalazar, thin drawn face dead white, eyes red and puffy.

"Julie?"

"I have to find Nick." She looked two beats away from collapsing into a sodden huddle of weeping. Roughly, she rubbed a hand across her cheek and mouth as though she had brushed against spider webs. "I need to find him."

"I saw him a minute or two ago."

"Where?"

"Going that way." Carena pointed.

"Excuse me," Julie said in her well-brought-up young lady's voice, "I have to go," and darted off, then turned. "He didn't kill her," she said with great conviction, and nipped away.

Carena watched Julie scoot down the slope. Julie was afraid Nick had killed Lynnelle?

Shaking her head, Carena headed for Adams Hall and let herself in. The hallways were dim and her footsteps had a hollow ring as she climbed the stairs. The emptiness and the gloom stirred hairs on the back of her neck. At her office, she unlocked the door, went inside and locked the door again before flicking on the light.

Her briefcase sat on the desk and she checked through quickly to see that it contained everything she needed. As she went back down the stairs, her footsteps echoed and she stopped twice to make sure the sounds were not made by someone following her.

Safely outside, she felt extremely foolish. The clouds were denser and the air colder. She shivered in the wind and by the time she got to the parking lot, she thought her nose must be frozen. A car pulled in ahead and Edie Vogel got out.

"Hello, Edie," she said, coming up behind her.

Edie whirled and gasped, her face going pale.

Good heavens, what do I look like that everybody turns pale when they see me. "How's your cold?"

"Oh, Dr. Egersund. It's better."

She didn't look better, she looked feverish with a blotch of red on each cheek and headachy with pinched muscles around her eyes. Her coat was open over a gray plaid skirt and red sweater. Carena wanted to tell her to button the coat before she got pneumonia. "Working on Saturday?"

"They want me to let them in her office," Edie said.

"Who?"

"The police. Dr. Kalazar's office." Edie's eyes strayed toward the admin building and back to Carena. "They found her."

"Dr. Kalazar?"

"In the well," Edie said with bewilderment. "How do you think they knew?"

Oh dear God. "Wait a minute, Edie. What happened to Dr. Kalazar?"

"She's dead. At the Creighton place. What do they want in her office?"

"I don't know," Carena said. How could I not have heard

224

about this? "I suppose any pieces they could fit together to explain what happened."

"Pieces? Dr. Kalazar didn't have pieces. She had everything always all together."

The old nursery rhyme about Humpty-Dumpty came to Carena's mind.

Edie picked nervously at the Band-Aid on her finger. "You think they'll want to—you know, talk to me? Ask questions?"

"I imagine they probably will. They ask a lot of questions." No wonder Julie had seemed in such a state of shock. Carena's mind made another nonsensical jump and she murmured, "The frost is on the pumpkin and the fodder's in the shock."

"What?"

"Nothing. I was just thinking about Julie." Wishing I hadn't let her go off like that. I should have stayed with her, or taken her home, or bought her a cup of coffee.

"Dr. Kalazar was really angry with her," Edie was saying.

"With Julie?"

Edie nodded. "About her boyfriend. Sometimes I could hear even when the door was closed. She told Julie she wasn't to see him. Do you think I should tell them?"

I'm a fine one to ask, being myself so honest with the police. "I don't know, Edie. Maybe you should."

Edie nodded uncertainly and walked off with a worried frown.

Carena got into the Volvo and headed for the supermarket, her mind trying to get a grasp on what Edie'd told her. Audrey's body was found in the well at the Creighton place. Someone had killed Audrey. Who? The same person who killed Lynnelle? It wasn't Caitlin. Caitlin didn't even know Audrey Kalazar.

With the shock and sorrow about Lynnelle's death and the worry over Caitlin, Carena hadn't given a whole lot of thought to Audrey's disappearance. She'd felt, as everybody felt and constantly mentioned, that it was not like Audrey. But Audrey dead? Somehow, Carena couldn't get her mind around it.

At the grocery store, Carena stocked up on dog food, soup, cheese, eggs, breakfast cereal, frozen vegetables and chicken. She loaded the bags in the trunk, wheeled the cart over to a row of others and drove home.

Carrying one bag of groceries, she went gingerly up the slippery walkway between the garage and the house. It should have been shoveled, previously trampled snow had turned to ice. In the screened porch, she heard the phone ringing in the kitchen. Setting down the grocery bag, she fumbled the key in the lock and dashed in.

"Hello."

Silence.

"Hello?" She heard breathing.

"Hello," she said again, sharper.

"Carrie?" The voice was faint, tentative.

"Caitlin?"

"They're here again. The dark angels. Singing. They're singing, Carrie."

"Caitlin, they're not real. They can't hurt you."

"Soft. And sweet. They want me to come with them. A quiet place. Sleep. In the well. Where it's safe."

A cold chill gripped her. "Caitlin, where are you?"

"The car."

"Car phone? Where's the car?"

"The crows. I can feel the crows. They're gathering. I can hear their wings. They scream at me. When I don't listen to the angels."

"Caitlin, listen to me. You can't hear them if you listen to me."

"The babies. They're crying. Hanging in the trees."

"No, Caitlin. I'll help you. I'll come and we'll sing. Loud. You won't hear crying. You have to tell me where you are."

"You can't help me."

"Caitlin—"

"You can't see them. A dark angel swinging. I have to fight them. I'm trying, Carrie. Babies hanging on the ropes."

"Caitlin, where are you?"

"I love you, Carrie." A click and the line went dead.

Carena broke the connection and started punching in a number, got it wrong and started over.

Phil answered.

"I just got a call from Caitlin."

"Where is she?"

"In her car somewhere. I thought she was in the hospital."

"What did she say?"

"Nothing. Dark angels and crows. Phil, what is going on?"

He was silent for a moment. "She got away."

"I don't understand."

"She left the hospital," he snapped. "Got up and walked out."

"Didn't they try to stop her? What kind of hospital—"

"They didn't know until she was gone."

Carena took a deep breath in an attempt to steady her voice. "When did she leave?"

"They don't know for sure. Sometime yesterday evening."

"Why didn't you tell me?"

"What could you have done?"

Carena didn't respond. Shrieking at Phil wasn't going to help.

"She's got her car," he said. "And money. She could be anywhere."

"What have you done?" Try as she might, accusation leaked into her voice.

"Everything I could."

"Have you talked with her doctor?"

"Yes. And the police are looking for her. You have any other suggestions?"

"No, Phil. I'm sorry. I'm just worried."

"So am I," he said more softly.

"Will you call me when you hear anything?"

He paused, then said tiredly, "Yes."

Carena hung up. At least, Caitlin was all right. *All right?* A laugh caught in Carena's throat. Hearing singing angels and talking crows? Well, functioning enough to drive and use the phone. The crows hadn't yet convinced her to slice her wrists. Alive then. Not dead or catatonic and curled up somewhere freezing to death.

Pressing her fingertips hard against her temples, Carena tried to recall Caitlin's exact words. Dark angels swinging. That was new. On a vine like Tarzan? Babies crying. Hanging in trees. And something about sleep, a quiet place. *In the well where it's safe.*

Oh dear God. Carena jumped up, looked around for her keys and snatched them from the counter by the phone. Alexa got to the door before Carena did and Carena grabbed up the leash, snapped it on the dog's collar and ran out.

She drove crosstown, then headed north, beginning to hear dark angels of her own scrabbling at the back of her mind. Caitlin wasn't violent. She hadn't killed Lynnelle. She hadn't killed Audrey Kalazar. Caitlin could never hurt anybody. Except herself.

Carena pulled into the long driveway, vaguely aware of tire tracks in the snow, and jounced around to the rear of the house. Alexa made little yips of excitement and her tail beat wildly.

"Lynnelle won't be here," Carena told her softly. "She's never coming back."

Alexa leaped from the car. Carena took a firm hold on the leash and looked at the house, dark against the gray winter sky. The air felt heavy with the promise of more snow on the way. She was glad of the dog's presence. There was nothing menacing about Alexa, but she was big and she did have big teeth.

Carena tried the front door, then the back. Both were locked.

Under the oak tree, she looked at the rope swing and wondered if that's where Caitlin's dark angels were swinging. She gave it a push. "Hear any singing?" she asked the dog. Alexa cocked her head.

The snow on the ground under the tree and across the open space before the woods was scuffed and trampled with trails of footprints, crisscrossed and overlapped. Left by the police activities, Carena thought. If Caitlin was out here somewhere, footprints weren't going to help find her.

Alexa frolicked toward the woods, leaping ahead, getting stopped by the length of the leash, scooping up snow with her nose, tossing it and shaking her head. Under the trees, the snow had a bluish color in the white winter light and Carena followed the layered footprints around trees and to the well. The old weathered boards were gone, replaced by fresh wood with shiny nails. Cautiously, Carena tested one corner with her boot, then she leaned her weight on it. Solid.

It was quiet under the trees, very little wind, occasionally a soft plop as a clump of snow fell from overhead branches. "Caitlin?"

Alexa, busily sniffing at the covered well, looked up at her. The dog seemed happy to be home and didn't behave as though there were anyone else around. Maybe I should turn her loose. Go. Find Caitlin. Hairy angel to the rescue. Her throat tightened around a half-laugh, half-sob.

"Caitlin?" she called again in a thick voice.

Damn it, Caitlin, where the hell are you? Please be safe. Apprehensive at what she might find and remembering Lynnelle's blond curls moving with the stream, Carena slogged to the creek. The muddy bank was frozen hard, the slate-colored water down below trickling endlessly by. Carena took in a breath of cold air. She'd been so afraid of seeing another sodden body.

Dog close by her side, Carena followed the trails of prints and scuffs left by the police, going one way, backtracking and going another. Despite her fleece-lined boots, her feet were cold. Despair pulled at her. She'd better get home. Phil might be trying to call. Maybe Caitlin had been found.

When they got back to the Volvo, the first snowflakes, big fat lazy flakes, started to fall. She opened the door to let the dog in. Alexa raised her head, then barked and Carena heard a car coming up the driveway. It pulled around the house and parked and a man she didn't recognize got out.

"Hello." He wore a brown suit and dark overcoat. Alexa took one look at him and didn't want to go anywhere near.

"I'm Herbert Ingram. Are you with the police?"

"Carena Egersund." She waited to see if her name meant anything to him.

He offered a hand to shake, pale against his dark sleeve. "You people told me you were through here and I could start packing up Lynnelle's things."

Carena nodded at the question in his tone. Ingram. He must be Lynnelle's stepfather. "This is Lynnelle's dog." Tail drooping, Lexi crowded against her knee.

"Oh yes, the dog," he said vaguely, looked at Alexa, then shifted his sad brown eyes to Carena.

She was struck by the enormity of the grief she saw there. He did love Lynnelle, she thought, and was somehow relieved by the knowledge.

"You knew her?" he asked.

"Not well."

"She was such a pretty little girl—" His voice trailed off and he cleared his throat.

Carena felt tears sting her eyes.

"I taught her to ice skate. When she was little."

"Was she a happy child?"

"Oh yes. Always. Yes." He smiled with a faraway look on his

face. "Until her mother died. She wasn't the same then. She was—almost like she was running away."

"Children grow up," she said gently. "They need to live their own lives."

"She wouldn't come home with me. She wanted to stay here. Here!" He turned to stare at the house. "This is her home, she told me. How could she want to stay here? Look at it."

He shook his head, one small shake in each direction, then he focused on Carena. His eyes blinked twice, then twice again. "You must forgive me. I keep going back and trying to make it different." He gave her a weak smile. "And I'm keeping you standing here in the cold. It's difficult to make myself go inside. Was there something you wanted from me?"

"To let you know I have Lynnelle's dog."

Alexa shifted nervously and gazed up at her with mute appeal.

"The dog," he repeated as though Alexa had just suddenly appeared. "Might I impose on you to keep it another day or two? Staying at the hotel, you see, there's no place to put it."

"Yes, of course."

She was about to give him her phone number when he said, "I do thank you. As soon as possible I'll make arrangements to have it put to sleep."

You damn well won't. Something of her thoughts must have shown in her face. Herbert's glance sharpened, muscles in his face seemed to tighten as though he suddenly remembered something.

"Excuse me," he said. "I'm afraid I didn't quite catch your name."

"Egersund."

"You're not a police officer. You're the one Lynnelle went to see that night."

Carena let that hang in the cold air.

"Why did she come to see you?"

231

"I don't exactly know."

"What did she say to you?"

Carena wanted to get away and get to a telephone and she'd just as soon he didn't ask her what she was doing here. "Not really anything. She mentioned she was trying to find her biological mother. I don't know why she thought I might be able to help." When Carena opened the car door, Lexi almost knocked her down scrambling to get in.

The streetlights came on as she was driving home and the snow fell with more seriousness. She drove into the garage, picked up the leash and with the dog at her heels made her way to the house.

Inside, she unsnapped the leash, hung it over the door knob, flicked on the kitchen light, and went right to the phone. No answer from Phil.

She put water on for tea, shrugged off her coat and tossed it over a chair, removed her wet boots and set them on the mat by the door. Alexa barked and Carena shushed her. When the kettle whistled, she put tea bags in the pot and poured water in.

At the table, she sipped peppermint tea and waited for the phone to ring. Snow collected on the window ledge and frost made patterns on the outside of the glass. She tried to call again, made another pot of tea and turned the radio on low. Every time she moved, Alexa jumped up, watched her and then lay back down with a sigh. Her restlessness was affecting the dog. Lexi barked again, went to her empty bowl and looked up hopefully.

"Food. You want your dinner." She put the bowl on the counter, stooped to get dog food and found a bare shelf. Oh damn, the groceries were in the trunk. Probably have frozen milk. She'd left one sackful on the screened porch, just outside the door. She retrieved it and plunked it on the table. With a sigh, she put on her coat and boots and slipped out to the porch, fending off the dog so she couldn't escape. Alexa barked furiously.

Carefully, Carena went down the steps and along the icy walkway that was even more treacherous in the dark. A noise made her start to turn, then a great white blizzard of pain exploded through her head. She slid down on frosty billows of white.

21

ELBOWS ON THE desk and head propped on her hands, Susan studied Dr. Fisher's autopsy report on Audrey Kalazar. Nothing much in it that she didn't already know. A bulb flickered in the overhead light. Death was caused by a depressed fracture of the occipital region of the skull. The weapon was something with an acute right angle point. Must have been a hell of a blow. What had a right angle and was heavy enough to do that kind of damage? No water in the lungs. Time of death was hedged around with all sorts of qualifiers—temperature of the surround, immersion in water, stomach contents, decomposition of soft tissues—and had occurred seven to ten days prior to examination.

Roughly, the same time as Lynnelle had been killed. Big news. Susan had assumed as much. Stretching her arms, she rotated her wrists and arched her back until her spine creaked. Nothing to indicate where Audrey had been killed. Not at the well, or in the woods. So. Audrey murdered, site unknown, body loaded into her own car, body disposed of and car abandoned in a field several miles away. The killer had a good long hike in the rain. Anybody I know have pneumonia?

Nothing turned up in the search of the woods either time.

Except a bauble of blue feathers from a key chain found by Carena Egersund. Was that pertinent? The bulb flickered. Damn bulb. Blue feathers. Blue birds? Did that bring anything to mind? Yeah. I didn't remember to fill the bird feeder this morning. Herbert Ingram liked birds, all kinds, presumably that included blue birds, and he had a muffler with blue birds on it.

She lit a cigarette and watched the smoke curl up toward the ceiling. Okay. Great strides forward. Shit. If I continue to work this diligently, I might conceivably have the answer by the time I'm eighty-six. Then I can scrape up Parkhurst from his nursing home, wheel him out to the appropriate cemetery and we'll read the Miranda warning to the perpetrator's tombstone.

Dr. Kalazar's suitcase had clothing enough for the planned three days away; underwear, pantyhose, nightgown and robe, one very proper calf-length dress of burgundy silk, a suit in a dark gray, silk blouse, toothbrush, comb and cosmetics. The purse had her wallet; driver's license, credit cards and two hundred dollars in cash. No airline tickets. The killer destroyed them? Why? The briefcase; pens, pads of paper, conference schedule and her speech. "The Roll of the Educator in Preparing Our Students for Today's Changing World."

Fascinating, Susan thought.

The bulb flickered. Goddamn it. She stood, stabbed out the cigarette, scattering ashes, and stomped out to the supply room for a new bulb.

Standing on the desk, she tried to remove the defective bulb by feel because if she looked at it, it blinded her. A truly smart person would have turned it off first. Using a Kleenex to keep from burning her fingers, she fiddled with it and finally twisted it free, then slotted in the new one and waited for a flicker. Ha. Success.

Assuming the bulb was defective and not the fixture. Dust coated the old bulb and she gingerly rubbed a clean streak along its length. Assumptions weren't necessarily true. Change it slightly and what have we got?

Oh my. Pieces that fell into place, answers that made sense of troublesome questions. Some, at any rate. Audrey's demand for flawless compliance. An airline reservation for Sunday instead of Saturday. Audrey's death. The odd lack of curiosity about Audrey's disappearance.

"View pretty good from up there?"

As she spun around, the bulb slid from her hand and exploded against the desk. A sharp sting pricked her cheek. She climbed down and dusted her hands together, muttering, "You need to wear cleats on your shoes."

"What were you doing?" Parkhurst pulled a handkerchief from his back pocket and held it out to her.

"Thinking," she said darkly.

"Hey, some people sing in the shower, others think on desks."

"Very funny."

He gestured with the handkerchief.

"What's that for?"

"You're bleeding."

"Oh." She touched a finger to her cheek and looked at the blood, then took the handkerchief and patted at the scratch.

"Anything interesting come to mind up there?" he asked.

"Oh yes. The voice of Frannyvan."

He raised an eyebrow.

"Maiden aunt," she explained. "Very smart lady. She used to say, what's the use of running when we're on the wrong road."

"I see."

She smiled quickly. "Old German proverb. Where she heard it, I don't know; she was Dutch. But it has finally occurred to me that we're not getting anywhere because we're on the wrong road."

"Is that right?"

"Drop the comedy and pay attention. We've been chasing

236

around finding motives for Lynnelle's death. Then Audrey's body turned up."

Shaking glass slivers from the autopsy report, she handed it to him. "Since Lynnelle's body was found first, we thought hers was the first death. Nothing in there confirms that."

"So?"

"Audrey was killed first."

Parkhurst glanced through the report. "Are we making assumptions again?"

"Yeah," she admitted. "But this time we're right."

He tossed the report back on the desk and crossed his arms.

"Audrey died because she was meant to die. Lynnelle died because she was in the wrong place at the wrong time. She saw the killer. Maybe with the body, more likely, just there. Out there in the woods, in the rain. When Audrey turned up missing, Lynnelle was going to remember."

"Why weren't both bodies in the well?"

"I don't know. I would guess Lynnelle appeared after those old rotten boards had already been replaced. They'd have to be taken up again. That meant more time. It was raining hard. The killer still had to get rid of Audrey's car and walk home. Also the dog was loose. Very friendly dog, but even so that had to be worrisome. Get your coat."

It was snowing hard when they came out of the police department. "I'll drive," Parkhurst said and steered her to the Bronco.

As they pulled away, the radio crackled with Marilee's soft southern voice sending an officer to check on a barking dog. A few seconds later, "Another fender bender, guys. You better sort that out first."

Cold, Carena thought. Freezing. She tried to move and hot bright pain exploded in her head. Headache, I have a headache.

Noises. Barking. Alexa barking. Voices. No. One. One voice. Whispering, mumbling.

"Oh God, oh God."

Constant mumbling.

"I'm sorry. Forgive me. Please. Oh God, please forgive me." Eyelids won't open. Important. Something important. Have to open my eyes. Arms won't move. Crying. Someone crying.

"I don't want to. I don't want to."

When she slitted her eyes open, light flooded in with needles of pain. She squeezed them shut, then tried again. Garage. I'm in the garage. No wonder I'm so cold. On the floor, lying on the floor.

A blurred figure sat cross-legged on the floor beside the Volvo. Breath hissed through bared teeth.

Carena tried to move, rolled onto her elbows and raised her head and shoulders. Pushing hard against the floor with her hands, she managed a sitting position. The effort made her dizzy, sparks of pain skittered across her skull. She moaned.

"You're awake." A gasp of horror. "You're not supposed to be awake. Oh God, what am I going to do?"

"You hit me." Carena slumped against the wall and peered at her hands. Tied. She tried to move her feet. Tied.

"You knew I killed Lynnelle."

"I didn't."

"You did!"

"Of course, I didn't," Carena said in her reasonable school teacher's voice.

"Yes, you did."

This can't be happening. We're squabbling like little kids. Did not! Did too! "How could I possibly know?"

"It just came out. I don't know how it happened. About the broken pumpkin."

"What pumpkin?" Carena was beginning to lose patience.

"Yours! She saw it. At your house!"

238

A pumpkin? At my house? On Halloween? I didn't have a pumpkin. I don't think I did. Wait. Yes, I did. A pumpkin, because they're so pretty. Just a pumpkin. I didn't carve it. It sat in the kitchen window until it rotted.

Carena felt herself getting angry. Lynnelle never saw it. She never came— Oh. The small ceramic figure of a crying ghost holding a broken pumpkin. Lynnelle had been charmed by it.

"That doesn't mean I knew anything." Carena's mind was filled with white cotton and back in there somewhere was a frantic voice shrieking, you're arguing with a killer who's trying to convince you you know she's a killer.

"I thought it maybe would be all right. You wouldn't realize."

Realize what? Carena tried to make sense come through the pain in her head. Lynnelle saw the ceramic pumpkin and mentioned it to her killer. The killer couldn't have known any other way. But that's silly. Not any kind of proof. Unless the killer had already stated she hadn't seen Lynnelle that night. Still wasn't evidence of anything, only the merest of indications.

"And then you said that about frost on the pumpkin."

Stupid habit of prattling quotations. Maybe back in my subconscious I did know and that's why the line came to mind. And maybe right now I should pay attention here.

Mumbles in that eerie whispery voice. ". . . liked Lynnelle. I did. She was my friend. I'm sorry. Oh God, I'm so sorry. If only she hadn't been there. Bad, that was bad. Why doesn't that dog shut up!" She slapped the floor with the flat of her hand.

Carena jumped and jarred loose slivers of pain. She's going to kill me. I should do something. Be scared. Get away. How? Against the opposite wall beyond the car, was an old push-type lawn mower, coiled garden hoses, screwdrivers, pliers. Screwdriver? How could I get it?

On this wall, a snow shovel, handle end on the floor, broad metal scoop propped upright, all the way down by the overhead door. She shifted and moved a tiny bit.

Steady muttering. "We have to wait. You weren't supposed to wake up."

"Wait for what?"

"The car," she screamed. "The car won't start. It has to be suicide."

"No."

"Yes. And then they'll think you killed Lynnelle and you were sorry and you killed yourself and then they'll stop asking *questions*." The voice grew shrill on the last word, then softened again to a thin hair-raising keen.

"And then it'll be over, it'll be over. Oh God, it has to be over." She rubbed her face in the crook of one arm. "It'll be all right. Don't worry. It'll be all right. It'll start. We just have to wait. And then it'll start and then I'll untie her."

Never thought I'd be glad the old Volvo wouldn't start. Carena twisted her hands and pulled hard, rubbing back and forth. Nobody's going to believe I killed myself. Not with marks on my wrists. Suicides don't tie themselves up. With all the twisting and pulling, she managed to move another half-inch closer to the shovel.

The bowed head jerked up, the eyes were hard and glistening. "She came to my house."

"Lynnelle?"

"Dr. Kalazar! Her face was all red and she kept shouting and waving the airline tickets. Wrong, I got it wrong, the date. The last straw. She kept saying, the last straw. I tried, you know. I tried. But I was so worried about Belinda and sometimes a mistake and— It was so hard to concentrate. And she said—and she said. And there she was in my house yelling at me. Don't bother. On Monday. Don't come back."

In her mind, Carena saw the nameplate on Edie's desk; Edith Blau Vogel. Blau was German for blue and vogel meant bird. Cold seeped in through her corduroy trousers and she clamped her teeth to keep them from chattering.

"I couldn't be fired. I have to have money. The detective—who's going to find Belinda and he's very expensive. I explained, you know. I did. I explained. I couldn't be fired. And I told her about Belinda. My baby. And I said please. I did. Please, I said. I won't— I'll be more careful— And I tried to tell her about Bob, about Bob—and she said—" Edie's voice flattened. "Anybody stupid enough to marry a man like that deserves what she gets."

Her shoulders slumped in huddled misery. "I didn't mean to," she whispered so softly Carena could barely hear.

"Belinda's little wooden stool. It's red. It's so cute. It has this little rhyme on it, all about brushing my teeth and watching TV and any job that's bigger than me."

Edie's white face seemed frozen in despair. "Scared. So scared. The old well. Nobody will ever find her. It was so awful. Dark. Raining. And she was so heavy. Cold." She shivered. "I had to take off the boards. Splinters." She looked at her right index finger and rubbed the Band-Aid. "And then—and then—Lynnelle. I didn't want to, but she was *there*."

I'm going to die, Carena told herself. Her sluggish mind viewed the situation with remote horror. Even if she could reach the shovel, she didn't know what she could do with it. Her feet were tied. If she tried to stand, she'd fall. Her hands were tied and so cold they were numb. She made another small slide toward the shovel.

Edie was enough aware that she pivoted a fraction on her rear. "I'm sorry," she said in a natural voice.

Carena's breath caught; the change in tone scared her as nothing else had.

"I don't want to. I hope it doesn't hurt." Tears ran down Edie's face.

Carena rolled onto her side in a fetal position, shoved hard against the wall with her feet and sprawled toward the shovel.

Edie leaped up. Carena got one hand around the wooden handle.

The shovel toppled, crashing against the floor. Carena slid her fingers up the handle and swung with a sideways arc. The edge of the scoop caught Edie just above the ankle. She cried out, stumbled to her knees and crawled toward Carena.

Carena scooted back, digging with her heels and tried to raise the shovel. Edie wrenched it away. As though in slow motion, Carena saw the shovel swing back and come toward her.

22

EDIE STOOD PANTING, legs spraddled, clutching the snow shovel, and watched Dr. Egersund. It's okay. She's not moving. Start the car first. Then untie her.

Gently, Edie laid down the shovel, rubbed her face in the crook of one elbow and backed to the Volvo, unwilling to take her eyes off Dr. Egersund. She felt for the door handle. The hinges squeaked. A sharp cry escaped her. Her heart pounded. This is the last. It'll be all over. Why doesn't that stupid dog shut up!

What if it won't start? It will. It has to. Her hand shook. Steeling herself, she twisted the key in the ignition. The starter whined; slow, weak.

Please start. Please. Oh God, please start. The motor chugged once. Yes, come on. She pumped the accelerator. The motor coughed. All right. All right. She held her breath, fed more gas.

The motor caught. She took a breath. It sputtered. She mashed the accelerator. It died. No! Gripping the steering wheel, she threw back her head and wailed.

Teeth clenched to keep them from chattering, Edie backed her own car up Dr. Egersund's driveway. Hard to see through the snow. She eased backward as near as she dared to the closed garage door. From the trunk, she pulled out Belinda's sled. She'd bought it for Belinda's Christmas. At Christmas time Belinda was— Belinda wasn't even there. Edie shoved the sled onto the rear seat, grabbed the old blanket and a roll of cord and went into the garage by the small side door.

Dr. Egersund was still there. She hadn't moved. Edie struggled to open the overhead door. I have to hurry. Dr. Egersund moaned. Edie gasped and whirled to stare at her. Dr. Egersund moved her head, sliding her cheek against the garage floor.

Hurry. Oh God, hurry. Finally, the latches clicked free and Edie shoved up the door. It rose a short distance and stopped. She shoved harder. The door banged against the bumper of her Ford. Oh no. Too close, I parked too close. What am I going to do? The light. I forgot the light.

Rushing to the switch, she flicked it off and stood a moment in the dark, breathing heavily. It's all right. She spread out the blanket and rolled and tugged Dr. Egersund onto it. It kept scrunching up.

Quickly, she covered Dr. Egersund's face, those half-open eyelids. She shivered, then tucked the blanket tight and wrapped cord around it, being very careful with the knots and telling herself how neat they were.

Opening the small door on the side of the garage, she peered out. What if somebody sees? No. It's dark. Kitchen light. Nobody's watching. She opened the door wide and went for the burden. The wind blew the door shut. She crouched and sobbed.

I have to do this. I can. I can. She blocked the door open with the handle of the snow shovel, grasped the burden and backed to the door. She toed it open and dragged the burden out. Kicking the shovel away, she let the door slam shut and pulled the burden around to the trunk of her car. With desperate effort, she heaved the top half in, hurriedly rolled in the legs and slammed the trunk lid. It shut with a solid thunk. Sagging against the Ford, she stared around wildly. It's okay. Nobody heard.

She jumped in the car and backed carefully out the driveway.

Parkhurst switched on headlights and windshield wipers, backed out of the parking space and turned to look at her. "Where we going?"

Susan clicked in her seatbelt. "Edie Vogel."

He headed left out of the lot. "Want to tell me why?"

"We want to ask her a few questions." Susan paused, trying to collect her thoughts. "Audrey Kalazar didn't tolerate mistakes. Edie made a big one. Airline reservations for the wrong day. What do you think Audrey would do when she found out?"

"Boot Edie's ass right out of a job."

"And Edie, right now, has some heavy expenses. Last time I saw her she had a Band-Aid on her finger. Maybe a splinter from rotted wood. She has a cold."

"So does half of everybody you run into. It's winter."

"And. Her attitude when I went to question her right after Lynnelle's murder. Edie was scared. She was resigned." Susan thought back to Edie's slack sad face. "She thought I'd come to arrest her."

Parkhurst pulled up at Edie's house. "Aren't we skating on some pretty thin circumstancial ice here?"

"Yes. But, I believe, if I'd asked the right questions the first time, she would have confessed. We'll ask them now."

"Not home," Parkhurst said, giving the doorbell another push.

"Damn it," Susan muttered. Edie's car was gone and the house in darkness; obviously, she wasn't home. Ringing the doorbell had been just a futile gesture of irritation.

"What now?" Parkhurst asked.

"Back to the department. We'll have her picked up."

In the Bronco, the radio chattered. "I have received yet another complaint about a barking dog," Marilee drawled. "Officer White, are you out there? Sixteen twenty-one Franklin Street. The neighbor is getting a mite testy."

Carena Egersund lived at sixteen twenty-one Franklin. Susan looked at Parkhurst, then picked up the mike. "Chief Wren," she said to Marilee. "I'll catch this one. We're on the way."

"Why are we doing this?" Parkhurst asked.

She waved a hand at the radio. "Everybody's busy." Pushing herself further into the seatback, she crossed her arms. She didn't know why they were doing this, except she was getting a bad feeling. A barking dog meant nothing. Dogs bark.

No lights were on in the front part of the house. The dog stopped barking when they came up on the porch and made little yips of welcome. The knock went unanswered.

"Try the back," Susan said.

The dog started barking again as they moved off the porch.

"Ben?" A middle-aged woman with a heavy coat thrown around her shoulders hurried up to them.

"Mrs. Farniss," Parkhurst said with a nod. "This is Chief Wren. You the one made the complaint about the barking dog?"

"It wasn't a complaint exactly. With the windows all shut up like they are, it wasn't that it bothered me. It's just she's had the dog ever since that poor girl got killed and it's never barked like this. I got to worrying. You know, with a killer loose and all. She's a good neighbor. I just thought I'd better call."

"Has anything unusual happened here?" Susan asked.

"I'm not sure." Mrs. Farniss looked slightly embarrassed. "Earlier, I thought there was somebody waiting, you know, kind of hanging around there by her back porch."

"What did this person look like?"

"I didn't really see. Getting dark and the snow and all. Then I thought maybe I was wrong." Mrs. Farniss clutched the coat tighter around her shoulders. "After a while I noticed the car."

"What car?"

"I just saw it driving away."

"It wasn't Dr. Egersund's car?"

"I'm not sure. I don't think so. But she wouldn't just go off without taking care of the dog. I know she wouldn't. I tried to phone and didn't get an answer."

"What kind of car?"

"I can't say I know anything about cars. And I couldn't see enough to tell anyway. Older, dark color."

"Was there one person inside," Susan asked. "Or two?"

"I don't know. It's snowing so hard and dark."

"What time was this?"

"It must have been just about six o'clock. I was about to get supper on the table."

"How long has the dog been barking?"

"Close to two hours. I tried to tell myself that nothing's wrong, but—" Mrs. Farniss shivered.

"You did the right thing in calling." Parkhurst put a hand under her elbow and gave her a gentle nudge toward her house.

"I hope she's all right."

"We'll check it out."

With the flashlight, Parkhurst tried to pick out tire tracks on the driveway; if there'd been any, they were obliterated by falling snow.

At the rear of the house, kitchen light spilled through the window. From the screened back porch, they heard the dog snuffling along the inside of the door. Susan tried the knob and found it locked. "I don't like this."

Parkhurst shrugged. "The lady's gone out. A friend picked her up."

"A friend who was lurking around earlier?"

"We've had a lot of calls lately reporting lurkers."

"Yeah." She shoved her hands deep in her pockets. "Let's check the garage."

Disappointed barking from the dog as they left the porch and headed for the garage. The overhead door was down. Parkhurst jiggled the handle, locked. The small door on the side was also locked. Brushing snow from the glass pane, he shined the light through. She bent closer to see.

"Car's here." He played the flashlight beam over the Volvo.

Didn't mean anything. She *could* have been picked up by a friend. Susan straightened, hunched her shoulders uneasily and tucked her chin in her collar.

"Well?" Parkhurst said.

She took the flashlight and, with her face against the glass, angled it down and to the right. Something lay on the floor that she couldn't see clearly.

Stepping aside, she handed back the flash. "Just inside, to the right. What is it?"

He crouched, peered through the glass, moved the light back and forth. "Wooden handle, looks like. Maybe a shovel or a rake."

She hesitated, took in a breath of cold air that hurt her lungs. "Open it."

He tipped his head and eyed her questioningly. She nodded. Raising a booted foot, he smashed it against the lock and the door popped open. Inside, he located the light switch and the sudden glare made her squint. It was a shovel, a snow shovel.

Melted snow had dripped puddles around the car; empty, keys in the ignition. She reached for them and bounced them on her gloved hand as she looked around the garage.

"Susan." Crouched on his heels, Parkhurst added the flashlight beam to the overhead light, pointing out a small dark smear.

She squatted beside him. "Blood?"

"Maybe. Not enough to get excited about."

"Maybe," she repeated, examined the keys and isolated one that looked like a house key.

Alexa yipped joyous cries of welcome when Susan opened the kitchen door and leaped around them in wild circles. Parkhurst knelt, whacked the dog's sides and fondled her head with both hands. Alexa slathered his face with adoring kisses.

"Dr. Egersund?" Susan called.

Rising, Parkhurst pulled off his gloves and used them to slap at the white hairs all over his black pants.

The light was on, bags of groceries—with things like milk and chicken and frozen orange juice that should be refrigerated—sat on the table. A black leather handbag hung by the shoulder strap from a chair. She looked at Parkhurst.

They went quickly through the house with the dog trotting at their heels. No signs of struggle, or break-in, nothing amiss but little puddles of tracked-in snow. Bloody hell, what happened? She opened the kitchen door.

"Watch it!"

Alexa shot out, knocking her aside, nosed open the screen and disappeared in the falling snow.

"Shit!" She dashed out. "Alexa, come back here!" At the end of the driveway, she looked one way, then another, took a couple of steps, then stopped. The damn dog was gone and she didn't even know which direction.

"Hey." Parkhurst put a hand on her arm. "How hard could it be to find a white dog in a snowstorm?"

She gave him a withering look, which he couldn't see in the dark, and tromped back to the Bronco. While he scooped snow from the windshield with a gloved hand, she got on the radio; pickup on Edie, lookout for Carena Egersund and the damn dog. "Anybody sees it, bring it in."

"Right away. Ten-four."

"We might as well head in," Susan said to Parkhurst.

They'd only gone a few blocks when the radio sputtered. She grabbed the mike.

"I spread the word," Marilee drawled. "Officer Yancy reported in he spotted Edie's car. Thirty minutes ago. Headed north out of town."

North? Susan looked at Parkhurst, pressed the transmit button. "We're headed north too. Get a patrol unit to the Creighton place."

The Bronco picked up speed once they left town. Snowflakes sparkled silver against the headlights. The silence was broken only by the hum of the heater, the double beat of the wipers and the whisper of tires cutting through snow.

Susan tried to tell herself that Egersund had simply forgotten her purse, had gone somewhere with a friend. Uh-huh, sure. She might forget her purse, but she wouldn't leave frozen peas on the table.

"No reason for Edie to axe Egersund," Parkhurst said, picking up on her thoughts.

Right. "No known reason." And no reason to think she was at the Creighton place, simply because she was headed that direction.

He slowed to make a left and they jounced along the driveway.

"No car," she said when they pulled around to the rear of the house.

No tire tracks either, but tracks wouldn't last long with the snow. When she slid from the Bronco, cold air made her catch her breath. Edie got stuck in a snow drift. Stopped for coffee along the way. Long gone into the next state. "Any bright ideas?"

He grunted, fanned the flashlight beam over the rope swing, across the unmarked snow on the ground and aimed it in the direction of the woods, invisible behind the swirl of snowflakes. From the set of his shoulders, she could tell he was as keyed-up as she was. He tromped a few paces, stood motionless, then tightened to attention like a sentry hearing a twig snap. Even his movements were tighter, direct and focused as he took two more steps. Turning, he motioned with the flash.

"Hear anything?" he asked in a soft voice when she joined him.

She listened. Wind. Sighing through the trees. Very soft. Almost like singing. Singing?

". . . falls the eventide . . . darkness deepens . . . help . . . helpless . . . abide with . . ."

The thin high sound drifting on the cold air was hair-raising. It seemed fragile, the way the sound of a finger running along the rim of a crystal glass seemed fragile.

Breathing in fast puffs of cold air, Edie opened the trunk. The hinges squealed. Didn't matter. Nobody could hear. She tugged her old rubber boots from beneath the blanket-wrapped burden and set them on the ground. Pulling off one shoe, she flung it way back in the trunk and pushed her cold foot into a boot, then put on the other one. The boots reached her knees. Leftovers from teenage. She'd used them on the farm when it was raining and muddy.

The wind brushed snow against her face and she rubbed her cheek with the back of a gloved hand. I have to do this. For Belinda.

She rolled the burden over the edge of the trunk and guided it as it flopped onto the sled. If she didn't think about what was in the blanket, it wasn't so bad. Think of it as a bale of hay. She used to move those around plenty when she was a kid.

She shifted the burden on the sled—the feet part dragged and she twisted them around and bent them up—picked up the big square flashlight by the handle and trudged toward the woods.

Under the trees the snowfall wasn't so thick. Hard-going, though. The ground was uneven and the flashlight sent shaky light around when she stumbled. She tugged and yanked her way, jerking the sled over tree roots when it snagged. Her arms ached and she had to keep switching the pull rope from one hand to the other. The hammer in her coat pocket banged against her thigh. The burden kept shifting and sliding and once even fell off.

Snowflakes stung her cheeks and clung to her eyelashes. She pulled her scarf low over her forehead to shield her face. Periodically, she stopped to rest or tug the burden back into position. Just a little way more. Keep going. Shadows hovered just beyond the beam of light. When she stopped and swung it around, there was nothing but falling snow. She heard sounds. Like somebody whispering. Wind through the trees. She plodded on.

There! Over there. By that tree.

Her heart pounded. She strained to see through the snow. No. It's all right. Nobody's there. She struggled onward. Unless it's Creighton's ghost. A laugh started somewhere in her throat and she pressed her lips in tight.

There's the well. It's almost over. This is the last. No more.

Dropping the pull rope, she bent and set the flashlight in the snow, pushing down firmly and rocking it slightly from side to side to make it level. She knelt and scooped snow from the boards.

The wood was new and nailed tight. They wouldn't think to look in here again.

With the claw end of the hammer, she pried at the edges; pulling hard, panting. Finally, she felt some give and there was a screech as she managed to raise a board. Working desperately, she wrenched out a nail, stuck it in her pocket so she wouldn't lose it, and started on the next one. The gloves made her hands clumsy. When the nails were out, she slid the board aside.

Despite the cold, she was beginning to sweat, but with one board gone, the others were not so bad. Her arms were trembling by the time the well was open. She started to get to her feet, then froze. She heard singing.

"On to the close, O Lord, abide with me."

A figure in a pale raincoat with the hood up materialized in the falling snow. Edie stared in terror. Tearing her eyes from the woman in the raincoat, she glanced at the blanket-wrapped burden on the sled. There's no such thing as a ghost.

"You finally came," the woman said in a soft creepy voice. "They've been screaming at me. The crows. The well, they screamed. I can't. I told them. I can't. I tried. The boards. You can, they screamed. A dark angel will come and help you."

Tears blurred Edie's vision and ran down her face.

The woman took a step closer. "Are you crying? The babies are crying. In the trees. Hear them? Hanging in the trees. Crying. I can't stand it any more. Even when the dark angels sing, I can hear the babies. Crying. Crying."

She looked down into the well. "A safe place. Long quiet sleep of peace where the angels are shining and caring. I'll see Lowell. I'll tell him about the baby. He never knew. We were friends and we helped each other. I kept the key. The only thing I have of his. We never—he was so unhappy—and we talked and—just that one time. It didn't seem wrong. And we held each other and—and after—and after—Lowell cried. He cried."

Edie watched, hypnotized, as the woman came closer and squatted to peer in her face.

"God sent the dark angels. Singing. Always singing. And then the crows. They laughed at me and they screamed you have to kill yourself. For your parents and Carrie, because they love you, so they won't suffer anymore. They said a dark angel would come. I've been waiting."

Somewhere in the back of her mind, Edie was aware of a dog barking.

Susan listened hard, trying to figure out where the dog was, sound seemed distorted, trying to see movement through the swirling snowflakes.

"This way," Parkhurst said.

She lengthened her stride to keep pace with his. There was a luminous quality to the falling snow. The footing was treacherous and the crunch of their boots sounded like an advancing army as they slogged beneath branches, heavy with snow, that closed overhead like a long black tunnel.

The dog barked again, closer. Slipping and stumbling, she followed Parkhurst. He stopped, placed a cautionary hand on her arm. Ahead was a dim glow of light.

Mouth close to her ear, he whispered with small puffs of warm air, "I'll circle around." He drifted away, almost immediately lost in the swirling snow.

Cold air burned her lungs. She felt she was struggling without gain as she weaved around trees, trying to move quietly and cover distance quickly. She couldn't hear anything over her own heavy breathing.

Then she stopped dead and stared.

Ahead in the small clearing, a flashlight resting on the ground gleamed through the dark like a beacon. Boards were gone from the well. Two dark figures, heads covered, crouched beside it, provoking the image of renegade monks performing ancient prayers.

The dog pawed at something on a sled, nudged and poked with her muzzle. Suddenly, the dog raised her head. She barked and came bounding toward Susan.

Oh shit! Susan started running. Her feet sank deeply into the snow. She floundered.

Edie jerked her head up, mouth pulled tight over bared teeth. Hands clasped together as though in prayer, she leaned forward.

"Noooo!" Susan screamed. The sound seemed to echo over and over, caught by the snow-laden branches, muted and twisted and thrown from tree to tree. She felt the sensation of time slowing down, of muscles stretching too tight over her chest, her face stiffening into vacancy and her mind growing still with horror.

Edie, head bowed, leaned out over the well, leaned further, seemed to hang suspended for an instant of eternity, then dropped, wordlessly, into the black hole.

23

THE FIGURE IN the hooded raincoat teetered on the edge of the well, peering in.

"No," Susan yelled, running toward her and tripping as the dog bounded in the way. Oh Christ, I'll never get there in time.

From the other direction, Parkhurst pounded up through the falling snow, tearing off his jacket. He shoved the raincoated woman aside. She stumbled back and fell on her rear. He threw his jacket down and started climbing into the well.

"Parkhurst!" Susan shouted.

The hood of the raincoat slipped back when the woman scrambled to her knees, crawled toward that black hole. The dog barked, raced toward her, then toward Susan. With a flying leap, Susan launched herself, hit broadside and knocked the woman down again. Using her own weight to keep the woman pinned, Susan grabbed at flailing arms and kicking legs.

"The dark angel." Fists battered against Susan's shoulders.

"Stop it!"

"Have to go with her." The tossing head caught Susan on the jaw, hard enough to make her teeth clack and her vision blur.

The dog pranced around them, barking, darting forward, then backing off. The woman fought like a captured cat and

Susan felt her grip slipping. She eyed the flashlight in the snow a couple feet away. *If I could reach it, would a good bash on the head knock her out?* Suddenly all resistance ceased.

Susan tensed. Not a quiver. Warily easing up from the heaving chest, she gripped a wrist in each hand. "What's your name?" She pulled the limp form to a sitting position.

The fighting cat now sat like a doll, lifeless. *Oh Jesus, what's this?* "Can you tell me your name?"

Still holding both wrists, Susan stood and helped the woman to her feet. Docile compliance. Seemed content to keep any position she was pushed into. Yanking the belt from the rumpled raincoat, Susan pressed down on unresisting shoulders until the woman was sitting and propped her against a tree. Hurriedly, Susan tied the cold hands, then pulled her own belt loose and tied the ankles. It wouldn't hold for more than a few minutes if there was a serious attempt to get free.

"Don't move," she patted an arm. Grabbing the flashlight, Susan shined it into the well. "Parkhurst!"

Nothing moved in the cold black water. *Oh shit. I've got four people here, possibly dead or dying. Where the hell is the back up?* Ripping off her trench coat, she flung it aside, jammed the flashlight through the top rung and put her foot on the second.

I don't want to do this. Placing her feet cautiously, she lowered herself down one rusty slippery rung and then another.

Just below, there was a great deal of splashing and Parkhurst's head popped up. He gulped in air and shook water from his face. One gloved hand held onto a metal rung and the other clutched Edie's hair. He pulled her face from the water.

"Hold onto her," he said through chattering teeth.

Susan lowered one more rung, held tight and reached down to grab Edie's coat.

Parkhurst draped Edie over his shoulder in a fireman's carry. "Move."

Susan clambered out, snatched the flashlight and held it so he could see better. He labored up one rung at a time. When he reached the top, she stuck the flash upright in the snow and grabbed Edie's shoulders, helped as much as she could as he staggered out and fell to his knees. They straightened Edie on the ground. He rocked back on his heels, shaking uncontrollably.

Scared and desperate, Susan wrapped his coat around him and started for the Bronco. Within seconds, she heard the siren. Thank God. Hurry up, guys.

She saw blue lights glimmer through the falling snow and ran to meet them. "Ambulance," she yelled, "then get over here."

When flashlights started bobbing in her direction, she went back to Parkhurst and knelt in front of him.

"I'm okay," he barely managed through chattering teeth.

"The hell you are." She stood up. "Yancy," she said to one uniformed officer. "Get him dry and warm. Right now. You radio for an ambulance?"

Yancy nodded, bent over Parkhurst and helped him to his feet.

"Car keys," she said.

Parkhurst tried to get them, but his hand was shaking so badly he couldn't get it in his pants pocket. Yancy fished out the keys and tossed them to her.

"Demarco, get that coat over Edie." Susan swung the flashlight over her own trenchcoat crumpled by the well and then over Edie lying with her slack face exposed to the falling snow. Edie didn't look good. Susan was very afraid Edie was not breathing. "CPR?"

"Yes, ma'am."

"Get with it."

The woman she'd left propped against the tree hadn't moved. Susan shined the light in her face, strong resemblance to Carena Egersund. Except for blinking her eyes, she gave no indication of awareness. Should the belts be removed? Get her on her feet so she wasn't sitting in snow? Susan decided not. She didn't want to risk one more person disappearing into that hellhole.

The dog, crouched beside the blanket-wrapped body on the sled, shot to her feet when Susan approached. Susan spoke softly. The dog whimpered anxiously as Susan struggled with the cord, but didn't snarl or attempt to bite. Susan peeled back the blanket from Carena Egersund's face; eyes closed, deathly pallor, dark bruise on one cheek. Leaning an ear close to the cold lips, Susan felt a faint whisper of breath.

An eternity passed before she heard another siren, then paramedics were swarming around. With deliberate care, they placed Edie on a narrow wooden backboard, secured her head and neck with a cervical collar and covered her with the padded blankets used for hypothermia victims. The trail of IV tubes meant she was still alive.

Susan forced herself to stay out of the way; inactivity didn't sit well and it took conscious effort. The paramedics used the same maddening slowness and same procedures to get Egersund on a backboard and carried her with great gentleness toward the ambulance. The dog got frantic and Susan almost strangled the poor thing hanging onto her.

Chilled to the bone, Susan watched a paramedic speak to the woman in the raincoat, get no response, then untie her, wrap her in a blanket and lead her docilely away.

Susan loaded the dog in Parkhurst's Bronco and drove to Brookvale Hospital. An empty ambulance, door still open and red lights flashing, sat at the emergency entrance. The hospital doors slid silently back as she walked up. She went in search of the doctor and waited for what seemed like hours sitting on a black-vinyl and chrome chair in a dim hallway.

Finally the doctor came through swinging doors at the end of the hallway and spoke with a nurse who nodded at Susan. Susan stood up.

"Chief Wren? Dr. Kyle." He led her along the corridor into a small conference room and slumped into one of the plastic chairs around a table. She sat down across from him.

"The Vogel woman didn't make it," he said. "We worked on her, but— I'm sorry."

"What about Parkhurst?"

"I clapped him in bed with my direst threats." Dr. Kyle smiled wearily. "He didn't seem too impressed. He'll be fine. We're treating him for hypothermia. Probably release him tomorrow."

She felt an easing of tension in her shoulders. "The catatonic woman?"

"Physically, she seems all right. Showing some effects of exposure. Mentally—" He shook his head. "That's not my field. You have any idea who she is?"

"No. She looks a lot like Carena Egersund. Maybe a sister. How is Egersund?"

"Concussion. Abrasions and contusions that are minor. Also effects of exposure. Just what went on out there anyway?"

Macabre scenes that would live on in nightmares. "Will she be all right?"

"Should be. Barring complications. I need to run some more tests. She's conscious now. That's a good sign."

"May I see her?"

He hesitated. "You can't subject her to questions."

"Okay."

"Just listen to what she says and then leave."

"Okay."

He rubbed his tired face and putting both hands on the table for leverage pushed himself to his feet. "She's been asking for you. Might be better for her to get rid of whatever's on her mind. You can have three minutes. If she gets agitated, I'll yank you."

Susan simply nodded and followed him into an elevator and along another corridor.

"Three minutes," he warned.

Lying in the bed with monitors and IV tubes, Carena Egersund looked very bad to Susan. Her face was almost as pale as the sheets, except for the dark bruise on one cheek. Her eyes, fixed on Susan, seemed too bright as they sometimes were with the seriously ill. Susan hoped the doctor knew what he was talking about.

"I have to tell you about Edie. She killed Lynnelle. She—" Those bright eyes filled with tears.

"I know," Susan said gently. "You don't have to tell me now."

"Audrey fired her. And Edie hit her with a stool, some kind of child's chair."

Susan recalled the square stepping block sitting by Edie's coffee table. "This can wait until you're feeling better."

"I don't remember much. Sort of a dream. Cold and being dragged along, and dark."

"Edie was pulling you on a sled." Susan yanked tissues from a box on the bedside table and handed them to her.

"I've been so worried—so—" Carena Egersund blotted at her face. "Caitlin is missing and—"

"Caitlin is your sister?"

"Yes. She's—she was— Lynnelle was her child, but she— Nobody knows where Caitlin is. I'm afraid—"

"She's here in the hospital. She's—," Susan started to say just fine, then changed it to, "not hurt."

"Here?" Much of the anxiety eased from Carena Egersund's face, leaving it slack and even more pale and corpse-like. "Oh thank God. I was afraid she'd hurt herself and—" The tears kept coming.

Susan thought it was time to leave. "I'll let you sleep now, but I do need to know where Caitlin lives, who to contact."

"Her husband. Phil Avery." Her voice now breathless, she gave Susan an address and phone number.

"I'll talk with you more later. Try not to think too much and just concentrate on getting well."

Worry came back to cloud her eyes.

"Is there anything you need?" Susan asked.

"The dog—Lynnelle's dog. She's in the house. She'll starve. She—"

"I'll take care of her. Don't worry."

Susan stopped at the nurses' station to ask where Parkhurst was, then took the elevator down a floor and paused in the open doorway. Parkhurst lay on his side with his eyes closed; face gray, dark circles under his eyes, dark stubble of beard.

She came in quietly and sat in the chair by the bed. Almost immediately, his eyes opened, gazed at her unknowing and then focused.

"Hi," she said softly. "How are you?"

"Fine." He flopped onto his back and doubled the pillow behind his head. "Edie?"

"She didn't make it."

He closed his eyes, took a breath and blew it out. "You know, Susan, we didn't exactly shine through any of this."

"True." They were almost too slow for Carena Egersund and would have been if it wasn't for the dog. Caitlin was in a padded room staring at the wall. Edie was dead. Her parents had lost a daughter, her daughter had lost a mother. Susan stood and hitched the strap of her handbag higher on her shoulder. "I'll try to spring you out of here tomorrow."

For a week, the *Herald* ran lurid headlines along the lines of "Creighton Well Claims Next Victim," "Tragedy Strikes Twice," "Is There a Curse On The Creighton Place?"

On the following Sunday morning when Susan scooped up the newspaper from the driveway, she noticed crocuses poking up green shoots through snowy slush and smiled at them ridiculously. Snapping off the rubber band, she unfolded the paper and glanced at the headline. UNSEASONABLE WEATHER.

The sun, so warm the air smelled sweet, sparkled through the trees with the bright light of premature spring. A pair of cardinals dipped and swooped like scarlet kites through the blue sky. After she took the dog back, she had the whole day free, and Daniel's clothes waited in the closet.